TW... TALES

Twisted TALES

BRANDON MASSEY

Kensington Publishing Corp.

http://www.kensingtonbooks.com

DAFINA BOOKS are published by

Kensington Publishing Corp.
850 Third Avenue
New York, NY 10022

Copyright © 2006 by Brandon Massey

All rights reserved. No part of this book may be reproduced in any form or by any means without the prior written consent of the Publisher, excepting brief quotes used in reviews.

If you purchased this book without a cover you should be aware that this book is stolen property. It was reported as "unsold and destroyed" to the Publisher and neither the Author nor the Publisher has received any payment for this "stripped book."

All Kensington Titles, Imprints, and Distributed Lines are available at special quantity discounts for bulk purchases for sales promotions, premiums, fund-raising, and educational or institutional use. Special book excerpts or customized printings can also be created to fit specific needs. For details, write or phone the office of the Kensington special sales manager: Kensington Publishing Corp., 850 Third Avenue, New York, NY 10022, Attn: Special Sales Department, Phone: 1-800-221-2647.

Dafina and the Dafina logo Reg. U.S. Pat. & TM Off.

First Dafina mass market printing: June 2006

10 9 8 7 6 5 4 3 2 1

Printed in the United States of America

Contents

Daddy's Little Girl 7

The Sting 28

After the Party 51

The Secret Door 59

Hitcher 80

Predators 102

Nostalgia 120

A Walk Through Darkness 143

The Monster 160

Death Notice 172

The Woman Next Door 187

Flight 463 214

Presumed Dead 236

The Last Train Home 255

Notes on the Stories 294

Daddy's Little Girl

"Nathan, I'd like you to meet my dad."

I offered my hand, and the bearish man in front of me swallowed it in his massive grip. Swallowed it and squeezed—hard. Pain snapped through my fingers and traveled up my arm. I tried to conceal my anguish when I addressed him.

"Nice to meet you, Mr. Payne. I'm Nathan . . . Hunter." I forced the words out of my mouth; it was a struggle to keep from whining like a puppy. He continued to smash my hand in his grip.

Mr. Payne grunted. He was the hairiest man I'd ever seen. He had an Afro, a grizzly black beard, crisp hairs covering his muscular arms, and on the back of his meaty hands hair so dense he probably had to comb it. No doubt in winter he didn't need to wear a coat. His natural fur probably served just fine.

He barely resembled his daughter. Stacy was short and petite, her skin as smooth as cream, her exotic features framed by long black hair. She stood beside us as we shook hands, and though a smile creased her lovely face, her eyes held a hint of apprehension.

I understood why. When we met a couple of weeks

ago, she had warned me that her father was over-protective and zealously guarded her from potential boyfriends. I'd wanted to see Mr. Payne as early as possible, to reassure him that he could trust me to treat his daughter well. But Stacy had postponed introducing us until our third date, which was our first dinner-and-a-movie outing. She worried that her father might chase me away, and she wanted us to get to know each other without his distracting influence. Now that I'd met Mr. Payne at last, she probably wondered what would go wrong.

I wondered the same thing, to be honest. It wasn't every day that you got a chance to meet a man who was supposedly guilty of murder.

We finally ended our handshake. My hand throbbed. This guy was *strong*.

"You've got a good grip," I said. "It must come from all of the working out that Stacy tells me that you do."

"I get my strength from other sources," Mr. Payne said. He had a baritone voice that originated from deep within his enormous chest. "Sources beyond your comprehension, young man."

What a strange response. Frowning, I noticed Mr. Payne's eyes. They were liquid black, with a wild gleam: the kind of eyes that belonged in a predator who took delight in torturing its prey before it consummated the kill.

I would have to be careful with this man. My superiors believed that I was capable of bringing Mr. Payne to justice with no problem, but I wasn't sure. My greatest advantage in this investigation was that neither Stacy nor her father suspected my intentions. But no veteran detective—especially one who specialized in my unique line of work—would risk dropping his guard and blowing his cover. The consequences could be deadly.

Although I'd finally met Mr. Payne, I could not ask him probing questions that might make him suspicious. I'd play it cool, date his daughter as though I was a regular guy, quietly gathering more clues . . . and when the picture was complete, I'd carry out my orders to bring the felon to justice.

I checked my watch. "I'm sorry, but we have to get going, Mr. Payne. It's been nice meeting you."

"You two will get a chance to talk some other time, I'm sure," Stacy said.

Mr. Payne grumbled. "You'll have her back by ten o'clock. My little girl has a curfew."

Stacy looked embarrassed. She was twenty-two years old, a grown woman. Was Mr. Payne serious?

"Ten o'clock is a little early," I said. "The movie might not be over by then. How about eleven?" I felt odd asking her father such a question.

Danger flared in his eyes. "You seem to have forgotten who is in control here, young man. You are dating my daughter, and I decide whom she dates, where she goes on her date, and when she will return from each date. Her curfew is ten o'clock. If you have a problem with that, not only will Stacy not accompany you this evening, I will permanently ban her from communicating with you. Understood?"

"Uh, well, sure," I said. "Ten o'clock. Yes, sir."

Stacy laughed.

"Oh, Daddy, you're too much." she said. "Nathan is the nicest guy I've ever dated." She slipped her arm through mine and smiled at him.

Mr. Payne's eyes softened when he regarded his daughter. I could see that he really loved her. Her mother—his wife—had died eight years ago, leaving him to raise Stacy on his own. Stacy was all he had left. I empathized, a little, with his overbearing attitude.

But when he turned to me, a threat flickered like fire in his eyes. I realized two facts. One: my investigation into Mr. Payne's crimes would end inconclusively if I botched the evening and Mr. Payne barred me from seeing his daughter—since she was my pipeline to his life. Two: Mr. Payne, as my superiors had warned me, was as scary as hell.

"Ten o'clock," Mr. Payne said. When I nodded and started to turn away, he said something else that I would not understand until later.

"I'll be watching."

As I drove to the restaurant, Stacy turned down the volume on the stereo and said, "My dad's something else, isn't he?"

I shrugged. "He's obviously concerned about your welfare. Kind of overbearing, I admit."

"In his eyes, I'm always Daddy's little girl. No guy I bring home is good enough for him. I could spend all night telling him how great you are, and he'd still treat you as if you'd crawled from under a rock somewhere."

"I felt like a suspected criminal."

"Ever since what happened to Mom, family has become extremely important to him. No man I meet will get in the family without Dad putting him through the wringer. He only wants the best for me."

"I guess that makes sense," I said. "If I had a daughter, I wouldn't want her spending time with a loser, either."

"You can't understand how Mom's death changed

things for him, for both of us." She shook her head. "You wouldn't believe it."

This could be a good opportunity to gain more information about her father's history. I said, "Want to tell me about it?"

"Not now, Nathan, it would spoil the mood. Later, I promise."

I clenched the steering wheel. Patience, I assured myself. I'd eventually uncover her father's secrets.

I glanced at Stacy. Secrets glimmered in her dark, beautiful eyes, and her mystique only made me want her more. This was something that complicated my investigation; I had never thought I would start to fall for her. More often, I'd wondered what I had gotten myself into when I accepted this assignment, and where it would lead.

We arrived at the restaurant, a popular steak house. She went to open her door. I touched her arm, stopping her.

"Answer me honestly, Stacy. Do you think I'll ever measure up to your father's expectations?"

Impulsively, she leaned in toward me and kissed me. Or *tasted* me, rather, since that was what her kiss brought to mind. Purring like a cat, she tasted my lips, chin, and cheeks as if I was a juicy slice of meat. Her kisses were like nothing I had ever experienced. There was something primitive and wild about them that made me want to explode.

She let go of me and licked her lips, as though tasting me still.

My heart pounded.

"You measure up to *my* expectations," she said. "In the end, that's all that will matter."

She winked at me, and we got out of the car.

Inside, the hostess guided us to a booth. Stacy slid

into one side. I was about to take the opposite side when she patted the space beside her.

"Tonight, I want you next to me."

I saw that compelling gleam in her eyes again. Of course, I did as she asked. She smiled at me, a subtle smile as mysterious as her gaze. I could not deny my suspicion that I was not the only one here who had ulterior motives—although I had no idea what she might have planned for me.

We ordered drinks, an appetizer, and steaks. I ordered the rib eye; Stacy requested the massive porterhouse. I looked at her, eyebrows raised. She'd always shown an enormous appetite—on our lunch dates, she ate more than I did—but could she put away that much meat?

It didn't take long for my question to be answered. After plowing through the appetizer of Texas Cheese Fries, then black bean soup, and then tossed green salad, Stacy cut into her steak eagerly. She made soft animal noises of satisfaction as she chewed, yet she ate gracefully, like a wolf that had mastered the use of silverware.

"Hungry tonight?" I asked.

She turned and blinked. Her eyes had a glassy look, as though she had been entranced by the food. "Oh, you mean the porterhouse. This is nothing, sweetie. I could eat two of these."

"You're kidding." I looked at the slab of thick, rare meat on her plate, and then I checked out her body. She wore a tight green sweater and a black skirt that showcased her taut, shapely figure. "Where do you put it all?"

"I have a high metabolism. So does Daddy. We eat like animals and don't gain a pound."

"I see."

"If you hang around me long enough, maybe you'll pick it up, like by osmosis." She gave me that enchanting smile again, hinting at things I could only imagine.

I excused myself to visit the restroom. After I took care of business, I went to the sink to wash up. As I stood there soaping my hands, Mr. Payne exited one of the toilet stalls.

I froze. "Uh, hi, Mr. Payne."

He glared at me as he walked to the sinks. "Have you been treating my little girl well?"

"We're having a great time," I said. What was he doing here? Had he followed us? I couldn't ask him those questions, so I said, "She sure enjoys steak."

"She takes after me." He washed his hands. "I love meat. The bloodier, the better." He stared at me. "Nothing tastes as delicious as the blood."

"Yeah," I said. The strange look in his eyes made me wonder if he'd like to slit me open and sample *my* blood. Quickly, I grabbed a towel from the dispenser and began to dry my hands.

Mr. Payne came over to me. He snatched the towel out of my fingers.

I gaped at him. I was suddenly aware of how big he was, and painfully aware that we were the only ones in there; the sounds coming from the dining room seemed to be miles away.

Did he know the truth about me? Was that why he was confronting me like this?

Towering over me, he grinned. It wasn't a friendly grin. It was a mouth-wide-open, predatory grin, letting me see his long, sharp canines, teeth that no normal man would have . . . teeth that belonged in the mouth of a carnivore.

I backed up against the wall.

"I'm watching you," he said. Saliva glistened on his teeth. "You try anything with my little girl, and you'll wish you'd never met her."

Tension had squeezed my throat like a garrote. I couldn't speak.

No ordinary man could have teeth like that.

Then Mr. Payne shut his mouth with an audible clap. He turned away as if nothing had happened and began to pick his Afro.

"Do you plan on keeping my daughter waiting much longer?" he asked. "Or are you as thoughtless and rude as I figured you are?"

Without a word, I got out of there.

Either Mr. Payne was on to me and was attempting to scare me off my investigation, or else he was only trying to scare me away from his daughter. Well, it wouldn't work. I had a job to finish, and I'd stick to it, regardless of how much he made my palms sweat.

Back at the table, Stacy had finished eating. Her plate was so clean it might have come right out of the dishwasher.

"Your father's here," I said. "I saw him in the restroom."

She sighed. "That figures. He's following me again."

"He's done this before?"

She nodded. "With other guys. I'm Daddy's little girl, remember? He doesn't want to let me out of his sight."

At the back of the dining room, the restroom door opened. Mr. Payne emerged, staring at me. He sat at a table across the room, but his location gave him a direct view of us. I could feel his glare stabbing like a knife into my brain.

"Take a look over there," I said to Stacy. "He's got a perfect view of us."

She didn't look. "I'll take your word for it. It's typical of him."

"Have you asked him to stop doing this?"

"All the time. But it doesn't matter, he does it anyway. He does it whenever he thinks I'm with the wrong guy, which is all the time."

"This is crazy," I said. "You're a grown woman."

"I know how we can get him off our backs, Nathan," she said. "Be patient, okay?"

"What are you going to do?"

But she would not answer; she only gave me that secretive smile.

On our way out, we had to pass by Mr. Payne's table. He had a huge cut of prime rib in front of him. The juicy meat oozed dark blood.

Nothing tastes as delicious as the blood.

Stacy, thankfully, didn't stop to converse. She said only "hello." I gave him the same brief greeting. But as I held open the door for her, I looked at him. He watched me, of course, a warning in his savage eyes.

You try anything with my little girl, and you'll wish you'd never met her.

You can't scare me away, I thought. I'm not quitting until I learn the truth.

Mr. Payne didn't say a word, but he held my gaze. Held my gaze as he raised a bloody chunk of meat to his long, sharp teeth.

At the theater, on Stacy's insistence, we took seats on the far left side, against the wall. We wouldn't have a great view of the screen. But we would have a great opportunity to get closer to each other. The feature film was a romantic comedy, and though I didn't plan on paying much attention to the story, I went to get popcorn for us.

Mr. Payne was in the lobby. He stood at the box office, buying a ticket.

This man was relentless. I understood what he had meant when, before we had left the house, he'd said to me, *I'll be watching you.* He was literally going to tail us all night.

He was messing up everything. I'd thought that I could gradually insinuate myself into Stacy's life—and, by extension, his life—and pick up all the clues I needed to complete my investigation. But Mr. Payne wasn't letting me take that path. He was committed to driving me away before I resolved anything.

I dashed back to Stacy. The theater had darkened; a preview of an upcoming film flashed on the screen.

"Where's the popcorn?" Stacy asked.

"I didn't get any. Your dad's here. I saw him buying a ticket."

"Oh, no." She covered her face with her hands.

"If he comes in for this movie, we're going to leave and see something else," I said. "I couldn't stand having him in here."

"Daddy has never gotten on my nerves this badly. I think he knows there's something special between us. He's scared of what it might lead to."

I frowned. "And what might it lead to?"

"Later," she said. "I'll explain later. Please trust me."

"Why don't you just tell me what's on your mind?"

But she had raised a finger to her lips. She motioned behind us.

I turned. I saw a tall, hulking silhouette in the

doorway at the back of the theater. There were two aisles, and we were near the left one; slowly, the figure marched down the right aisle, head swiveling back and forth, looking for either a seat—or for us.

"That's him?" I asked in a whisper.

"I think so."

I grabbed her hand. "Come on, let's go see something else."

Masked by darkness, we slipped out of there. I did not look back to see if Mr. Payne saw us leave. I had the bizarre notion that if I glanced in his direction, he would be watching me. Like a creature of the night, he seemed to have heightened, almost extraordinary senses.

We entered the theater at the end of the hallway. It was a horror flick, and it was dark inside. Lucky timing for us; the opening credits had just begun.

We found seats in the same area as before. Far left corner, against the wall. Stacy took the seat near the wall, and I sat beside her. I put my arm around her. She snuggled closer.

"I forgot to ask you," I said, "do you like horror movies?"

"I love them," she said. "Especially monster movies. This is one of those, isn't it?"

"Yeah, something about a werewolf." I recalled the lurid poster beside the theater entrance.

She grinned. "Ooooohh, that's perfect. I only hope it's realistic."

I was about to ask how a film about a werewolf could possibly be realistic, but then she kissed my lips—no, *tasted* my lips, and I didn't care about asking her questions. I didn't even care about her father. I cared only about being with her.

She laid her head on my shoulder. I stroked her lustrous hair.

Maybe we were falling in love. The idea worried me. How could I resolve my case if I was in love with her? Love would make it difficult, if not impossible, to carry out my assigned task.

Rather than mull over the situation, I immersed myself in the movie. It was a gory show about a pack of werewolves tearing through a quiet Illinois town. The acting was terrible, the dialogue was stilted, and the plotting was choppy, but it nonetheless got a huge response from the audience, especially Stacy. Every time a werewolf ripped out someone's throat, she whooped, and she sighed with something approaching ecstasy at every drop of spilled blood. I got the weird feeling that she rooted for the werewolves to prevail over the humans.

But I didn't complain. We explored each other's bodies quite a bit during the show. At several points, we became so entangled that I wasn't sure whose limbs were whose. We might never have done any of that if she hadn't been so engaged by the film. Not only was I curious to see if this new level of intimacy would loosen her tongue on family matters, I also, I admit, looked forward to becoming better acquainted with her body.

As the closing credits rolled down the screen, the theater lights brightened. Hands entwined, we stood. I led the way to the crowded aisle . . . and then I glimpsed a familiar shape in the corner of my eye. I spun.

It was Mr. Payne. He stood two rows behind us. He glared hatefully at me. I realized, with despair, that he had witnessed every kiss, every forbidden touch that I had shared with his precious daughter.

Mr. Payne pointed a long finger at me. "You!"

I shrank back. People around us looked, curious and alarmed.

Stacy gripped my hand. "Daddy, you shouldn't have followed us!"

"I'm only looking out for your best interests, sweetheart," he said. His eyes burned into me. "I should kill you."

"Will you relax?" I said. "We just watched a movie!"

"Bullshit. I saw you. You were all over her!"

The crowd snickered. Humiliation flushed my face. I hated that he had chosen this place to cause a scene.

Mr. Payne charged toward us. The crowd fled out of his path like antelope fleeing a lion. Indecision, disbelief, and fear had rooted me in place. I stood there holding Stacy's hand, while fury seethed in her father's eyes. His hands clenched and unclenched, as if in eagerness to crack my neck.

Spurred to move, I pulled Stacy backward. As though she weighed no more than a Barbie doll, Mr. Payne grabbed Stacy by the arm and yanked her toward him. She cried out, her hand slipping out of mine. Using one huge arm to cradle his daughter against him, he thrust his other arm toward me.

"Stay away from my little girl!" He shoved me. I flew backward, tripped on something, and hit the floor.

I lay sprawled in the aisle, gazing at the ceiling.

Clearly, agreeing to this assignment had been a mistake. Mr. Payne was too volatile for me to get close enough to him to learn the truth. The safe, slow-moving course of action sanctioned by my superiors was not going to work. If I was to succeed in my mission, I'd have to break protocol.

I was more certain than ever that Mr. Payne was a killer. With his tendency toward violence and his fiery temper, I could believe that he had slaughtered several men, as the rumors indicated. All in the service of protecting his lovely daughter.

By the time I got out of the theater, Mr. Payne was screeching out of the parking lot in a black jeep. Stacy was mashed against the rear windshield, crying out my name.

I raced to my car. I was about to jam the key in the ignition, when I noticed the front of my shirt, in the area of my chest where Mr. Payne had pushed.

A couple of buttons had been torn off. Dark blood—my blood—stained the cotton. The blood had clotted and the small wound didn't hurt. In fact, I hadn't noticed the injury until now, maybe due to my dazed shock. But I thought of Mr. Payne's long, sharp nails. Nails like claws.

Mr. Payne had left me no choice. I opened the glove compartment.

Inside, a revolver awaited me.

It was already loaded. With silver bullets.

When I arrived at Stacy's house, she answered the door. She ushered me inside.

"I'm so glad you came," she said. "I'm sorry about what happened."

"Your father went nuts," I said. "Is he here?"

"He's out running."

"Running? At this hour?"

"He does it all the time," she said. "I usually go with him, especially when there's a beautiful full moon, like there is tonight. But I was mad at him for what he did to you, so I stayed in."

"When will he be back?"

"Later." She smiled seductively. "Relax, Nathan. We have plenty of time to pick up where we left off."

She led me to the sofa. She sat on my lap, put her arms around my neck, and leaned toward me. I put my finger on her lips.

"Not now," I said. "We have to talk."

"What's wrong?"

I was going to put everything on the table. "Do you remember Daryl Williams?"

She suddenly drew back. Anxiety lit up her eyes.

"Who is he?" she asked, her quavering voice betraying the fact that she knew who I was talking about.

"You dated him three months ago," I said. "You went out with him a few times, until your father apparently decided that he didn't like him. Someone discovered Daryl's body in a forest. His corpse had been mauled, like a pack of wolves had attacked him."

I drew the crime-scene photograph out of my jacket pocket and held it in front of her face. She gasped. She climbed off my lap, her hand covering her mouth.

"Nathan," she said. "I'm sorry. I . . . I don't know what to say."

I whipped out another grisly photo.

"How about David Taylor, a guy you dated last year? Remember him? Yeah, this rotted corpse with its neck chewed in half doesn't resemble him at all, but I think you know who I'm talking about. Your father hated him, too."

Tears shimmered in her large eyes. She hugged herself.

"Where did you get those pictures from?" she asked shakily.

"Doesn't matter." I didn't enjoy forcing her face

into this dirt, but it was necessary to stop these games. "We know what's been going on."

"I'm so sorry." Tears rolled down her cheeks. "Daddy can't control himself. He gets crazy when he doesn't like the guys that I date—"

"Don't make excuses for him. Your dad is a blood-crazed killer. He's only using his desire to protect you as an excuse to indulge in these wild killings. He has to be stopped."

"What do you mean, stopped? Are you a cop?"

"I am a cop, but not the kind of cop that you might think."

"What do you—"

A howl pierced the night, silencing her. I did not know exactly where the howl had come from, but I knew *what* it had come from—and I knew it was not far away.

I gripped Stacy's shoulder. "If you like me as much as I like you, you'll tell me everything. No more secrets, Stacy."

Her eyes were wary. "But he's coming, Nathan. Do you have any idea what he'll do if he finds you here?"

"I'll take the risk. I have to know the whole story."

She slumped on the couch. Stared at her lap.

I pulled over a chair, sat in front of her.

"I'm waiting," I said. I was trying like hell to convince her that I wasn't afraid.

She said, "Eight years ago, on a family vacation in Arizona, my mother was killed."

She paused and looked at me, as though checking to see whether I believed her. I said nothing, only nodded.

She continued. "My dad and I found her body. It was torn to pieces. Before we could even think about what to do, my father and I were attacked, too. But we weren't killed. We were bitten and turned into . . . Well, you know what we became, don't you, Nathan?"

"Yes," I said.

"What happened to my mom scarred both me and my father pretty deeply, but my father's pain is more obvious. He became obsessed with protecting me, with making sure that I never ended up like my mom. Pretty foolish for him to worry about that, considering the abilities I have, but in his mind I'm just Daddy's little girl, like I've always been."

"Go on," I said.

"He's as obsessed with protecting me as he is with making sure that I hook up with the right guy. I mean, the right guy, whoever he turns out to be, will have to become one of us. He'll have to become part of the family, in every way. That's why he's been giving you so much hell, Nathan. He doesn't think you're right for me, and he's trying to scare you off."

"Without resorting to killing me, I presume," I said.

She winced. "Daryl and David were sweet guys," she said. "But they were much more aggressive than you are. Daddy didn't like that at all. He tried to make them leave me alone, but the harder he tried, the pushier they became. Daddy had finally had enough. So he . . ."

"Slaughtered them," I said. "There are others, Stacy. I don't have photos, but I know that Mr. Payne has been busy 'protecting' you for at least the past five years. Over a dozen innocent guys have paid the price for being interested in you."

"He's not a killer, Nathan. Please don't make him sound like he's evil."

I touched her face. I felt bad for her. She was immersed in denial.

Another howl shattered the night. It was getting closer.

I glanced at the windows, at the shadows surrounding us. He would be there soon.

Stacy straightened. "How did you learn so much about us?"

"Word gets around," I said. "When someone has been as reckless as your dad has been, others notice. I pursued a relationship with you because I was asked to learn the full story."

"You mean you dated me only to learn about my father?" she asked. "You used me?"

"Hold on, don't get mad. Yes, I first wanted to date you to find out about Mr. Payne. But when it became obvious that we clicked so well, I started to fall for you."

She smiled a little. I could not return her smile. I was conscious of the howls. They were getting much closer.

"So who sent you to me?" she asked. "What kind of police do you work for?"

Just as I opened my mouth to tell her an angry roar filled the air. A huge, dark shape hurtled like a torpedo through the living room window, shattered glass flying everywhere.

The intruder landed in the far corner of the room, an area thick with shadows. I glimpsed a hairy, hunched form, like a big man on all fours, and I heard husky breathing issuing from the beast.

Stacy grabbed my hand. "Come on. If you want to live, we've gotta get to my room!"

We ran to the staircase. Behind us, the creature growled. I looked over my shoulder.

The animal had moved out of the shadows. In spite of the glossy coat of gray fur, the long snout, and the sharp, canine teeth, I recognized who it was. The eyes gave it away.

Mr. Payne—the werewolf.

"Hurry!" Stacy pulled me upstairs. We scrambled into her bedroom, and then she slammed and locked the door.

"Do you want to be with me?" she asked. Her eyes blazed.

"Be with you?"

She grasped my shoulders. "Do you want to be with me? Forever?"

I stammered. "Stacy, I have to do something."

"What?"

I opened my jacket, revealing the gun holstered on my hip. I pulled the revolver out of its sheath.

Stacy retreated a few steps. "Please, put away that gun, Nathan."

"Sorry, but I'm only following orders." I grabbed the doorknob and flung open the door.

"No!" she cried.

Ignoring her, I moved to the staircase. Mr. Payne, the werewolf, bounded up the steps. The beast leaped over three and four risers at a time. It snarled, saliva flying in thick ropes, eyes aflame with inhuman rage and hunger.

My hands trembled. He was so *enormous*. If I missed, I was finished.

The werewolf sprang toward me.

I squeezed off one, two, three shots, the revolver booming like a cannon. One misfired round plowed through the railing; one smacked into the creature's chest; and the third drilled it between the eyes.

The beast shrieked. Leaking blood like a busted water hose, the werewolf rolled down the stairs. It crashed to the floor with an impact that reverberated through the house.

Then, silence. The creature lay on the floor unmoving. Dead.

I closed my eyes.

I hadn't handled my assignment in the neat, thoroughly documented manner that my superiors would have preferred, but they would accept my work. They would have to accept it. I was one of the few detectives in the world qualified to handle this kind of case. The scarcity of individuals in my position provided job security.

"You killed him," a guttural voice said from behind me.

It was Stacy. She was crouched in the doorway. She had begun to metamorphose, too: pretty nose lengthening into a canine snout, claws pushing through the tips of her slender fingers, coarse hair covering her creamy skin . . .

"I had to kill him," I said. "Unchecked beasts like him make it more difficult for all of us. He was violating the code."

I thought I saw confusion on her rapidly transforming face.

I wanted to explain, so I said, "Our power lies in our secrecy. Your father was killing at will, and that isn't allowed. Kills have to be carefully planned and concealed, or else the safety of our entire species is threatened."

She dropped to the floor on all fours. She raised her long neck, stretched her jaws wide. Her thick tongue swept across her rows of sharp teeth.

She howled.

"I'm responsible for enforcing the laws for us," I said. I looked at the revolver in my hand. "According to the law, I'm supposed to slay you, too. I'm not allowed to leave witnesses."

I studied Stacy's werewolf form. She regarded me with her dark eyes, panting softly, expectantly.

She was gorgeous.

I tossed aside the gun.

"But you know what? To hell with protocol. There's a full moon tonight. And I don't know about you, but that tiny steak I ate earlier left me hungrier than ever . . ."

The Sting

There were only two things in the world that really frightened Anthony Morris: snakes, and winged insects with stingers, like wasps.

When Anthony reached the outside entrance to their hotel room, he spotted a wasp as long as his index finger batting against the top of the door. With each soft bump against the wood, the insect emitted a loud buzz, as if grunting from its efforts to get inside.

Anthony's first impulse was to spin around, race across the walkway, plunge down the stairs, and wait in the car until the wasp flew away. His wife, as slow as ever, was still in their Mercedes, fiddling around with her camera, purse, and who knows what else. They had spent all day under the merciless Mississippi sun at a family reunion picnic; he could use the excuse that he wanted to find an ice-cream shop, to get a cool respite from the heat, and she would never know the true reason why he'd returned to the car. Although they had been married for three years and had known each other for five, Anthony had managed to conceal his embarrassing phobia. Letting Karen discover how deeply he feared wasps would be as bad as getting stung.

Well, not quite as bad. As a child, he had been stung several times by wasps, yellow jackets, hornets, bumblebees—all of them had gotten him at least once. Nothing else matched the agony. He believed that his admittedly paranoid fear of the insects intensified the pain of being stung. The last time a hornet had attacked him, he had nearly passed out.

In the parking lot below, a door thunked shut. Karen was on her way.

Wings fluttering, the insect had attached itself to the door. Anthony could not believe the sheer size of the wasp. Maybe insects were bigger in Mississippi, because the thing was huge. Its stinger—he thought he could actually see it—seemed to glimmer in the twilight, like the tip of a deadly needle.

From his readings about wasps, he knew that once they plunged their stinger into you, they would still survive. Unlike bumblebees, which left their stingers in your skin and soon died, a wasp retained its weapon, and could return to punish you again. And again, and again.

He shivered.

Okay, be a man about this, he told himself. *I'm thirty years old, a successful lawyer, admired, respected, envied. It's only a stupid bug. Kill it.*

Keeping his eye on the quivering wasp, he slipped off one of his Nikes. In a furious burst of energy, he hammered the shoe against the door.

Got it! The wasp crunched underneath the shoe sole and drifted harmlessly to the pavement.

And the verdict is: life in bug hell.

"See ya, sucker," he said, and chuckled. He kicked aside the insect's carcass.

As he put on his other shoe, his wife climbed the last step of the landing. With what he hoped was a nonchalant motion, he slid his room key into the narrow slot, unlocking the door.

"It's hot as hell in here," he blurted. "And I turned on the air conditioner before we left for the picnic. What a shitty room. I told you we should've stayed at the Hyatt."

Karen trudged toward him, her normally cheerful face lined with fatigue, and browned from a full day in the sun. Her oversized purple T-shirt, which read MORRIS FAMILY REUNION 2006 in white letters, was rumpled and probably damp with perspiration. She had pulled back her hair into a bun; several strands stood up like unruly weeds.

Anthony hated to see his wife looking worn-out like this. All she'd want to do is take a shower and flop across the bed. No loving for him tonight.

"One more night in here won't kill us," Karen said as she walked inside. "I only need a shower. When I hit the mattress, I'm going to pass out. Put an ice bag on your head if you need to."

"Very funny," he said. "I'm going to suffer heat exhaustion in here."

"Serves you right. After what you pulled at the picnic today, you aren't getting any sympathy from me."

At the picnic, Anthony had been appointed gatekeeper, responsible for checking in relatives and family friends and giving them name tags. It was a humiliating, tiresome task. He was an attorney, for God's sake, not some shiftless high school dropout—like some of his cousins. He hadn't driven seven hours from Atlanta so he could sweat in the heat and be a receptionist. He had agreed to do it only because

Ma Dear had asked him herself, and with her being ninety-two years old and this possibly being her last reunion, well, he felt obligated to comply with her wishes.

Of course, Ma Dear had asked him to do it only because she wanted to give him a lesson in humility. When folks reached Ma Dear's age, all they thought about was trying to dispense their so-called wisdom. He was sure she was thinking, I'm gonna make Tony pass out name tags, that boy's too proud and needs to be humbled.

He was humbled, all right. He did the job so well he was certain they'd never ask him to do it again. Everyone whom he didn't recognize—and there were many such people—had to prove they were a legitimate relative or friend. No exceptions.

"I was only doing my job," he said to Karen. "Rules are rules. Was I supposed to let in every stray person who comes off the road claiming some vague kinship, salivating for a plate of ribs and potato salad? Then you'd be complaining that because of me, there wasn't enough food left for the real family members."

"Yeah, sure, you only did your job," she said. Sitting on the bed, she pulled off her sneakers and socks. "You had an interrogation going on there. But the elderly lady was worst of all, Anthony. What you did to her was terrible."

Karen made it sound as though he had robbed the old woman. A short, stout lady wearing dark shades, a big hat, and a flower-patterned dress, had waddled up to the picnic. A frail young woman was leading her, which made him wonder whether the old lady was blind. In a scratchy voice, the woman said her name was Sis Maggie.

"Sister who?" Anthony had asked. "You don't look like the sister of anyone in my family, old girl."

Sis Maggie's face puckered up like a prune. "I'm a friend of the family, young man. Been knowin' your people from way back."

"What people of mine do you know?"

In a halting voice, Sis Maggie proceeded to run down a list of names: Junebug, Little Tommy, Lillie Mae, and other names Anthony had never heard in his life. He didn't have the patience to listen a minute longer. He cut her off in midsentence.

"Listen, I've never heard of those people," he said. "Either they're all dead, or you're at the wrong family reunion. In any case, you wasted your time coming here. Have a good day."

Sis Maggie frowned in confusion; so did her skinny guide girl. "Young man, listen here—"

"The exit to the park is over there." Anthony pointed. "If your eyesight is too bad to see it, I'm sure your little nurse there can find it for you."

Muttering under her breath, Sis Maggie and the girl huffed, turned around and shuffled away.

A handful of people had gathered around the sign-in table. Their mouths hung open in shock. Anthony only smiled. He had balls, all right. No one could pull one over on him.

Minutes later, one of Anthony's aunts ran to him and told him he'd made a big mistake by turning Sis Maggie away. No, his aunt said, she ain't really a friend of the family, but she lives in these parts, and only a fool dares to disrespect her. The old woman has been known to work with roots—and she holds terrible grudges.

Anthony only laughed at this backwoods' superstition. Talk about ignorant. If Sis Maggie was so bad, let her work some roots to conjure up some ribs of her own. She wasn't getting any from his reunion.

"It's over now," he told Karen. He sat on the bed. "Drop it."

Karen rolled her eyes. She stripped down to her bra and panties, and the sight of her shapely body made his heart skip a beat. He reached for her as she walked past him. She swatted his hand away.

"None for you tonight," she said. "I'm tired, and you've gotten on my damn nerves. Make friends with your hand."

"That's cold," he said, watching her shuffle into the bathroom. He used the edge of his shirt to mop the sweat off his face. Waves of heat pressed upon him like heavy pillows, squeezing sticky sweat out of his pores. On the other side of the room, the air-conditioning unit rattled. Piece of shit. This is what he got for buying into the "family reunion" hotel package: two miserable nights at a cheap hotel. He had wanted to stay at the Hyatt, but Karen had insisted on staying here with the rest of his family, so his relatives wouldn't think he assumed he was better than them. Who cared what they thought? Most of them envied his success anyway. It was lonely at the top.

Sighing, he used the remote control to click on the television.

In the bathroom, Karen screamed.

Two yellow jackets had taken hold of the bathroom. While Anthony and Karen watched from outside, the door open only an inch, the insects circled between the mirror and tub. Big suckers.

"They flew out of the drain when I turned on the

water." Karen huddled beside him, a bath towel wrapped around her. "You have to kill them, Tony. I'm allergic to bee stings."

"Allergic?" He frowned. "Are you serious?"

She nodded, her eyes huge and scared. "The last time I was stung, six years ago, I was helping Mom in the garden. A hornet got me on the arm, and my face swelled up like a balloon. Mom had to take me to the emergency room."

Anthony sneered. His wife was allergic to stings; he was scared to death of the beasts that could sting you. Weren't they a well-matched couple?

He certainly wasn't going to share the secret of his phobia with her now. It was time for him to be the man of the house. Moments like this defined marriages.

"Go back in the bedroom, honey," he said. "I'll take care of this. I'll let you know when I'm done."

She smiled gratefully and left.

He peered into the bathroom. The yellow jackets soared through the air leisurely, as if they owned the place. In the tub, hot water continued to gurgle from the faucet; if Karen had stopped up the drain, the tub surely would have overflowed by then. A fine vapor, borne of the steaming water, had begun to cloud the room.

The insects' buzzing seemed to thrum in his eardrums. Two yellow jackets. Christ.

Although the room was as humid as a tropical rain forest, he grabbed his jacket from the closet, slid it on, and zipped it up. He was wearing shorts, so he threw on his jeans, too. He slapped on his Atlanta Braves cap.

It was as much bodily protection as he could manage at the moment. He would've preferred a beekeeper's suit.

He found a copy of *USA Today* sitting by the door. He rolled it up, fashioning it into a billy club.

Then, he crept into the bathroom.

Hot vapor churned in the air. The gurgling water in the tub was thunderously loud.

But the yellow jackets were gone.

"You can't hide from me, you bastards," Anthony muttered. They were in there, somewhere. He could feel them watching him, waiting to attack.

His fingers tightened on his newspaper club.

Moving quickly, he stepped to the tub and switched off the faucet. He wanted to clear the air.

As he was turning away from the bathtub, a yellow jacket zoomed toward him from above, like a miniature fighter plane.

Crying out, he swung the club wildly. The paper smacked the insect and knocked it into the mirror, but in the process of swinging, Anthony lost his balance, slipped on a patch of water, and tumbled into the bathtub.

"Shit!"

Hot water splashing everywhere, he rapped his head against the edge of the ceramic basin. He would have passed out, but fear kept him awake. There was one yellow jacket left, and it was waiting to make a move on him.

"Is everything okay, Tony?" Karen asked from the other side of the door.

"I'll be out in a minute!" he shouted. His cap had flipped off, and he pulled it on again.

Soggy and dripping, his head aching, he dragged himself out of the tub. He caught a glimpse of himself in the foggy mirror—Anthony Morris, Esquire, going through hell over a couple of bees—and he was briefly embarrassed. But his embarrassment faded when he heard the loud, angry buzzing.

It was coming from right on top of his head.

Underneath his baseball cap.

Shouting and cursing, he snatched off the hat. He saw the yellow jacket creeping inside the cap. Gritting his teeth savagely, he smashed the edges of the cap together in his hands, to squash the evil insect inside.

"I've got you now, bastard! I've got you!" He laughed maniacally.

The insect buzzed furiously, trying to escape.

Anthony moved to the toilet. Like a man handling a hot potato, he flipped over the hat and cast it into the water. Then he flushed the toilet.

The sight of the bee being sucked out of the hat and into the bowels of the sewage system was one of the sweetest things he'd seen all day.

The departed yellow jacket's fallen comrade lay on the vanity at the base of the mirror. Dead. Anthony captured it in a wad of tissue and, after removing his cap from the toilet, flushed away that one, too.

He grinned. "You fools don't know who you're messing with."

He peeled off his wet clothes. He was quite pleased with himself. It had been a tough battle, but he had won. He always won, in the end.

Now that he had saved the day, he thought with a smile, Karen would feel obligated to give him some loving before she went to bed.

He left the bathroom.

And found Karen pressed in a corner of the room, her hand covering her mouth, her attention fixed on something near the ceiling light.

"They came out of nowhere," Karen said in a shaky

voice. "One minute, I was watching TV, the next, I heard buzzing above me . . ."

There were four or five hornets up there. Gigantic ones, each the size of his pinkie. They flew in a tight circle, buzzing.

Anthony felt as if his legs had been swept from under him. This couldn't be happening. Were there hives in the walls?

"We're getting the hell out of here," he said. "Throw on some clothes and grab your stuff, honey. I'm going to talk to the manager."

By the time Anthony finished chewing out the manager on duty at the front desk, not only had the manager given them a new, upgraded room on the other side of the hotel, he had agreed to charge Anthony for only one night's stay, not two. One of the many advantages of being a top-notch attorney was knowing exactly what to say to make virtually anyone fear a lawsuit. He had mastered the art of hurling legal jargon to terrify, to reduce the average citizen to a blubbering, eager-to-please fool.

Their new room was a deluxe suite, but it still wasn't as nice as the Hyatt. Anthony didn't care anymore. He only wanted to sleep and drive home tomorrow. At least the air conditioner worked.

When he turned the handle in the tub, the water flowed cleanly. No bees.

No wasps or any like creatures buzzed around the lights, either.

The room appeared to be safe.

However, something nagged at him. As he showered, he began to think.

Why hadn't they seen any bees last night? The

night before, not one bug had invaded their room. Why so many today? If there were, indeed, hives in the room's walls, wouldn't the hateful insects have revealed themselves from the start?

Anthony knew he was an especially smart man— brilliant, even. He had graduated summa cum laude at the University of Georgia, and third in his class at Emory Law School. He was accustomed to being envied for his intellect and flawless education. In his opinion, a handful of people, like him, were simply better equipped than the average person to achieve success and solve problems. He was a member of the vaunted Talented Tenth, one of the leaders of the ignorant masses.

But even his refined intelligence could not explain this bee situation. He didn't like being unable to explain things. Ignorance was not bliss—it was weakness.

Karen was asleep by the time he stretched out beside her on the bed. He was too worn-out to ask for any loving.

He clicked off the bedside lamp and lay with his hands folded behind his head. One minute, he was gazing at the dark ceiling, pondering the inexplicable insects . . . and the next, he was dreaming. In the dream, he was once again at the family reunion picnic, serving as gatekeeper. The old woman, Sis Maggie, suddenly appeared in front of him, this time without her guide girl. He asked her why she was there when he had already told her that she wasn't a friend of the family. And when she parted her lips to answer, a swarm of hornets poured out of her mouth, buzzing madly, and they enveloped him like a storm cloud; covered his face and neck and arms and legs and crawled up his nostrils and into his ears and between his lips, stinging and stinging and stinging—

He erupted from the nightmare, shouting and flailing his arms.

"Baby, you okay?" Karen touched his shoulder.

He was panting, dipped in cold sweat. He thought he felt insects creeping over his arms, and he rubbed his skin. Nothing there. Just a dream.

But he thought he heard a faint buzzing, as if the creatures from his nightmare had followed him into the real world. Was he imagining the sound?

"Tony?" she asked, sitting up.

"I'm fine," he said. "It was only a dream."

"About what?"

"Oh, that old heifer who came to the picnic, Sis Maggie. It's nothing, go back to sleep."

"You pissed off that root woman," Karen mumbled, drifting back to sleep. "Now she's sending you nightmares . . ."

"That's nonsense."

But Karen had fallen asleep. Anthony, however, was too wound up to rest. Keeping the light off, he slid out of bed.

The ghostly buzzing did not subside, which meant that it was not a figment of his imagination. He turned around, trying to determine the source of the noise. He walked toward the window. The buzzing grew louder with each step.

Hands trembling, he parted the curtains.

Honeybees covered the window. Dozens of them. They wriggled and swarmed across the glass, their strange, beady eyes fixated on him.

It took all of his strength for him to stay on his feet.

"This is impossible," he said, in a whisper. "It's night,

bees aren't nocturnal creatures, they're supposed to be asleep . . ." His voice trailed off. His throat was tight.

Slowly, he put his hand against the glass.

The bees buzzed angrily. They stabbed their stingers against the window.

They were eager to get him, to sting him to death. Just like in his nightmare.

Legs trembling, he snatched the curtains shut.

The buzzing ceased.

Terrified, but curious, he peeled away part of the curtain.

The window was clear. It gave him a view of the parking lot, the highway beyond, and the pale moon above. There were no bees, anywhere.

Which was impossible. The insects could not have vanished instantaneously.

Chills overcame him. He stumbled to the bed and wrapped himself in the sheets.

His aunt's voice came to him: *You shouldn't have done that to Sis Maggie, Tony. That old woman is known for working roots—and she holds terrible grudges.*

Backwoods superstitious bullshit, Anthony told himself, over and over. *Bullshit, bullshit, bullshit. I'm too smart to believe that nonsense. I'm too good for that. There has to be a logical explanation, there has to be.*

But by the time he finally fell asleep, an hour later, he still had not found it.

"Tony, did you get any sleep last night?" Karen asked, as they got dressed the next morning. "Your eyes are bloodshot."

"This bed kept me tossing and turning." He slid on his Nikes and began to tie them. "This mattress is like a slab of rock."

Her eyes were concerned. "Hmmm, I slept fine. You think it's because of the nightmares you were having? You kept waking up—"

"No," he said, and yanked the shoelaces so tightly they nearly snapped.

Karen sighed loudly and went into the bathroom.

He knew that she was annoyed at him for not sharing what was on his mind. Well, tough. He wasn't the kind of guy who talked about his emotions— as far as he was concerned, doing so was a sign of weakness. He dealt in facts. If it couldn't be proven, it wasn't worth his time.

So if it looks like an old, evil woman has slapped a curse on me, is that worth my time?

He shut down that train of thought before it inched forward any further.

He finished dressing, downed a cup of the vile-tasting coffee they supplied in the hotel room—due to him getting so little sleep, he'd need to slam his system with caffeine to stay awake—and grabbed their luggage to take down to the car.

"Be ready to go in five minutes," he told Karen, who was still messing around in the bathroom. Of course, she probably wouldn't be ready in five minutes. The woman was so habitually slow she'd be late to her own funeral.

When he opened the door, before stepping out, he checked both ways for bees, wasps, anything like that. All he saw was a monarch butterfly fluttering nearby. Good.

He reached the parking lot without incident, too.

Their black Mercedes Benz sedan shimmered in the morning sunlight, the shiny surface pearled with dew. A glance around the parking lot confirmed that he owned—by far—the most expensive vehicle on the premises. It was a reassuring feeling, like finding out that an old, favorite pair of slacks still fit comfortably. He was back in charge.

Smiling, he pressed the button on the key chain to unlock the trunk.

He had lifted the trunk lid a couple of inches before he heard the furious buzzing, coming from deep inside. As if a monstrous hive awaited within.

No, it can't be. Yesterday was just like an unexplainable, bad dream. It can't be happening again today.

He quickly slammed the trunk shut. He took a step away from the car.

"What is happening to me?" he muttered. "What in the hell is happening?"

He remembered what happened last night, after they had switched hotel rooms. They had not found any bees in the room, but he had dreamed of that hag, Sis Maggie; and saw a swarm of hornets pour from her black mouth.

And then he had looked out the window and found it completely covered by bees, in the middle of the night. When he looked again a moment later, the insects had vanished. As if he had been hallucinating.

He would have preferred that the bees had been real. The possibility that he was losing his mind was terrifying.

"I am not going insane," he told himself. "I'm too smart for that, I graduated at the top of my class from Emory Law, I'm a top-notch corporate attorney, I earn over—"

"Tony, I thought you'd be ready to go. What are you doing?"

It was Karen. He hadn't realized that she had approached. She stood in front of their car, wearing a puzzled expression.

He stammered. "Uh, I was—"

"Come on, we have to go or we'll be late for breakfast." She plucked the keys out of his hand and pressed the button to unlock the trunk. "Why didn't you load the bags in the car?"

He had frozen, his gaze riveted on the trunk. Karen reached for the lid.

"Don't do that!" he shouted.

He was too late. Karen had opened it.

But the trunk held only a couple of small plastic bags, a pair of Karen's sandals, and an Igloo cooler.

No buzzing beehive.

As was their family tradition, the day after the big cookout, they always had Sunday breakfast for those who would be driving out of town that day. His Aunt Janice hosted the gathering at her home in Hernando.

Tony sat in a quiet corner of the living room, a paper plate heaped with congealing eggs, cold bacon, and stiff grits sitting at his feet. He had no appetite. How could he eat when he was clearly in danger of losing his mind?

He couldn't wait to get home and lose himself in the familiar world of his law office, where order ruled.

Ever the busy hostess, Aunt Janice spotted him and came over, probably to nag him about isolating himself from the rest of the family, most of whom were enjoying breakfast outdoors.

"I just talked to your wife, Tony," Aunt Janice said. "She tells me you were having nightmares about Sis Maggie."

He dragged his hand down his face. Karen could never keep her mouth shut.

"I'm fine, all right? I just need to get back home."

Aunt Janice's brow creased. "These nightmares are a bad sign, sugar. You ticked off that old woman yesterday, and I told you that she works roots and holds terrible grudges. She's worked some kinda evil spell on you."

"Evil spell? Come on, don't tell me that you believe that backwoods superstitious crap."

Aunt Janice shook her head. "Doesn't matter whether you believe it or not—that old lady's powerful. You'd best find her and apologize, that's the only way you might put an end—"

"I've heard enough of this nonsense, I'm ready to hit the road," he said, and stood abruptly. "Where's my wife?"

"She's outside—"

Anthony marched out of the house. He found his wife on the patio, sipping orange juice and talking to one of his younger cousins, a girl who was only twenty-three, a college dropout, and had something like five or six kids. Relatives like her were an embarrassment to him. He couldn't even remember the girl's name.

Karen was probably blabbing about his nightmares to her, too.

A breeze blew, carrying the aroma of smothered potatoes to him, and his stomach growled, unexpectedly. He hadn't eaten a thing since last night. He needed to eat something before they left.

I'll grab a quick bite to eat, he thought. *Then we're getting the hell out of here.*

The breakfast food was spread on a long table at the edge of the patio. He picked up a paper plate and reached for the potatoes, which simmered in a lidded silver pot.

When he removed the cover, he discovered that the potatoes were infested with crawling wasps.

He yelped.

Like missles, the wasps launched off the pungent base of smothered spuds and buzzed through the air.

Anthony stumbled backward, waving his arms wildly, violating every rule of how to respond to angry wasps.

But they didn't attack him. They darted toward his wife.

"Karen, look out!" he shouted, but his voice, strangled by terror, came out in a hoarse whisper.

Probably drawn by the sight of him waving his arms, Karen looked up.

By then, it was too late.

She dropped her glass of orange juice. It shattered when it hit the patio, a nerve-jarring sound.

But it wasn't as bad as her scream when the wasps attacked her.

At a medical center in town, Karen lay on a bed, pumped up with drugs to counteract the wasps' venom. Her face was puffy, as if her skin were made of self-rising flour. She hardly resembled the pretty woman that he had married.

Karen was asleep, and had been for over an hour. Anthony paced across the room. Numerous relatives, including his Aunt Janice, were huddled around the bed, speaking in hushed tones.

In his rational mind, Anthony had dismissed the wasp attack as coincidence. The things just happened to be in the potatoes, and they were drawn to his wife, maybe because of her perfume. It was a terrible occurrence, but there was nothing particularly unusual about it.

You're lying to yourself, a pesky voice in his mind whispered. *Those wasps were the work of the root woman. She sent them to torment you. Admit it. You don't know what the hell you're dealing with.*

He put a lid on that voice. It was nonsense. He was an educated man and ought to know better.

At least his wife's prognosis was encouraging. According to the doctor, she should be recovered and ready to leave for Atlanta by tomorrow.

Still, he hated the thought of spending one more night in this wretched place of suffering, one more night of bad dreams about that old woman—

Anthony caught a snippet of his family's conversation. He stopped in his tracks.

"Did you say something about Sis Maggie?" he asked.

Aunt Janice bobbed her head. "You've got to apologize to that woman, Tony. She did this to you and your wife."

Hot blood surged to Anthony's face.

He pointed to the door. "Everyone, get out. Now."

"But—" Aunt Janice started.

"Out!" Anthony was trembling.

His family quietly shuffled out of the room. He shut the door.

"Apologize to Sis Maggie," he mumbled. "I don't apologize to anyone. Sis Maggie can kiss my ass."

Karen's eyelids fluttered. He rushed to her side.

She said something in a whisper. He leaned down closer, to hear her.

"What did you say, honey?" he asked.

"This is . . . your fault, Tony," Karen said in a weak

voice that nevertheless carried an undercurrent of anger. "Do . . . what your aunt says."

He rose, his back rigid.

Karen blinked slowly, but resentment glinted in her red-rimmed eyes. Even his wife agreed with his family. Okay then.

"Fine," he said at last. "I'll find out where the old heifer lives and get this over with."

Anthony was deep in the country, driving on a narrow, bumpy road. Aunt Janice had given him directions to the old hag's house. No one offered to come with him. They were scared.

"Ignorant fools," he muttered. He drew to a halt at a STOP sign, and consulted the directions that lay on his lap.

He was about to turn left, when he looked in the rearview mirror and saw a black cloud rolling toward him.

A swarm of bees.

His fingers clutched the steering wheel in a death grip.

I can't take any more of this. Why won't they leave me alone? I'm on my way to apologize to the old heifer!

The buzzing was thunderous. The Mercedes hummed in unison with the insects.

He jammed the accelerator. The tires shrieked, and the car swerved crazily to the left. He barely avoided plunging into a ditch.

The bees chased after him.

You bastards aren't going to catch me. I didn't spend seventy grand on this car for nothing.

Teeth gritted, he kept the gas pedal mashed to the floor. The engine roared.

The swarm receded, and soon became a black dot in the mirror.

But the bees were still out there, pursuing him. He had to take advantage of his lead.

Thankfully, Sis Maggie's place was around the next bend. He veered around the curve, and found himself in a long, dusty driveway. An old black Cadillac was parked in front of the tiny house.

"Let's get this over with," he said. He rocked to a halt beside the Cadillac, and hurried out of the car.

He glanced down the driveway.

The dark swarm rumbled around the corner. Hundreds of bees.

He was certain that they would sting him to death.

He raced to the front door. He twisted the knob.

He didn't bother to knock. To hell with good manners. He didn't have time.

The door opened. He plunged inside, slammed the door behind him.

He found himself in a cramped, dark living room. A shadowy shape sat in an overstuffed chair in the corner.

The air smelled strongly of exotic spices and herbs. Stuff he couldn't even name.

The shape across the room shifted.

"Sis Maggie?" Anthony asked, hesitantly.

"What do you want, boy?" the elderly woman asked. Her voice was brittle. "Did you bring me a plate of ribs from yesterday?"

"Uh, no." He struggled to find words—a new experience for him. Usually he knew exactly what to say to get what he wanted from someone. "I've been having, uh, this problem . . . with bees."

Sis Maggie leaned forward on her cane. "You

think I worked some roots to make them bees and such give you hell?"

He shrugged. "My family seems to think that's the case."

"I wanna know what you think."

I think it's a bunch of backwoods superstitious bullshit, he wanted to say, but didn't. *And I think they believe you're some kind of witch, but in reality you're just an old, ugly woman who badly needs dentures.* But he didn't say that, either.

What he said was this: "Honestly, I don't really know what to think. But I know why I came. I'm here to apologize, Sis Maggie. I treated you badly yesterday, and I'm sorry. I hope that you can forgive me."

Sis Maggie cackled, as if he had said the most humorous thing in the world.

Her anorexic-looking guide girl appeared in the hallway, glanced at Anthony, and looked at Sis Maggie with concern.

Wiping her eyes, still laughing, the old lady waved her away; the girl withdrew.

"I'll take away the bees," Sis Maggie said. She chuckled. "I know they were scaring you somethin' terrible. Everybody's scared of somethin'. Some of us are scared of a whole bunch of things."

"Thank you," he said. He blew out a deep breath.

Sis Maggie giggled, like a child. He didn't see what was so funny. Maybe she was just plain crazy.

"Well . . . good-bye," he said. He bowed slightly, and turned to the door.

She was still giggling when he stepped outside. Old, demented woman. He doubted whether she really possessed any magical powers at all. She was just strange. Here in the Deep South, ignorant people probably equated strangeness with someone having supernatural gifts—being able to give the evil eye, work roots, or some such nonsense.

However, the swarm of bees had vanished.

He climbed in his Mercedes. He drove out of the driveway and rolled back onto the road.

No bees followed him.

"It's over," he said. He laughed, but it was a stress-relief laugh. "I can't wait to get the hell out of this place."

He reached to crank up the air conditioner. Refreshing, cool air hissed from the vents.

Then he frowned.

Something behind him was hissing, too.

He looked over his shoulder.

He immediately felt as though someone had poured ice water down his pants.

An emerald green snake was coiled on the backseat.

Cursing, he wrestled the steering wheel, forcing the car to the shoulder of the road.

Before he could reach for the door handle, a creature—long, black, and serpentine—slipped out of the dashboard air vent. Hissing.

Snakes, snakes, oh, shit, there's nothing worse than snakes, not even bees and wasps and hornets can compare to snakes.

And he knew then, in a horrible instant, why Sis Maggie had been laughing when he'd left. She had not lifted the spell. She'd only changed it. To torment him with his number-one fear in the world.

Something warm and oily slithered up his leg.

Another one wriggled under his shirt collar, slid down his back.

Anthony lost all conscious thought, forgot all his years of fine education and legal training. He opened his mouth, and screamed . . . and screamed . . . and screamed . . .

After the Party

When Terry was halfway along the twisting, dark country road, he looked in his rearview mirror and saw a frightening sight: the flashing blue lights of a police cruiser.

"Damn, I don't believe this," he said. "He better not be coming for me."

But at two thirty in the morning, his was the only vehicle on the desolate road. It was a pretty fair bet that the cop was coming for him, and him alone.

Terry took one of his hands away from the steering wheel, blew into it. His lips curled. The sour smell of alcohol was thick on his breath.

"Shit," he muttered. But he wasn't surprised. At the Halloween party, he'd had a lot to drink. Three Heinekens . . . two Rum and Cokes . . . two Hennesseys . . . and more. His memory of exactly what he had drunk was foggy—as it always was when he was smashed.

On the stereo, an Outkast song thumped at a bone-jarring volume. Listening to loud music was one of his tricks to make it safely home after he'd had too much to drink. It kept him alert.

But the music wasn't enough to save him tonight. He should have known better than to be out on the road in a drunken daze on Halloween night. Johnny Nabb (his uncle referred to all cops by that dubious name, and Terry had picked it up) would surely be out in force, cruising for suckers like him.

He'd fallen right into the trap. Shit.

The cop car veered up to his rear bumper, and sounded a sharp horn that made Terry jump. The beacon's blue lights whirled around, shining into Terry's car like some crazy disco strobe light.

Biting his lip, Terry slowed his Nissan Maxima. He pulled to the shoulder of the road.

With a trembling hand, he shut off the stereo.

The last time he'd been pulled over was two years ago, for speeding. He'd gotten away with a fine and a slap on the wrist from the judge. He'd never had a DUI, in spite of driving home drunk at least a dozen times. DUI was a serious trespass in Georgia.

But if you got away once without being caught, you always thought you could pull it off again. His apartment was only twenty minutes away, after all, and the country road was a shortcut, and it wasn't as though he was falling-down drunk. He floated in that dreamy, slow-motion world that existed somewhere between Tipsyville and Truly Wastedland.

But he was definitely over the legal limit, and he knew it.

He should have accepted Nikki's invitation to stay at her place for a while, to sober up. But she'd gotten on his last nerve at the party, following him around as if she were a lovesick puppy and getting all in his mix while he tried to hang with his boys. He couldn't tolerate another minute of her company. Clingy females like her made him sick. They reminded him of his mother.

Still, her company would've been better than his upcoming date with Johnny Nabb.

Behind him, the police car waited like a hungry beast, headlights glaring. The cop was probably running Terry's license plate through the system. He wouldn't find anything, but the thought didn't comfort Terry. Driving While Black was enough to land your ass in jail for something—anything Johnny Nabb could dream up to nail you. And his being drunk didn't help his case at all. Although he was rapidly sobering up.

The worst part was that he was still dressed in his costume. He'd gone to the party as Blade the Vampire Slayer. He had the long black-leather jacket, the boots, the gloves—all the gear. Instead of a real sword, a plastic blade dangled from a loop on his belt.

He could only imagine being hauled to the county lockup dressed like this.

He never should've gone to the stupid party in the first place. He should've rented some horror movies and stayed home. But he'd been excited about showing off Nikki, who, for all her clinginess, was fine as hell, and looked great in her tight, black-leather vampiress outfit.

The fellas had asked him about her all night, and it had stroked his ego to respond, "Yeah, man. She's mine, I've got that girl strung out on me . . ."

What the hell's taking that cop so long? he asked himself. The asshole still hadn't gotten out of the car. He was probably sitting back there chomping on a doughnut, knowing that he was making Terry sweat and enjoying every second of it.

God, he hated cops.

Not a single vehicle had passed since he'd been pulled over. Thick, dark woods crowded both sides of the road. There were no streetlamps out here, and a cape of purple-black clouds concealed the moon. The only light radiated from the police car's headlights.

Anything could happen out there, between him and the cop. And no one would know.

Okay, don't think about stuff like that, he warned himself. *You're freaking yourself out. There's still a way out of this.*

He remembered the Certs in his cup holder. His hands shook so badly it took three tries for him to pop the mint into his dry mouth.

He might not fool Johnny Nabb into thinking he was sober, but he had to try.

Behind him, the cruiser's door finally swung open. A tall, beefy cop climbed out. He strutted toward Terry's car, as if he had the world on a leash.

Remember, be respectful, and enunciate crisply, Terry told himself. *You can talk your way out of this. You've got to convince this cop that you're sober.*

The police officer tapped on the glass with a fat finger.

"Mister, please roll down the window, will ya?" The cop had a thick Georgia accent.

Terry pressed the button to lower the glass. Chilly air swept into the car.

"Yes, sir?" Terry asked.

"I spotted ya weaving over the line back there." The cop hooked his thumb behind him, then bent closer. "You been drinkin', buddy?"

"No, sir. I'm only tired, it's late."

"Where ya comin from?"

"Um . . . a party."

The cop's penetrating blue eyes raked over him. "A costume party? What you got on there?"

"Uh, I'm supposed to be Blade. You know, the vampire slayer from the movie?"

"The flick with that black boy, Wesley something?"

"Yeah, that one."

The cop grinned. It wasn't a pleasant smile. "Gimme your license and registration, Blade."

Here we go, Terry thought. *I'm fucked. First, I hand him this stuff, next he'll be asking me to get out of the car to take a Breathalyzer test, which I'll fail, and after that, I'll be riding in the back of his cruiser on the way to the Clayton County Jail.*

Terry dug the registration out of the glove compartment and slid his driver's license out of his wallet.

The cop snatched the items out of his grasp and stuffed them into his pocket without so much as a glance at them.

Something isn't right here, a voice cautioned in the quiet, sober part of Terry's mind. *Something about this policeman isn't quite right.*

But when the cop stepped back and commanded Terry to get out of the car, Terry hesitated only a second before he obeyed. He was a law-abiding citizen, and the policeman was an authority figure. No black man in his right mind resisted arrest or caused conflict with an officer. Look at what had happened to Rodney King.

"Wait by the car, Blade," the officer said with a smirk. He strolled back to the cruiser.

Terry stood beside the car. He didn't feel drunk anymore. Nothing sobered you up as much as knowing that you probably were going to jail.

Beyond the circle of light cast by the cop car's

headlamps, the night seemed to shift, like a living thing. Terry found himself staring at a spot in the dark woods, maybe a hundred yards away. He had the oddest feeling that something was out there, watching him, just as he was watching it. He felt the weight of a sentient creature's gaze, like a pressure on his forehead.

It's an owl, he thought. Or a raccoon. Something like that. The forest is full of living shit.

But he shuddered.

He was almost relieved when the cop returned.

"Okay, tell it to me straight," the officer said. "How much did you drink at the party?"

Terry shrugged. "A couple of beers. Not much."

"That's all, eh? The punishment for DUI is stiff in Georgia, buddy. But there are worse things than a DUI. Much, much worse." His pale lips twisted into a strange smile.

"I've never had a DUI," Terry said. "You pulled up my record, you know it's true."

"You mean, you've never been caught," the cop said.

Terry didn't respond. Why had he thought he could fool this guy? Johnny Nabb put the hook on suckers like him all the time. He wasn't special.

The cop threw open the door to Terry's car. He removed the key from the ignition, and then slammed the door.

"Are you taking me in to the station?" Terry asked. "Aren't you supposed to give me a sobriety test first?"

Without answering, the cop pressed the button on the key chain to activate the door locks. The locks snapped down.

"Do I have to get someone to tow my car?" Terry asked.

The cop wound up his arm like a baseball pitcher. He hurled the keys into the woods. They tinkled somewhere in the darkness.

"Hey, what the hell are you doing?" Terry asked.

A deep laugh bellowed from the policeman. Laughing, he turned to Terry, and in the bright light, Terry saw the purplish bite marks on the side of the cop's pale neck: two small puncture wounds positioned on the jugular vein.

Terry didn't believe his eyes. Surely, he wasn't as sober as he thought he'd become. He had to be imagining things.

"The master will be pleased with you," the policeman said, in an oddly formal voice, as though he was repeating words that he had memorized. "Quite pleased, indeed."

"What are you talking about? What's going on? Is this a joke?"

Chuckling, backing away, the policeman shook his head. "Good luck out here, Blade."

"Where are you going? I thought you were arresting me!"

Still laughing, the cop hopped in his cruiser.

"You can't leave me out here!" Terry ran toward the car.

The vehicle sped forward. He jumped aside and grabbed at the passenger door handle. But his sweaty hands slipped away.

The patrol car shot down the road. Soon, the red taillights dwindled into darkness. Deep silence fell over the night.

"Help!" Terry shouted. "Someone help me!"

His shouts echoed into the woods, uselessly. There was no one out here to help him. He was alone.

Well, not quite alone.

His gaze shifted to the dark patch of forest that had claimed his attention earlier.

Something had been out there watching him. It was still watching him. He felt it as surely as he felt the cold October air on his face.

"Who's out there?" he asked, in a cracked voice.

The darkness did not reply. But something out there, a large, shadowy shape, edged closer.

Within a heartbeat, it was rushing toward him.

I don't believe what I'm seeing, but it's got to be real, because now I'm pissing my pants.

Weak-kneed, he reached down, and drew his flimsy plastic sword . . .

The Secret Door

"All I can say is, I hope you do a better job up here than that last loser did," Mr. Green said.

He marched down the wide, carpeted corridor like a drill sergeant on his way to boot camp. Mark, pushing the wheeled cart stocked with janitorial supplies, struggled to keep up.

It was a few minutes after seven o'clock in the evening. The hallways and offices of Adams Laboratories were silent. The only sounds were the occasional squeaking of the wheels on Mark's cart, and, distantly, a vacuum cleaner humming somewhere else on the fifth floor, another janitor at work.

The cold March night pressed against the large windows on his left. Mark caught his reflection in the glass—hunched over a trash can, wearing a blue CORPORATE HOUSEKEEPING uniform, sweat gleaming on his dark brown face—and quickly looked away.

Even after working there for three months, he had never quite gotten used to seeing himself as a janitor. Being somewhere like this in his first year out of high school hadn't been in his plans.

"There's honor in honest work," he said, under hi'

breath. It was one of his mom's favorite sayings and repeating it usually bolstered his mood, but that time, it made him think poignantly of her, five months dead, and such a tide of grief washed over him that the cart abruptly felt as heavy as a barrel of bricks.

He drew in a deep breath, regained his strength.

The corridor terminated in a dead end, a featureless gray wall. Mr. Green halted in front of the nearby men and women's restrooms. Light shone on his bald pate; he had an almost perfectly round head that reminded Mark of a polished bowling ball.

"You'll start with these," Mr. Green said crisply. "They're like the restrooms on the third floor, which you were doing before. There are a total of six restrooms on this level that you're responsible for cleaning. The layout of this floor is exactly the same as your previous floor."

Mark nodded; none of this was news. Practically every level of the ten-story building was the same, down to the location of the soda machines in the vending areas. Mr. Green had an annoying habit of explaining matters with which his employees were already well familiar—one of the many reasons why Mark disliked the man.

Mr. Green pointed at the blue door across the hallway. The door, nestled within a recessed, shadowy space in the wall, resembled the entrance to a secret tunnel.

"That's your supply closet. The key you already have will fit in the lock. Now, let me tell you something." Mr. Green cleared his throat, yanking up his baggy slacks over his swollen belly.

Leaning against the cart, Mark waited.

"The loser who worked on this floor before you

had the bright idea that just because the supply closet was pretty well hidden, he could dick around in there during his shift and whittle away the time." A cruel smile twisted Mr. Green's face. "Don't you even think about it. He wasn't slick. I caught him in there once, playing a goddamn Game Boy. I docked the loser's paycheck pretty good for that."

There was another thing Mark disliked about Mr. Green: he showed no awareness of each employee's work record. Mark was a top performer who always finished his restrooms early and pitched in to help others, but here this guy was, talking to him as if he was some lazy bum who needed to be micromanaged. Man, this guy worked his nerves.

"You don't have to worry about me doing that," Mark said.

Mr. Green tapped his temple with his sausage-thick finger. "The king has a thousand eyes, Markie. Remember that. Don't ever let me catch you slacking off."

The last time I checked, my name was Mark, not Markie, he wanted to say. But he only asked, "What ever happened to Bobby, anyway?"

"The jerk off quit in the middle of his shift," Mr. Green said. Indignation colored his face red. "Left his supplies in the middle of the hallway, and walked out. No one even saw the loser leave. I had to come up here myself to clean the restrooms!"

Mark shook his head, as if this was the worst thought imaginable, when in fact he would love nothing more than to see Mr. Green on his knees scrubbing a toilet bowl.

Mr. Green clapped his hands. "Now, no more small talk. It's time to get to work. You're already behind, Markie, and I was thinking of you dropping

down to the third floor when you're done to clean
some offices there, too. You're so good you can do
the work of two people!"

Grinning like a shark, Mr. Green patted Mark on
the shoulder and strode down the hallway.

"Asshole," Mark muttered under his breath. Sighing, he pushed his cart closer to the janitor's closet.
He needed to load up on disinfectant, toilet tissue,
and other supplies. Once he started cleaning, he
didn't like to stop to restock his cart.

An elevator beep echoed down the corridor, most
likely the sound of Mr. Green leaving.

Mark unlocked the closet door.

It looked like an ordinary supply closet. Lit by a
bank of pale yellow fluorescent lights, it was an eight-
foot by ten-foot room, with a scuffed tile floor. Large
cardboard boxes containing rolls of toilet tissue were
stacked along the walls, as high as the ceiling. Bottles
of disinfectants were arranged in neat groups across
the floor, and boxes of garbage bags, paper towels,
soap, and other items stood in random piles.

There was nowhere to sit and play a Game Boy,
even if Mark had been so inclined.

As he began to stock his cart, his thoughts wandered into a favorite daydream: He was fabulously
wealthy, living the charmed life of a best-selling nov-
elist. He owned a mansion in a tony Chicago suburb
and drove a Mercedes coupe. He'd purchased a
nice house for his still-alive mother, and she had di-
vorced his stepfather. Invitations to exclusive parties
flooded his mailbox. He did book signings around
the country, and at every store, eager fans lined up

in droves to get his signature on his latest top-selling masterpiece. He had a beautiful wife who—

Suddenly, as he was pulling a twenty-pound box of toilet tissue away from a stack, it slipped out of his grasp and crashed onto his foot.

"Ouch! Dammit!"

He propped his smashed foot atop the next box in the stack. He removed his shoe and sock. A red blotch throbbed on his big toe. It would develop into a helluva bruise, but at least his toe wasn't broken.

"Too bad it's not broken, maybe I could sue." He chuckled. What would Mr. Green have thought of that?

He checked his watch. Twenty minutes after seven and he hadn't even started cleaning yet. He had to get moving. The injured toe wouldn't slow him down much.

He had put his shoe back on and was about to move away when he glimpsed a small, shiny object wedged between the stack of boxes and the wall. The shadows back there were too deep for him to discern exactly what he was looking at.

He nudged the boxes a few inches, being careful not to knock them over. Then he reached into the blackness, grabbed the object, and brought it into the light.

It was a Game Boy.

Frowning, Mark held the miniature video game player in his hands.

According to Mr. Green, he had once caught Bobby, the last janitor to work on this floor, nested inside the supply closet, playing a Game Boy. It only followed that this belonged to him. No one else would have a reason to go into the room.

Why would Bobby have left this in here? Game Boys weren't cheap. It wasn't the kind of thing you forgot and left behind—no matter how much of a rush you were in to quit your job.

He peered behind the boxes, wondering if Bobby might have forgotten something else back there, too.

He didn't find anything else, but he noticed something odd: there seemed to be an indentation in the brick wall, about four inches deep. The niche began at the floor, and was about three feet high.

Mark pushed the boxes farther away from the wall, to get a better view of the area.

Shifting the boxes revealed that the recessed section was about three feet wide, too. Like a large trash chute.

Mark knelt, and laid his fingers against the depression.

"Oooh." He jerked his hand away. The bricks were as cold as a slab of ice.

Was there some kind of cooler back there? No, that didn't make any sense. Who would build a cooler in a supply closet?

He heard, suddenly, a soft hiss, like air escaping a sealed tomb.

Then, a grinding-scraping sound. The recessed panel appeared to be gliding away, receding into the darkness—as if it was a door that had been activated by his touch.

Keeping a safe distance, he stared at the portal—if that's what it was—his heart knocking.

Cold air billowed from the aperture. His breath fogged in front of him.

I'm not seeing this, he told himself.

It was not possible for there to be a door on this wall that led to anywhere. This was the far east side of the building, the very end. Knocking out the wall would place him above the parking lot.

Yet when he gazed inside the doorway, it seemed to possess depth, as if the darkness beyond the entrance stretched on for a great distance.

He heard, faintly, a wind whispering in the tunnel.

He ripped open a box of toilet tissue. He lifted a roll, and set it spinning like a wheel through the portal.

A few seconds later, a soft thwack echoed back at him, clearly the sound of the object losing its momentum and falling onto its side somewhere deep within.

As he was trying to reason how this could be possible—and finding no explanations—the panel floated back into its slot in the wall with a soft scraping sound, though the indentation remained.

The roll of tissue remained on the other side. Wherever that was.

For the rest of his shift, Mark avoided the supply closet. He drove home in a daze, around midnight.

The Game Boy lay on the passenger seat beside him.

While at work, he'd taken the allowed fifteen-minute break in the vending area on the fifth floor. As he leaned against the wall chewing a Snickers bar and sipping a Coke, Sandy, a stout, middle-aged white woman who cleaned the offices on the floor, wandered inside.

"Break time for you, too, huh?" Mark asked.

"Damn right," Sandy said in a smoky voice. She stretched. "My back's killing me."

"Hey, I was wondering if you knew Bobby, the guy who used to work on this floor?"

She fed quarters into the soda machine. "Nah, not

really. Know he split town, though. I heard that the day after he quit, his girlie called here looking for him. Sounds like the dude just decided to drop out of sight without telling anybody." She cracked a wry smile. "You guys do shit like that sometimes. Hell, I wish my old man would." She barked a laugh.

Mark responded with an obligatory chuckle, but anxiety had begun to gnaw at him. It chewed at his nerves throughout the rest of his shift and during his drive home, too.

Bobby had vanished, leaving behind only his Game Boy.

But where had he gone?

The image of the improbable doorway spun through Mark's thoughts.

At half-past midnight, Mark parked in the driveway of his house.

Lights burned in the front windows, a reliable sign that his stepfather, Willie, was home, and maybe awake. Mark had hoped that the guy would be out with one of his women.

Maybe he'll be asleep on the couch, Mark thought.

His hopes were dashed when he stepped through the front door and found Willie standing at the gas stove, spatula in hand, cooking bacon and eggs. Six feet tall and soft-bodied, he wore a silk shirt with the sleeves rolled up to his elbows, dark slacks, and shiny Stacy Adams. The mingled scents of Halsten cologne and cigarette smoke hit Mark like a smack to the face.

Willie had been out partying again.

"Hey," Mark said.

"What's happening, potna?" Willie asked, turning around. His Jheri curl sat like a wet mop on his head. He grinned. "Chase any giant turds down the toilet tonight?"

Willie asked him similar crude questions almost every night when Mark returned home from work. He found Mark's job to be a source of endless amusement.

The ridiculous part was that Willie didn't even have a job. Fired from his auto factory position, he hadn't worked in almost a year. When Mark's mother died of breast cancer, the life insurance proceeds had been split between Mark and Willie. Mark had planned to use his share to pay for college, expecting Willie to cover the house utilities and incidentals. Instead, Willie had purchased a new Cadillac Escalade and spent another twenty thousand dollars customizing it. Although Willie was fifty-one years old, he got the thrill of his life driving a vehicle outfitted with twenty-six-inch wheels, and mini-TVs in the dashboard and headrests—and picking up young women, too.

It fell to Mark to pay the utilities and maintenance costs. Fortunately, the mortgage was paid off, and Mark's mother had had the foresight to bequeath the house to him. Mark, technically, had the power to kick Willie out. But sometimes he imagined simply leaving this place for somewhere else rather than showing freeloading Willie the door. He could go to school somewhere faraway, like Oregon, maybe even Hawaii. Anything to get away from this guy.

"Being a janitor is only a temporary thing for me," Mark said. "It's a stepping stone."

"The only stepping up you'll be doing there is cleaning the snot off some vp's desk," Willie said.

"It's just a part-time job while I go to school. Not my real career."

Willie scratched his potbelly. "Oh, yeah, you're gonna publish them books, right? Make a living sitting in a room dreaming up shit. Almost forgot, there's a letter on the table for you, James Baldwin."

Mark picked up the envelope. A sinking sensation dropped through his stomach. Willie had already opened the letter.

When he removed the correspondence and saw the salutation that began "Dear Author" he didn't bother reading any further. It was yet another rejection of his mystery novel, from a literary agent in New York. He crumpled the letter into a ball.

Willie grinned.

> *"Dear Turd-Chasing Author,*
> *Your book is BULLshit!"*

Laughing, he stuffed a strip of bacon in his greasy mouth.

"Don't open my mail again," Mark said softly.

"Why? It ain't like somebody gonna be sending you a check for that shit. You oughta let me screen the mail for you. I don't think your fragile ass can handle the rejection."

"Just mind your own business," Mark mumbled, and left the kitchen.

He tried to avoid looking at the house as he rushed to his bedroom. The place was filthy—clothes, junk, and clutter everywhere. Mom, a neat freak, would be turning over in her grave if she could see it.

Someone stepped out of the bathroom and into the hallway. Mark almost shouted in surprise.

It was a girl. Willie's guest for the night, presumably. She wore a tight red blouse that emphasized her huge breasts, and leather jeans that hugged her thick thighs like plastic wrap.

She looked as if she was Mark's age.

"Hi," Mark said, and brushed past her.

"Hi yourself," she said. She smiled flirtatiously. He could feel her gaze on his back as he walked away.

Mark wondered, not for the first time, why his mother had ever married Willie. They'd been married for less than a year when his mother died; soon after they wed, Willie was fired from his job, leaving his mother to pay the bills. Now, only a few month's after her death, Willie already was seeing other women. It was disgusting.

Mark's bedroom was the cleanest, quietest area in the house. But tonight, even the sight of his room failed to soothe him.

The manuscript of his first and only book sat in a pile on his desk, beside his computer. He'd spent fourteen months writing and revising the novel, pouring his soul onto the pages. But the rejection letter he'd received was number sixty-three. No one in the publishing business gave a damn.

The beginnings of a headache thumped behind his eyes. He flopped onto his bed and stared at the ceiling, hands folded behind his head.

"I hate this," he said.

Leaving Illinois State to return home and go to a community college had been a mistake. But a few months ago, as he struggled to deal with his mom's death, coming back to the familiar house seemed to be the only decision that would enable him to retain his sanity. He'd craved to be around people, places, and things that he knew, loved.

He opened the moon-shaped silver locket that he wore on a chain. Inside, there was a photo of him and his mother together, taken when he was only four years old and she was barely twenty-five. They looked so happy and carefree.

Mom had worn this locket for years. After she

died, Mark began to wear it himself. Some days—days when gray clouds of grief hung over him—the locket felt like a lead weight, heavy with cherished memories. But he never slipped it off, no matter how badly he felt. It was his special connection to her, an umbilical cord to her eternal spirit.

"I wish you were here," he said, gazing at her youthful face. "I need you right now, Mom . . . I just don't know what to do."

At times like this, he wished that communicating with the spirits of the deceased was a real thing, something that he could do. He longed to talk to his mom again, to hear her soft voice and let her wise words guide him.

He could imagine what she would say to him: *Tough it out, honey. Make lemonade out of lemons. Nothing worth having comes easy. Trouble don't last always.* His mom had been a walking encyclopedia of old-fashioned, motivational sayings.

In the room next door, mattress springs began to squeak, rhythmically. Soft female cries of pleasure pierced the air, punctuated by piglike grunts.

Mark's stomach lurched.

He closed the locket. He reached for the portable CD player on the nightstand, slipped on the headphones, and switched on some music. Stevie Wonder's soulful voice piped into his ears, singing, "Ribbon in the Sky."

Mark fell asleep thinking about the doorway in the supply closet, wondering where it led . . . and if it was somewhere better than here.

The next evening at work, Mark closed the door to the supply closet behind him, and moved the boxes away from the wall to give him an unob-structed view of the portal.

He was on his break. He'd finished cleaning half of the restrooms for his shift and had left the wheeled cart on the other side of the building. He hadn't come here to get supplies. He'd come here to explore.

He'd brought a heavy-duty, twenty-five-foot meas-uring tape with him, which he'd found in Willie's toolbox at home. (In Mark's opinion, Willie's only redeeming quality was his skill at fixing things.) He'd brought a big yellow flashlight, too.

Mark approached the wall. Kneeling, he pressed the panel.

As before, it was ice-cold to the touch. But the soft hiss came, and then the bricks slid away into dark-ness, revealing the doorway. Frosty air drifted from the entrance.

Taking care to avoid crossing the threshold, Mark methodically fed the measuring tape inside, listen-ing for the click of the end hitting a solid object. Five feet . . . ten . . . fifteen . . . twenty . . . twenty-five . . .

He reached the end of the tape. It still had not tapped against a wall on the other side.

"Just impossible," he said.

He flicked the button on the tape holder, automat-ically reeling the tape back into its metal housing.

Still avoiding passing over the threshold, he shone the flashlight within. He couldn't see any surface at all; the light did not reflect off any objects. He saw only a vast region of unrelieved blackness.

He switched off the flashlight.

Now, he thought, *it's time for me to make a decision.*

He could step away from this hole, slide the boxes back into place, and walk out and forget that he had ever seen this phenomenon.

Or he could go inside.

Mark was a lifelong lover of horror movies. But one of the things he hated—and he saw it happen so frequently in films that it had become a genre cliché—was when a character did something supremely stupid. Like walking into haunted woods at night armed only with a flashlight. Or investigating strange noises in a cellar that obviously concealed the killer. Such moments made him want to shout at the screen, "You idiot, you deserve to die!"

He thought he was pretty smart. But he wanted to see what lay beyond the doorway, as stupid and dangerous as it seemed. His curiosity was like an ache in his gut.

Just stick your hand inside first. There's no risk in that.

He chewed his lip.

Then, he slowly placed his arm inside.

He didn't know what he'd been expecting—in his vivid imagination, he half-feared that some toothsome creature on the other side would take a bite out of his hand—but the reaction he received was far outside the realm of his expectations.

A pleasant coolness enveloped his arm, made his skin tingle.

And he heard music.

The music was as clear as if he was wearing headphones. It was melodic harp music; the soothing notes felt like honey on his ears.

He heard voices, too. Lovely voices sang a song so pure and angelic that his heart raced, swelled with transcendent joy.

His eyes slid closed as rapture swept through him.

Happiness beyond anything he had ever experienced cascaded through his spirit, washing away all of his troubles and worries and sorrows. Eternal bliss awaited him if only he stepped deeper inside, climbed all the way in, moved forward, and didn't look back. . . . It was a good place over there, a fantastic place, a place where he desired to be . . .

Someone rapped on the closet door.

Abruptly, as if awakened from a dream, Mark snatched his arm out of the gateway. Dizziness tipped through him.

"You in there, Markie?" It was Mr. Green.

"Just a minute," Mark said in a slurred voice. Fighting to get his balance, he quickly shoved the boxes in front of the secret doorway.

Mr. Green unlocked the door and banged it open.

Mark spun around.

"What the hell are you doing in here?" Mr. Green asked.

"Uh . . . I came in here to get some paper towels," Mark blubbered.

Mr. Green's eyes narrowed. "You been whacking off? You're panting."

"No, of course not. I came in here . . . on my break. Decided to use my time to get some more supplies. Always on the job, you know?" Mark laughed, but it sounded strained even to him.

Mr. Green's frown sharpened. "You've been up to something, and it's not work. I have a sixth sense for these things. That's why I'm the boss."

"Just work, honest," Mark said.

Mr. Green smiled derisively. Mark had never been a convincing liar.

"Your break's over," Mr. Green said. "Get back to work. If I catch you in here again tonight, you're fired."

* * *

When Mark arrived home, the driveway and the street in front of the house were full of cars. Lights blazed in the windows.

"I don't believe this," Mark said.

He heard the music long before he reached the front door. It was an Otis Redding song that Willie was always blasting.

The house was so crowded with people that Mark had to struggle to get inside. Cigarette and reefer smoke clotted the air, blended with a heavy dose of funk.

Mark coughed, shielded his mouth.

The rooms were full of folks talking loud, drinking, and dancing. Mark recognized a few of the partygoers as Willie's friends, but even they were basically strangers to him. People looked at him as if he didn't belong there, as if he was a kid who had wandered into a grown folks' party. And it was his house.

He had to find Willie and put a stop to this. Right now.

He found Willie in the master bedroom. He was lounging on the bed with two young women, smoking weed and sipping Hennessey.

"Hey, potna!" Willie sat up. He laughed at nothing in particular, waved the reefer in the air like a magic wand. "Want a hit of this?"

"I want all of these people out of here," Mark said. "You didn't say anything about throwing a party tonight."

Willie waved his hand. "Aww, man, stop trippin'. Come on over here and chill with one of these fine young ladies. Moppin' all that piss off the floor's stressed you out, man."

Right then, if Mark had possessed the nerve, he would have clocked Willie in the jaw.

Instead, he said only, "I'm going to my room." He backed away, head tucked down.

Laughing, Willie shrugged and put his arms around the women; like a prince in a harem.

Mark hurried to his room, eager to get inside and lock the door against this craziness—and was shocked to see four guys in there. Sprawled on his bed and the floor, they had turned on his PlayStation and were playing Madden Football. They shouted at the screen and at each other, thoroughly engrossed in the game.

Someone had balanced a can of Colt 45 on top of his book manuscript.

Mark's mouth had dropped open.

"You want next, brotha?" a scruffy-looking guy asked him. "It's gonna be a while, we got us a tournament goin'."

"No, thanks," Mark said softly. He took his CD player off the nightstand. One of the men looked at him suspiciously. "This is mine," Mark said, wondering why he felt he had to justify himself to these graceless people who had invaded his private space.

He retreated to the basement. In a junk-filled corner, near the washer and dryer, he found an old recliner that his granddad used to relax in, years ago. Mark dropped into the chair, tilted his head back.

Dust sifted through the air. He sneezed.

Creaks and thuds issued from the ceiling. Upstairs, they had turned the living room into a dance floor.

Mom never would have tolerated this. She would have kicked all of those people the hell out, granting them some choice cuss words along the way.

But Mom was gone. The house belonged to him now.

Although she might as well have given it to Willie.

* * *

The next night, Mark again cleared the boxes away from the secret door in the supply closet.

It was a quarter after seven. He hadn't even started cleaning his assigned restrooms.

But he wasn't worried about them, or Mr. Green, either. Not anymore.

He pressed the icy panel. The wall floated away.

Beyond, the mysterious darkness beckoned.

He moved to within a foot of the portal, and got on his knees. Cool sweat streamed down his face, turning icy when kissed by the frigid air blowing from the doorway.

The magic door led to a marvelous place. He was certain of that; the mere memory of the divine music stirred his spirits. Music that sounded so good had to come from somewhere wondrous. It was from somewhere better than here, this cold world, where beloved mothers died in their prime, and sorry, weed-head stepfathers squandered life insurance money on flashy cars and chased women half their age and slept with them in beds that still carried the scent of their dead wives and ridiculed their stepsons who were only trying to make an honest living working as janitors, and mocked them for collecting rejection letters on first novels from faceless literary agents who didn't care; this hateful world, where nothing was fair and nothing seemed worth living for anymore, and every day was gray and every night like a black void, because the one he most loved in all the world was gone, gone forever, and he couldn't even tend the home she had left him, couldn't even preserve her legacy, because he was too damned scared to stand up for himself . . .

Weeping, Mark thrust his arm inside the passage. Coolness covered his skin. The heavenly music struck up, pleasure surging through his nerves like a drug-induced high.

An involuntary gasp of joy escaped his lips.

He edged closer, put his foot inside.

The music increased in volume.

He dipped his head, to squeeze inside . . .

. . . and the silver locket dropped off the chain and clattered against the floor. Striking the floor made it pop open to the photograph of Mark and his mother.

He paused. Stared at the picture.

His mother's wise eyes penetrated him.

He no longer heard the music, though it continued to play in the back rooms of his mind. But he heard, quite clearly, his mother's voice. Her words broke into his thoughts as if she was standing beside him.

Where do you think you're going, Mark?

"Mom?" he asked.

It looks like you're running away from your responsibilities.

"I . . ." he started, and couldn't find the words to finish his sentence. Shame sat like a lump in his throat.

Did I raise you to be a quitter, Mark?

He swallowed.

"No," he whispered. "No, you didn't."

He reached to pick up the locket.

That was when he heard something in the darkness beyond the doorway, coming toward him with a sound like sharp claws cutting across ice.

His heart clutched.

The thing scuttled toward him, viper-fast.

Frantic, he backpedaled away from the door.

On the other side, something monstrous howled. It was a roar of anger, of hunger. An utterly alien cry.

Mark's blood ran cold.

He scrambled away to the opposite wall.

Staring into the blackness, Mark glimpsed a vision out of a nightmare: a rippling mass of green-black scales, a flash of luminous yellow eyes, and a maw of large, jagged bones that only could have been a mouthful of deadly teeth.

Then the panel slid back into place in the wall, keeping the creature at bay on the other side. A final, furious shriek echoed in Mark's ears.

Then, silence claimed the room.

He was safe.

"Jesus, Jesus, Jesus," he chanted. His knees shook so badly that he had to sit on the floor.

He had been grasping the locket tightly. When he opened his fist, the edges had etched a red circle in his palm.

Hands trembling, he slipped the locket back onto the chain. How it had fallen off just in time to save him from wandering through the gateway, he had no idea.

No, that wasn't true. His heart knew the truth, even as his rational brain labeled it impossible.

His heart knew a lot of things, including what he had to do next.

Steady again, he got to his feet. He moved the boxes to conceal the door.

It was only a temporary measure. He was going to return here on the weekend and seal the doorway with a layer of bricks.

Afterward, he walked out of the supply closet. Mr. Green marched down the corridor. His eyes gleamed with suspicion.

"What were you doing in there, Mark? It's a half

hour into your shift and you haven't started on the first pair of restrooms!"

"I'm going home," Mark said. "Dock my paycheck, whatever. I promise to come back to work. But first, I've got to kick someone out of my house."

Hitcher

"Get your nose outta that damned book and check out that piece," Raheim said.

Sitting in the passenger seat of Raheim's Chevy Tahoe, I looked up from the sci-fi novel that I was reading and pushed up my glasses on my nose.

"What?" I asked.

"Look what's coming up on the side of the road. Damn, Scottie, sometimes I gotta wonder whether you even *like* women."

I ignored his comment—there was a long story behind it—and looked out the window.

"Oh," I said.

Raheim laughed.

It was early evening, the sun dipping into the horizon. We were cruising on a winding rural road outside Atlanta, on our way to see Raheim's girlfriend and her friend, with whom she was hooking me up. I had never met this "hookup" date and had no idea what she looked like, but Raheim claimed that she was cute. Not as cute as *his* girlfriend, Shonda, of course, but in Raheim's words, "better than you could do on your own, Scottie, so you better thank me."

The woman on the side of the road made even Raheim's girlfriend look homely by comparison.

Raheim slowed the truck as we drew closer, giving me a clear look at her. The woman stood near the open trunk of a black Honda Civic; I noticed that the hood yawned open, too. She looked to be in her mid-twenties. Her skin was the color of coffee, and her hair flowed to her slender shoulders in lush waves. She wore tight black jeans and a red halter top that ended at her midriff.

As I looked at her, my mouth grew dry. Embarrassed by my own reaction, I had to glance away.

The woman turned and watched us as we rolled closer. She waved, and gave us a smile that gave me heart palpitations.

Raheim quickly pulled over in front of the Honda.

"You're stopping?" I asked. "We're running late for our dates."

"Shonda can wait. Ain't no way in hell I'm passing this up."

I couldn't say that I blamed him. But I hated to be late for anything, and especially for a date with a new woman. I guess it was the gentleman in me.

"Maybe you should call Shonda and tell her we're running late—"

"No." Raheim flipped down the sun visor and examined his dark brown face in the mirror. He smoothed his well-trimmed goatee. "After I see what's poppin with this thing here, I might not *wanna* see Shonda tonight. You dig?"

"But what about her friend?" I asked. I really wanted to ask, *What about me?*

"She was fat, anyway." Raheim shrugged. "You ain't missing nothing."

"But you'd said she was cute."

"Her face is." Chuckling, Raheim slugged me in the arm—a playful but painful gesture—and opened the door. "Watch your big brother at work, Scottie. Watch and learn. And keep your mouth shut."

He hadn't needed to say that. I was tongue-tied around most women, anyway.

Raheim got out of the Tahoe. So did I. Darkness gathered around us like an old friend. Forestland lined both sides of the road, and deep in the woods, the night creatures had begun to conduct their concerts.

I shuffled closer to the Honda. Raheim strutted into view on the other side of the car, broad shoulders thrown back proudly, acting every bit of the famed University of Georgia linebacker that he'd been in his younger days. He met the woman near the rear of her car and started talking in a smooth, playa patter that I envied but never could replicate. The woman listened, her lovely eyes sparkling. She shook my brother's hand. Then she glanced in my direction, gave me a smile.

Blushing, I looked away.

I looked under the Honda's hood. I didn't know a thing about automobiles, but at that moment, I wished I had majored in automotive engineering, instead of biology. I could have fixed the woman's car and won her everlasting gratitude, and possibly a date—

Something shifted in the front passenger seat.

The windows were tinted, concealing the Honda's interior. But I had seen . . . something.

I leaned closer to the glass.

A small, pale hand brushed across the window.

I let out a startled sound and stumbled backward. My feet got tangled together, and I lost my balance and hit the gravel on my butt. Shame burned my face. I'd always been a klutz.

Raheim laughed. "What the hell you doing over there, man?"

Her face concerned, the woman came over to me.

"My son's in the car," she said in a soft voice. "I'm sorry, he must've startled you. He seems to enjoy doing that."

She offered me her hand. Her eyes were kind. Caring.

Suddenly, I was in love. Just like that. I had never been in love before—I'd had plenty of crushes on women, but infatuation wasn't the same thing. I knew that I was in love with this woman. I felt the emotion stirring at the deepest level of my heart. It was love at first sight.

She helped me to my feet.

"My name is Elana," she said.

My lips were so dry that I struggled to form words. "Scottie," I finally managed.

She smiled. I smiled, too.

Coming around the car, Raheim grunted and said, "So are we gonna take a stab at fixing this car, or what?"

Raheim got a toolbox out of the Tahoe, set it on the ground in front of Elana's car, and began fiddling under the hood. Leaning against the car, Elana watched him.

I watched her.

I wondered if she felt the same, sudden connection to me that I'd felt to her. Emotionally, I believed that maybe she did; I couldn't forget our shared smile. But logically, I thought the idea was ridiculous. Why would she be in love with me? I was a thin, book-ish guy who, much to Raheim's chagrin, sucked at sports. I was almost thirty, but had little experience with women, and none with a woman of her caliber. It was pure delusion for me to think that she felt any-thing at all for me—other than pity.

As Raheim worked under the hood, my gaze wan-dered from Elana's perfect form to the passenger window. Like a strange sea creature that rarely sur-faced, her son remained hidden behind the smoky glass. I was curious about the kid, but didn't want to appear to be nosy. I had once dated a woman who had a small child, and she had been very protective of him, consenting for me to meet the kid only after we'd dated for over two months. A month later, the woman had dumped me, declaring me "poor father material." I'd been crushed.

But eventually, I'd moved on—to yet another heartbreaking encounter. Rejection had followed me since I was a teenager. It was tempting to give up, to relegate myself to a depressing life of lonely bach-elorhood. But I nursed a hope that, one day, I would meet someone special—and she would think I was special, too.

"Try to start it now," Raheim said to her. Straight-ening, he wiped his hands on a towel.

Elana got inside the car. She turned the key in the ignition.

The engine clicked but didn't catch.

"Shit." Raheim tossed the towel on the ground. Anger compressed his features. He seemed to be per-sonally offended that he had been unable to fix the car and save the day.

Elana slid out of the car. "Well, you tried." She

looked from Raheim to me. "Thanks for stopping for me. Guess I'll call a tow and wait."

"You can call a tow, but we aren't leaving you alone out here," Raheim said. "We're in the boonies, and it's dark. Get in the truck and I'll drive you and your kid home."

For once, I agreed with Raheim. Elana glanced at me, as if seeking my approval, and I nodded.

"You guys are so sweet." Her smile was magnetic. "I don't know how I can ever repay you for being so kind."

Raheim winked at me, and I knew exactly what he was thinking: *I have a few ideas for what you can do.*

My stomach turned. Raheim wasn't worthy of a woman like Elana. In his mind, women had been placed on Earth to cater to his desires—sexual and otherwise. And because of his looks and charisma, he found a lot of women who were willing to give him just what he wanted. But Elana seemed different, better.

But that wouldn't stop Raheim from making a run at her.

"I've got to get my son," Elana said. She opened the passenger door. "Come on, sweetie. These nice young men are going to give us a ride home."

The boy got out of the car, and—how can I say this without sounding like a weirdo?—I suddenly felt cold. As if an icy breeze had wrapped its fingers around me.

The kid looked to be about nine or ten. He was shorter than usual for his age, and very thin. He wore a black pullover—with the hood draped over his head—jeans, and sneakers. Although the voluminous hood concealed his face in shadow, I saw a flash of ghastly paleness, and dark, glimmering eyes.

Even Raheim seemed affected. Worry crinkled his features.

There was something about this kid that made me uncomfortable. But I couldn't say anything. If I dared to voice my opinion I would lose whatever remote chance I had with Elana.

Elana took his hand—I noticed that he wore dark leather gloves—and they walked toward the Tahoe. She smiled at us.

"You can ride up front with me, Elana," Raheim said. "Your boy can ride in the back with Scottie."

Great. I didn't want to sit anywhere near this creepy kid; I would've rather let a cobra coil on my lap, but what could I say? I was in love with Elana. I'd have to accept her kid, too. A mother and her child were, as one woman had told me, a "package deal."

As Raheim got behind the wheel, I opened the rear passenger door. Elana helped her son inside. I began to wonder if the kid suffered from some kind of strange medical condition. She treated him as delicately as a ceramic figurine that might shatter if bumped or dropped.

But it would be rude to ask her a question like that. Besides, her bare arm grazed against my hand as she helped the boy inside, and the brief contact sent electricity jazzing through my veins, plunged me into pure erotic sensation, and wiped all questions out of my head.

Elana bent deeper inside, securing a seatbelt over her son. Her butt was only inches away from the front of my jeans, and her halter top rode above her waist, giving me a glimpse of a tattoo painted on the small of her back: a lush black rose.

I wanted to drop to my knees and kiss those rose petals.

"There you go," she said, her son safely belted on the seat. She flicked a strand of hair out of her eyes and turned to me. Her perfume, a scent that reminded me of wildflowers, filled my head.

"Excuse me," she said, in a voice so low it might have been a whisper. "I need to get inside."

"Oh, yeah." I stepped back. "Sorry."

She brushed against me again—deliberately, it seemed—as she opened the door and climbed into the front seat.

She likes me, I thought. I went around to the other side of the SUV and got in. *I think she really likes me.*

I was so enamored of the possibility that Elana would reciprocate my love that I didn't immediately realize that her son was watching me with his strange, dark eyes.

The kid was staring at me. At first, I ignored him, gazed out the window as Raheim steered back onto the road. But I felt the kid's attention on me still.

Either his mother hadn't given him good "home training," as my mama would say, or he had some kind of problem.

I looked at him. The hood had slipped back a bit, revealing more of his face. His skin was pale; he looked like an albino. He had a small mouth, with narrow, red lips. A thin nose. And not a single hair on his head; he was completely bald.

I shifted in my seat.

The boy's eyes glinted like cold metal. He hadn't said one word since I had first seen him, but an intense intelligence shone in his gaze. Whatever his problem was, mental incapacity wasn't one of them.

"My name's Scottie," I said. "What's your name?"

The boy's lips parted, but he didn't speak. His tongue slithered out, and slowly probed his lips as if in search of crumbs. Finding none, it disappeared inside his mouth again.

He kept his gaze on me throughout this strange display. His small, gloved hands had balled into fists.

The kid was creeping me out.

"His name's Johnny," Elana said, hooking a glance over her shoulder at me.

Driving, Raheim said, "The boy can't talk for himself?"

I wanted to shrink in the seat. Although I was admittedly curious about the boy's odd state, good manners sealed my lips shut. But when Mama had been teaching us good manners, Raheim hadn't been paying attention.

"Not that it's any of your business, but my son has a condition," Elana said.

"What kinda condition?" Raheim asked.

"Raheim, come on." I leaned forward between the seats, being careful not to touch Johnny. "It's really none of our business."

"Don't tell me what I can and can't ask, boy." Raheim glared at me in the rearview mirror. "I just asked the girl a simple damn question."

I pressed back in the seat. Johnny, the subject of discussion, sat there indifferently, as if used to having his "condition" debated in front of him.

Elana paid me a thankful look, then turned to Raheim. "I really don't want to talk about it right now."

"Is the kid a mute or something?" Raheim asked.

I wanted to disown Raheim as my brother.

"Please," Elana said. "Can we change the subject?"

"Fine, whatever," Raheim said. "Where'd you say you live?"

She sighed. "About five miles down the road. Not far."

Raheim nodded. The tension drained out of the air. I wanted to reach forward and pat Elana on the shoulder, but I resorted to simply sitting back and looking out the window, avoiding Johnny, though I felt him watching me again.

What was wrong with this kid?

I felt a sting on my forearm, the telltale sensation of a mosquito bite. I raised my hand to smack the insect before it buzzed away.

But Johnny was faster.

He shot his hand forward and snared the insect between his thumb and forefinger. As I watched, stunned at his swift response, he pressed his fingers to his lips, pink tongue sliding out to capture the mosquito, and then he licked his fingertips, closed his eyes, and exhaled with obscene pleasure.

The gag reflex gripped my throat. Stifling the urge to vomit, I moved farther away from the boy, cowering against the door.

Johnny's stomach made a squeaky, settling noise. I envisioned the crushed mosquito traveling through his digestive system. Another shudder of revulsion rocked me.

I looked at Elana. She gazed out the window, too, studiously avoiding my brother. I couldn't understand how such a beautiful woman had given birth to such a monstrous child.

I couldn't wait to drop him off at home.

Ten minutes later, we parked in front of Elana's house.

It was a cozy brick ranch, sitting at the end of a

narrow gravel lane. Elms and maples sheltered the house. Flowerbeds and colorful azaleas fronted her home. A vegetable garden thrived nearby, leafy green plants waving in the night breeze.

"Nice place," I said.

"Thanks." Elana smiled at me. "It's not much, but it's home."

Gazing at the house, Johnny whined softly, like a puppy. He gnawed on his thumb. After the mosquito incident, he had been quiet and still for the rest of the drive, but now he seemed eager to return home. I was just as eager to get away from him.

"Anybody live with you and your kid?" Raheim asked, probing, I knew, for her relationship status. Not that it would stop him from pursuing her—I'd seen him hit on women who wore wedding bands.

"No. It's just me and Johnny."

She sounded genuinely lonely. It was hard to believe that a woman as gorgeous as her lived alone with her kid.

"You're too fine to be single," Raheim said. "You need a real man in your life."

Elana laughed lightly. "Thanks for the ride home, guys. Would you like to come inside for a drink? It's the least I can do to thank you."

She looked at me as she finished her sentence, but Raheim responded; I was too shocked to say a word.

"A drink sounds great," Raheim said. "Give us some time to get to know each other better."

"Yeah," I said, lamely.

I was shocked that Elana felt comfortable inviting us into her home. She didn't know us; we could be escaped convicts, for all she knew. She was either really naive, or extremely friendly. I preferred to believe the latter. She was a sweetheart. She'd been looking at me often, speaking to me as if she valued my opinion, and no other woman, save my mother, had ever treated me like that. She seemed to truly like me.

But Raheim was going to get in the way. He always got what he wanted, and left me with nothing.

We climbed out of the Tahoe. Johnny allowed Elana to guide him. I was still thinking about how swiftly he had captured the mosquito. If the kid could move that fast, why was his mother helping him walk?

The question bounced around in my head.

Elana led Johnny across the walkway, to the front door. Raheim and I followed a few paces behind. Raheim's attention was riveted on Elana's butt so intensely I imagined her flesh must have felt hot.

Raheim spotted me looking at him looking at her, and he winked, lecherously.

If I was a stronger man, I would have punched him for his disrespect. It was one thing to admire a woman's beauty; it was another to drool over her as if she were the main course at a dinner party. But that was Raheim for you.

Elana opened the front door and ushered her son inside. Raheim shouldered me aside and went in.

The place was even cozier inside. Warm colors, comfortable furniture, lots of green plants, and open space. I immediately felt at ease.

Apparently, Raheim did, too. He went to the sofa in the living room, plopped on the cushions, stretched his legs in front of him, and crossed his arms behind his head.

"What you got to drink?" he asked.

Elana frowned. "Well, make yourself at home,

why don't you? I'll be back in a few minutes to get your drinks. I have to get Johnny settled first."

As she took her son away down the dark hallway, I sat in an upholstered chair across from Raheim. I looked around, noting the numerous framed photographs that sat on end tables and hung on the walls. Photos of Elana with similarly beautiful people. They had to be her relatives; attractiveness must run in her family. Except for her son.

"Her son isn't in any of the pictures," I said.

Raheim shrugged. "Can you blame her? Who'd wanna take pictures of that weird-ass kid? He doesn't look like he's hers."

It was a crude comment, but I agreed with his last statement. Johnny didn't look like her flesh-and-blood child at all. Maybe she had adopted him?

"I'm gonna make a move on her," Raheim said. He ran his fingers along the armrests, as if massaging Elana's legs. "You can either stay in here and learn from the playa, or you can go back in the truck. Up to you."

"We have dates," I said. I couldn't think of anything else to say that might persuade Raheim to leave. "We're already running late. Shonda and her friend will be mad at us."

"Then go. Tell them I was sick or something, and come scoop me up in the morning."

The thought of Raheim spending the night with Elana made me desperate.

"I'll hang around," I said.

"If I didn't know any better," Raheim said, cocking his head, "I'd think you wanted a piece of her, too. Wanna bust a nut for the first time in a dime piece like her?"

"What?"

"Come on, Scottie. I know you're a virgin."

"No, I'm not." My palms had begun to sweat.

"Liar." Raheim chuckled. "Who've you fucked?"

"It's none of your business."

"Because you ain't never had none." Raheim laughed. "What woman would want you? You and Elana's kid are like peas in a pod, man."

I had grown up suffering Raheim's merciless teasing and had developed an armor to fend off his insults— but at that moment, my defenses faltered and, I believed, deep in the core of my soul, that Raheim was right. I *was* a virgin, a few episodes of awkward, heavy petting being the extent of my sexual experience. I had never had a serious girlfriend. Virtually all of the women that I encountered designated me as "just a friend."

What woman would want you?

Tears pushed at my eyes. I could not cry, *would not* cry, not in front of Raheim, not in Elana's house. Giving in to tears would make my humiliation complete— and Raheim would never let me forget it. He still teased me about the time I'd wet the bed when I was six years old. He had a flawless memory for stuff like that.

I sucked in a shaky breath.

"I'm fine the way I am," I said, with as much conviction as I could muster. I didn't know if I believed what I was saying, but I wanted to sound as if I did.

"Whatever, man." Unconvinced, Raheim waved his hand dismissively. "All I know is you better stay outta my way."

Elana strode into the living room. She had refreshed her red lipstick and brushed her hair. Fixed herself up. I wanted to believe that she'd done it for me.

"Sorry that took so long, guys," she said. "What

would you like to drink? I have tea, coffee, Coke, water . . ."

"A Coke would be great," I said.

"Got any beer?" Raheim asked.

Bunching her hands on her waist, Elana frowned. "Hmmm . . . I think there might be a couple bottles leftover from a cookout I hosted a few months ago."

"Will you check, sweetheart?" Raheim asked, in a too-familiar tone that rankled me. "I'd like that."

"Be right back," she said. She headed toward the kitchen, swinging her hips.

Watching her, Raheim shook his head and rose. "I can't wait any longer. Time to do the damn thing. She owes me more than a drink for all my help."

"Where are you going?" I stood, too.

"Sit down and watch cartoons or something," Raheim said. He hitched up his jeans and strolled toward the kitchen.

Anxiety clutched me. My brother was going to be alone, in close quarters, with Elana. I could feel my chances with her—whatever slim chances I had—slipping away.

But I sat down, like an obedient little brother.

I heard their voices drift to me from the kitchen. Raheim was talking in his smooth, playa patter. Elana was laughing and responding to him, but there seemed to be an undercurrent of tension in her voice.

She wasn't interested in Raheim, I thought. She was interested in me. But I'd been too afraid to make a move.

I cracked my knuckles. A remote control for the television sat within easy reach, but I didn't turn on the TV, for fear of missing something that was said in the kitchen.

When Elana clearly said, "Stop," I rose again. My heart throbbed.

There are some things that I've done of which the memories, years later, still shame me. One evening when Raheim and I were teenagers, we had the house to ourselves, our parents out for one of their "date nights." Never one to waste an opportunity, Raheim invited over a girl that he knew, a cute cheerleader who'd had a crush on him for years. While I sat in my bedroom reading an *X-Men* comic, I heard Raheim in his room, tussling with the girl. At some point, she said, clearly and firmly, "No, Raheim. Stop."

I'd sat still, clutching the pages of the comic book, knowing that I should knock on Raheim's door and intervene.

But I did nothing.

The girl cried out, repeatedly. Raheim's headboard began to thump against the wall. The girl's cries faded. When she left the house some time later, her eyes were red, and she didn't hug Raheim good-bye.

I knew what had happened. But I didn't say anything to Raheim, or anyone else.

I'd always regretted my behavior, my unspoken compliance with my big brother.

Standing in the living room of this sweet woman's house, listening to her tell my brother "stop," I made a decision: This time, I wasn't going to back down. I was going to help her.

I swallowed. I marched across the living room, toward the kitchen.

As I walked, I spotted Johnny in the hallway, swathed in darkness. He wore Spiderman pajamas; I had a pair like that when I was his age. He had a hungry look in his eyes—the same predatory glare I'd seen when he devoured the mosquito.

"I'm going to stop him," I said.

Johnny didn't say anything, and I wondered why I had spoken to him at all. I suppose I wanted to reassure him that his mother would be okay.

Johnny clenched his small hands into fists. He no longer wore the gloves. His fingers were thin, his nails long and, oddly, quite sharp.

Johnny was tense, but he made no move to follow me. He must have believed that I was going to save his mother.

Now I couldn't back down.

I squeezed my hands into fists, too, and then I stalked into the kitchen.

Raheim had wedged Elana into a corner, between the sink and the stovetop. He pawed her hips with one of his big hands, and roughly stroked her hair with his other. She was squirming, to no avail, to escape the circle of his arms. A bottle of Budweiser stood on the counter beside them, frothy suds oozing down the neck.

Raheim didn't hear me enter, but Elana saw me. Hope bloomed in her eyes. As I realized that she believed in me, thought I could help her, my resolve strengthened.

"Get away from her, Raheim," I said. "She told you to stop."

Raheim turned. His face was full of surprise.

"What are you doing in here, Scottie? Go back in the living room."

"No." I stood my ground. "Leave her alone."

Raheim's eyes sharpened like daggers.

"I'm warning you, turn around and leave," he said, in a low, dangerous tone that I recognized from the brotherly beatings he'd given me over the years. "This ain't none of your business."

Physically, I was no match for Raheim. He was at least three inches taller than me and outweighed me by over sixty pounds—and every ounce in his favor was muscle. He could bench-press four hundred and fifty pounds with the ease of a hydraulic press. I struggled to do twenty push-ups.

Nevertheless, I couldn't back down. Elana needed me. And I needed her.

"If you've got your hands on her, then this *is* my business," I said.

I hadn't anticipated the punch. Raheim swung at me so fast that one moment, I was looking at him grope Elana, the next, his fist was crashing into my jaw.

I fell backward and collided with the refrigerator like a drunk. Its magnets clattered to the tile floor. Dazed, I slid to the floor on wobbly knees.

Raheim seized the front of my shirt. "What the fuck is wrong with you? You know better than to challenge me!"

I tried to loosen Raheim's hold on me, but his hands were like steel clamps. He hauled me to my feet and pinned me against the wall. His breath was hot, his nostrils flared. The last time I'd seen him this angry with me, he had broken my arm (our parents believed me when I told them I'd fallen off my bicycle).

On the other side of the kitchen, Elana hugged herself. "Johnny!" she cried. "Now!"

Even in the maelstrom of my fear, I had the clarity of mind to wonder why she was summoning her strange son.

I received the answer to my question a moment

later, when I saw Johnny on the threshold of the kitchen.

Dressed in his pajamas, the kid might have appeared harmless in any other situation. But anger—or hunger—had transformed him into a fearsome spectacle. His dark eyes burned like coals. His hands flexed, his long nails curved, like claws.

His mouth bristled with sharp teeth. Like fangs.

Distracted by my terror, Raheim let me go and whirled to face the boy.

"What the fuck . . . ?" Raheim started.

Johnny's swift attack cut off the rest of Raheim's sentence.

The boy leapt across the kitchen like a jumping spider. He hooked his arms and legs around Raheim's torso and plunged his teeth into Raheim's neck. Raheim screamed as blood spurted, spraying the child's face. Johnny devoured the blood, sucking. Raheim attempted to throw him off, tried to pry the boy away from him, but Johnny tightened his hold on him. And still he continued to suck.

His eyes rolling up to expose the whites, Raheim sagged to the floor.

I was sickened by what I was seeing. I could have done something, saved my brother.

Instead, I ran.

I dashed out of the kitchen and bolted out of the house. Elana called after me, but I didn't stop. I ran to the Tahoe—and was at the door when I realized that I didn't have the keys. Raheim had them. I'd have to go back in the house to get them.

The prospect of going back in there to face that bloodsucking child was about as appealing as crawling through a snake pit.

I would have to travel by foot. Maybe some kind

soul would give me a lift, just as we'd helped Elana and her demon-boy.

A revelation flitted at the edge of my thoughts.

What if Elana had planned to bring us to her home? What if she'd intended, from the beginning, to feed us to her son?

A gorgeous woman like her was sure to catch a man's attention. No red-blooded man would be willing to leave her stranded in the middle of nowhere, waiting for a tow truck when she lived only a few miles away. Any man would do as we had done: give her a ride home.

Having her son along would elicit even more sympathy.

As the truth settled over me, I decided that I had to get as far away as possible from this house. I started running across the driveway, toward the road.

"Scottie, wait!"

It was Elana. She rushed out of the house.

Every logical molecule in my body urged me to keep running. But my blind, crazy love for her brought me to a halt.

She ran to me.

"I'm so sorry you had to see that," she said. "Even after all these years, I haven't gotten used to watching Johnny feed."

"You set us up!" I said. "You planned all this! You were going to feed both of us to that monster kid!"

"No." Elana took my hand in hers. She kissed my fingers, and in spite of my confusion and terror, I got a warm, tingly sensation. "Not you. You're special to me, Scottie."

"What do you mean?"

"Do you believe in love at first sight?" she asked.

My heart thundered in my chest.

"I do," she said. "I think you do, too. I felt it when I first touched your hand."

She loved me, too. Just as I'd yearned to believe.

But years of rejection resisted the evidence in her eyes, in her touch, in her voice.

"You mean it?" I asked.

She stepped forward and kissed me. On the lips. Only in my wettest dreams had I ever been kissed like that. She tasted my tongue, twined her hands around my waist, and pulled me closer to her, rubbing against the bulge that had appeared at the front of my pants.

"I mean it," she said. "I want you to stay with us."

"You do?"

"I've been praying for a man like you." She ran her hands along my arms. "Johnny . . . he wants a father."

I saw, over her shoulder, her son step onto the porch. Blood stained the front of his pajama top. He watched us, silently.

"What is he?" I asked.

"He's my son."

"But the blood-drinking . . . the teeth . . ."

"It's his condition," she said. "He was born that way. He hates it. He hates everything about himself, Scottie. That's why I don't keep pictures of him around the house—I used to do that, but he'd smash the frames. His self-esteem is so low . . . because everyone is scared of him."

Johnny's head hung low. He shuffled back inside the house.

Although Johnny was monstrous, I empathized with him. I knew how it felt to despise yourself.

"But you're killing people to feed him," I said.

"Only men who deserve it," she said, with steel in her voice. "Only bad men, like your brother."

Someone else might have come to my brother's defense. I couldn't. She was speaking the truth.

"Come back inside, Scottie," she said. "Johnny needs you. *I* need you."

A woman had never needed me. Ever. And this glorious woman was telling me that she needed me, and I knew she meant it.

"Okay," I said.

We went back inside the house together.

At night, I hid in the shrubbery on the side of the road.

Dressed to kill, Elana popped the hood of the Chevy Tahoe that had once belonged to my brother. She made a show of looking underneath the hood, and then leaned against the side of the SUV, as if distraught.

Within minutes, a young man in a pickup truck pulled over. He got out of the truck and strutted to her, cocky and flirtatious.

Gripping a stun gun, I watched my wife—yes, we had married—interact with the guy, waiting for her signal that he was the one for the night. She wore a smile as she spoke to the stranger, but I knew that her smile was meant for me. We had a special relationship, a family that others might have deemed weird, and even repulsive—but I didn't care about that. It was *ours*.

It felt so good to be wanted, needed.

It felt so good to be loved.

Predators

Olivia Strong had been living in the neighborhood for three weeks when she became aware that the man was watching her.

Olivia was renting a three-bedroom, two-story contemporary house in Fairburn, a southwest suburb of Atlanta. It was located in one of those cookie-cutter subdivisions that had popped up all over metro Atlanta in recent years: a playground, swimming pool, and man-made lake were among the amenities, but the community was so new that none of the elm trees sprouting from the lawns were taller than eight feet. She lived alone with her dog, a perky Bichon named Mimi.

It was when she was outdoors walking Mimi, early one May evening, that she realized he was watching her.

She felt his attention on her before she actually saw him. He lived with his mother in a ranch-style home, halfway down the block from Olivia. As she walked by the house, she saw the gauzy curtains on a bay window stir, as if blown by a breeze. She fixed her eyes on the road ahead, following his movements with her peripheral vision. She detected a slight parting of the curtains, evidence of a spy within—but more acutely, she *felt* his gaze on her. It was a sensation like fingers pressing gently—and insistently—on the back of her neck.

Of course, Olivia was used to catching the eye of the opposite sex (and here in diverse Atlanta, the same sex, too). She was a honey-brown sister, five-five, with the lithe body of a dancer, the result of rigorous exercise. She had soft brown eyes, shoulder-length auburn hair, and a megawatt smile. Men tended to look at her quite frequently, and the tank top and shorts that she wore encouraged an admiring glance.

But this was different.

This was the surreptitious stare of a voyeur. The leer of a man who was undressing her with his eyes, visualizing her participating in a depraved sexual fantasy. This was creepy.

The man who lived at 1408 Riverview Drive was a convicted rapist. His name was Lonnie White.

As Olivia strolled past, Mimi trotting alongside her, anxiety rippled through her stomach.

"Keep walking," she muttered under her breath. "Don't let him know that I feel him watching me."

But it was difficult. She had to fight the compulsion to run screaming back to her house, lock all of the doors, and never venture outside again. She gritted her teeth. She had to do this.

She kept walking until she reached the cul-de-sac at the end of the block. Then she turned around and began walking back. She prepared herself to pass his house again.

This time, she saw him. He'd opened the garage door. He emerged from the cavernlike darkness of the garage like a creature stepping out of its lair. He held a push broom in his large, meaty hands.

Brown-skinned, Lonnie stood around six feet two, with the hulking, flabby build of a football player gone to seed. He had dark eyes set in a clean-shaven face that looked as soft as a young boy's. He wore a wooly Afro, and he was dressed in a T-shirt that read, WHITE FAMILY REUNION 2002, and faded, paint-spotted Levi's.

He looked harmless, really. Like the good-natured, neighborhood man-child who offered to cut your grass for ten dollars. Or the mild-mannered, former high school classmate whose name you could never remember. But Lonnie White was a monster— a modern-day predator. He had served six years in prison for rape, and was reputed to have been responsible for many, many more sexual crimes, but they hadn't been able to pin additional charges on him. He'd been unemployed and living in his mother's house for four months now. Olivia doubted that any of the neighbors knew who he really was.

But she knew better.

As Olivia neared, Lonnie set about sweeping the driveway, though it already looked clean to her. Mimi began to growl, which was atypical. Her dog was usually friendly to everyone.

Mimi knew better, too.

Lonnie stopped sweeping. "Now that's a cute dog. Does she bite?"

He had a soft, mellifluous voice, with a gentle Georgia accent. Not the sinister voice of a vicious criminal. It was unnerving.

Olivia forced herself to smile. "No, she'd never bite. She's completely harmless."

Lonnie grinned. He had perfectly straight, white

teeth—they belonged in the mouth of a better man. "What's her name?"

"Mimi."

By now, Mimi was barking.

"Feisty little thing, ain't she?" Lonnie asked. He leaned against the broom.

Olivia tugged Mimi's leash. "I'd better get her home."

"You take care, miss. I'll see you around."

Lonnie watched her as she walked all the way back to her house. She could feel it. She had to bite her tongue to keep from screaming.

An hour later, Olivia was watching television with Mimi on her lap when the doorbell rang.

Mimi hopped off Olivia's lap and raced to the door, barking.

"Go lie down," Olivia said to the dog. Rebuked, Mimi slunk away, a growl rumbling deep in her throat.

Lonnie was at the door. He'd changed into a polo shirt and clean jeans.

She had expected him, but her heart picked up speed.

"Evening, miss." He held a plastic grocery bag in his hands. "My mama asked me to give you this, since you was new to the neighborhood. A welcoming gift."

It was a pecan pie from Kroger. The price tag was still on the plastic lid.

Olivia accepted the pie. "Thank you, this is a nice gesture."

"My name's Lonnie." He stuck out his hand, which was large enough to palm a basketball.

Olivia hesitated. How many women had he pinned down with this hand as he violently thrust into them? How many horrified screams had that palm muffled? How much innocent blood had spilled through those fingers?

Striving to conceal her revulsion, she shook his hand. It was clammy, like shaking hands with a waterlogged corpse.

"I'm Olivia."

He held on to her fingers a beat too long to be neighborly. She shoved her hand deep into her pocket, wishing she could wash it.

"Nice to meet you, Miss Olivia."

She caught a whiff of cheap cologne. He'd splashed on far too much, had taken a bath in the stuff. It made her want to gag.

"Is the man of the house home, too?" he asked. "I'd like to say my greetings."

Clever. Fishing for information.

"There's no man of the house," she said. "It's just me and Mimi."

"Ah, gotcha." He chuckled, but she could see the machinery working in his brain. "You one of those independent women, huh? Live in a house by yourself and all?"

"I guess I am, Lonnie." She added: "A good man is hard to find."

"Keep your eyes peeled. Never know where you might meet him. He might just come knocking at your door one day." He blushed slightly, and lowered his gaze, as if ashamed at his own brazenness.

"Wouldn't that be something?" she asked.

Lonnie shifted from one foot to the other. He wanted to come inside, she sensed. But she wasn't ready for that—yet.

"Thanks for the pie," she said. "It was nice meeting you. Tell your mother I said hi."

"I sure will."

He stood on the doorstep, without moving.

Her heart boomed so loudly she wondered if he could hear it.

"Yes?" she asked.

He smiled hesitantly, like a shy teenager.

"Aw, nothing," he said. "You have a good night."

"You, too."

She closed the door.

Lonnie remained on the doorstep for a half a minute before he turned and shuffled away.

Olivia sighed. Then she went to the kitchen and tossed the pecan pie in the wastebasket. And she thoroughly washed the hand that had shaken his.

That night, Olivia took a bath before retiring to bed. Submerged in the garden tub, she luxuriated in the scents of lavender and vanilla, sipped a glass of Chardonnay, and performed what had become a nightly ritual: writing in her diary. She balanced the journal on the lip of the tub.

> *May 7*
> *Today, I finally spoke to Lonnie. He looks the same—like a harmless oaf. It's no wonder that he's fooled so many women.*
> *Now that he's met me, I don't think it will be long before he will try something. It's inevitable. He can't control himself.*
> *He never should have been released from prison. I'll call everyone first thing in the morning.*
> *The clock is ticking . . .*

Olivia stepped out of the tub and dried off with a thick, warm towel. Leaving the towel on the floor, she walked out of the bathroom and into the bedroom.

She enjoyed the feeling of cool air caressing her bare flesh, but she was not doing this for mere sensory pleasure.

Before bathing, she'd pulled back the thin curtains on the large bedroom windows. Not all of the way, but wide enough to give someone a tempting peek, a tantalizing glimpse.

Someone like Lonnie.

He would be watching her house. With binoculars. That was the way he stalked his prey. He'd admitted it during his trial.

She paraded past one of the windows, her breasts bouncing.

Watch me, baby.

She walked in front of another window, as if moving about the bedroom cleaning or looking for something.

Mimi lay on the bed, head cocked, watching her quizzically.

"You think he's enjoying this?" Olivia asked the dog. Mimi wagged her tail.

Olivia approached a window, acted surprised to notice that the curtains were parted, and cinched them together—but not before giving anyone watching a full frontal view.

That'll get his heart racing.

She strolled to the other window and pulled together the curtains on that one, too.

She'd left her nightgown on the bed, near the first window. She dressed, slowly, positioning her body to provide a luscious silhouette viewable from outside.

By now, he probably was masturbating.

She cut off the lights.

She sat on the bed and waited for a few minutes.

Then, she crept to the window and peered through the curtains.

A tall, husky black man with a cap pulled over his head ambled down the street, binoculars in his hand, like a kid walking home after his favorite movie.

She'd pegged him perfectly. The pervert.

"Show's over, Lonnie," she said. "Come back for the sequel, tomorrow night."

But as it turned out, she would see Lonnie earlier than that.

The next day was a Saturday. Unlike most people, Olivia did not sleep in on the weekends. She rose at dawn and exercised in the fitness room she'd set up in the finished basement. She put herself through a punishing, two-hour workout. Aerobics, weight lifting, and knocking around the hundred-pound heavy bag.

Afterward, she showered and made several phone calls. It took an hour for her to call everyone that she needed. By the time she finished, it was nearly ten o'clock.

She changed into a cherry-red bathing suit. It was going to be in the low 80's, a nice day for taking in some sun rays—though she was not really interested in a tan.

She lay on a lounge chair in the backyard, wearing sunglasses, sipping a tall glass of sweet tea, and listening to an India Arie CD. Girl-power songs about loving yourself and taking control of your life. She periodically checked her watch. It wouldn't be long.

Barely an hour after she had begun sunbathing, Lonnie poked his head around the corner of the house.

He wore the same family reunion T-shirt and paint-soiled jeans he'd worn yesterday. He was getting comfortable with her. Or perhaps he was just filthy.

"Good morning, Miss Olivia." He gave her a half-wave. "I rang the doorbell, then I heard the music playing and figured you was out back here."

"Hi, Lonnie." She put on a plastic smile. She shifted on the lounge chair, to best display her legs and cleavage to him. "You're an early riser on the week-ends, I see."

Lonnie's lips had parted. He stared at her body. *Gawked* really. His eyes had glazed over, and she was sure that he hadn't heard a word that she'd said.

He had an erection, too. One of his hands slid into his pockets and slowly stroked its length.

Revulsion curdled her stomach. He was cruder than she had thought.

She cleared her throat. "Lonnie?"

He blinked. His eyes swam back into focus, and he snatched his hand out of his pocket, shamefaced, though his erection remained.

"Good morning, Miss Olivia," he said, clearly not realizing that he was repeating himself.

"What can I do for you?"

"Umm, I was gonna offer to cut your grass," he said. "It looks kinda high, and since you ain't got no man here to cut it for you, I'd be happy to do it."

As he spoke, he didn't meet her eyes—he kept his attention focused on her body, his gaze crawling across her hungrily. Olivia felt as if spiders were creeping across her flesh, but she forced herself to stay calm.

"That would be nice of you," she said. "How much would you charge me?"

"Aww, it'd be free—for you. Little way for me to welcome you to the neighborhood."

She didn't bother reminding him that he had already given her a welcome gift—the pecan pie—last night. Neither did she say that nothing in life was ever free.

She only said, "That's sweet of you, but I won't ask you to do it for free. How about I cook dinner for you tonight? Would that be a fair reimbursement?"

Lonnie gulped. "You'd cook dinner for me?"

"Certainly. What do you like to eat?"

He wiped sweat from his forehead with the back of his hand. "I love me some catfish. That's what my mama cooks, every Friday. Fried catfish and French fries. When I was in the pen—"

He stopped, laughed nervously. She watched him, waiting for him to continue.

You can't fool me, Lonnie. I know your life story, you sick bastard.

"When I moved away from home for a little while," he said, "I missed Mama's fried catfish most of all."

"Fried catfish it is, then—though I can't promise that I cook it as well as your mama does."

He giggled, like a child. "What time we gonna eat?"

"How about eight o'clock?"

He bobbed his head. "I'll be there. Want me to bring some hot sauce?"

She smiled thinly.

"I'll have all the heat you need, Lonnie."

Giggling deliriously, he hurried away to get his lawn mower.

Olivia returned inside the house.

There were preparations, beyond the food, to be made for tonight.

* * *

Lonnie rang the doorbell at a quarter to eight o'clock. Well in advance of their dinner date.

Olivia had been prepared for his overly eager arrival. She checked her hair in the mirror one final time, made sure that her short skirt and blouse looked good, and answered the door.

Lonnie wore a dress shirt and slacks. He carried a glass jug of Carlo Rossi blush wine.

"They had a sale on wine at the store," he said. "I got me three jugs of this—left the other two at the house. I can get another one if we drink up all of this."

"That's so thoughtful of you," she said, taking the jug. "I'm sure this one will be sufficient, Lonnie."

He moved closer, his bulk filling the doorway. Once he crossed the threshold, that would be it. This would move from a case of subtle manipulation to an eventual life-or-death struggle. There would be no turning back.

But that was what she had signed up for.

"Come on in," she said.

"Thanks, Miss Olivia." He walked inside. He looked around, appreciatively. "This sure is a nice place you got here."

"Thank you." She showed him into the living room and handed him the remote control for the television. "Make yourself comfortable. What would you like to drink?"

Sitting on the sofa, he smacked his lips. "How about you crack open that jug of wine? I got it nice and cold."

"Certainly."

"Where's that little cute dog?" He looked around.

"I put Mimi in the basement, so she won't bother us. We can have a quiet evening to ourselves."

His grin was so large it seemed it might consume his face.

"I'll go get that drink for you," she said. "Dinner will be ready in a little while."

She strutted down the hallway, toward the kitchen, swinging her hips sexily. She heard him make a low whistle.

When she got into the kitchen, she opened the wine, and took two glasses out of the cabinet.

She also removed a bottle of pills from the cabinet. A powerful sedative that could be absorbed in liquid without leaving a trace. After a few sips, Lonnie would be in La La Land. And then this would finally be over for her.

She shook two of the pills into one of the glasses, and splashed wine over them. She filled another glass, her glass, with wine, too.

Then, drinks in hand, she sashayed down the hallway and into the living room.

Lonnie was gone. The TV was on, to the evening news.

Terror leapt in her chest. Where was he?

She heard the faint creak of a floorboard, behind her. She spun.

"Sorry, Miss Olivia," Lonnie said, and clouted her upside the head with a blunt object.

Olivia awoke sometime later to find herself lying on the sofa. Her head ached. Rough rope bound her wrists and ankles. She had been stripped to her bra and panties. Her clothes lay heaped in a pile on the carpet.

The large clock hanging above the fireplace read

fifteen past eight. She'd been unconscious for . . . what? Twenty minutes?

She was alone in the living room. But she heard Lonnie's heavy, thudding footsteps moving around upstairs. Searching through her stuff.

She had underestimated him. Once he entered her home, she should not have allowed him out of her sight, not for one second. The sisterhood had warned her about that.

She had made a rookie mistake, and she might have to pay the terrible consequences.

From where she lay, she could see the phone, lying on an end table. A red light on the cradle would indicate whether someone had called. The light was not lit.

That meant they had not called to check in yet. They had no idea of the danger she was in.

When an entrapment date was set, the sisterhood was supposed to call during the event, to confirm that the operative was safe. But they never promised precisely when they would call, to prevent the operative from furtively glancing at the phone and possibly alerting the prey that something was afoot.

If they called and she did not answer, they would dispatch back-up assistance immediately. But they might call five minutes from now—or two hours from now. You never knew when.

You assumed such risks when you signed up for the job.

As a last resort, there was a panic device that, once activated, alerted the sisterhood that you required emergency assistance. Resembling a tiny key chain, you wore it around your neck on a lanyard, and pressed the button only when absolutely necessary.

Lonnie had taken off her lanyard. It probably lay

in the mound of clothes on the floor. Out of her reach. It didn't matter, since she was tied up.

How was she going to get out of this?

She tried to loosen the knots, but she was bound tight.

Lonnie began to come downstairs. He was reading something. Her diary.

Tension tightened her stomach another painful notch.

"Hmmm," Lonnie said. Flipping through pages, he crossed the living room and sat at the foot of the sofa, near her feet. He glanced at her. "Ain't this interesting? Sound like you know all about me, don't it?"

"Lonnie, please, I'm sorry. I wasn't going to hurt you."

"Then what was you planning, then?" He removed the bottle of pills from his shirt pocket, shook it. "You was gonna give me some of these so I'd fall asleep, then you was gonna call some folks here to catch me, wasn't you?"

"No, it's not like that—"

"That's what you wrote in here!" He flung the diary across the room. It struck the wall and fluttered to the floor like a dead bird. "I ain't going to prison again, uh-uh. I'll kill myself before I go back to that place."

"I want to get you help, Lonnie," she lied. "That's all. That's what we do. We help people like you."

"Help me? Ain't I heard that before?" Lonnie laughed. He put his meaty hand on her thigh, rubbed. He leaned closer to her. His breath stank.

The phone rang.

Olivia wanted to whoop for joy.

If she didn't answer the phone within four rings,

they would assume the worst and would be busting down the door within ten minutes.

Lonnie paused. Indecision flickered on his face.

"Who's that calling?" he asked. "That's your folks?"

Stall, stall, stall.

The phone rang a second time.

"I don't know," she said. "I can't see the caller ID from here."

Lonnie cursed under his breath.

The phone rang a third time.

Lonnie lumbered to his feet and hurried to the phone. It rang a fourth time.

He brought the phone back to her. But it had fallen silent.

She contained her excitement.

Lonnie studied the caller ID display.

"Oh, it was only my mama. Must've been calling to check up on me." He grinned. "My mama's real overprotective."

Shit!

There would be no last-minute rescue, she realized. She was going to have to find her own way out of this situation.

Lonnie placed the phone on the coffee table behind him. He knelt beside her. He rested his fingers on her thigh again. His hand felt like a piece of cold, dead meat.

"You got real nice lips," he said. "Can I kiss you?"

Oh, God, I can't deal with this. This is too much.

But denying him would only infuriate him. When Lonnie White was angry, he could be extremely violent. She remembered the photos she'd seen of his last victim. The woman had required major surgery to reconstruct her face.

"Well . . . okay," she said. A plan had begun forming in her mind.

Lonnie's face floated above hers like a low moon. He opened his mouth, guided his lips to hers.

She clamped her teeth on his tongue and bit down hard. Warm blood squirted into her mouth.

Lonnie howled. He fell on the floor, holding his mouth, blood spilling between his fingers.

She spat out the tip of his tongue. It landed on the sofa like a giant pink comma.

"How's that for a tongue kiss, you sick bastard!"

Lonnie was shrieking. He tried to rise off the floor.

Olivia lifted her legs in the air, parted them as much as the ropes around her ankles would allow—and brought them down over Lonnie's head, like a vise. She had him trapped between the juncture of her thighs, in a scissor hold.

He beat against her legs, but her muscles were strong, the result of months of rigorous training.

She squeezed.

Lonnie emitted a garbled scream.

She rolled onto her side, gaining more leverage. She intensified the hold.

Lonnie's face was turning blue. His bloody tongue lolled from his mouth.

"How's it feel?" she screamed, spittle spraying from her lips. "Feel good, fucker?"

Finally, Lonnie's face went slack. His eyes slid shut. He had passed out.

Her leg muscles throbbed, but she slipped her thighs over his head. She moved her feet through the clothes on the floor, found the emergency alarm, and pressed it with her foot.

They would be here very shortly.

Olivia lay back on the sofa. She started to cry.

* * *

Less than ten minutes later, the front door opened. They didn't announce their presence by knocking.

Three tall, husky women entered. Two of them were white, and the other, the tallest woman, was black. They wore dark blue sweat suits—they resembled a team of college basketball players on their way to a game.

They quickly came to her. The black woman cut the ropes away from Olivia's ankles and wrists. The other two busied themselves with Lonnie, who was still unconscious.

"You handled yourself well," the black woman said. Olivia remembered her from the sisterhood training classes. Her name was Kenya. "Mr. White here's out cold."

"Thanks, but it didn't go quite as planned," Olivia said.

"Hardly ever does," one of the white women said. "Doesn't matter. You got the job done."

The other woman brought a syringe out of a small black case. She stabbed it in Lonnie's hip. Lonnie jerked, but did not awaken.

After the injection, he would not wake up, Olivia knew, until several hours later. By then, they would have already transported him to The Garden.

The sisterhood, which bore no name and operated in secret, was composed of female rape victims. Women disgusted with society's habit of releasing convicted serial rapists back into the general populace, to prey again. Women who had decided to take the law into their own hands. Women who vowed to dispense their own special brand of justice for predators like Lonnie White.

You could spend your life as a victim, or you could do something about it.

When Olivia had been raped, sixteen months ago, by a man much like Lonnie, a member of the sisterhood had contacted her and offered her justice. Olivia had accepted the offer, and never turned back.

That guy who'd raped her had gotten out of jail after only seven months. The sisterhood had located him, and set the bait. He'd taken it—as they always did. They took him to The Garden, too.

No one ever left The Garden alive.

The two white women were transporting Lonnie out of the house. Typically, they parked in the garage and inserted the predator in a secured van.

"Freshen up and hit the road," Kenya said. "You've got to clear out of here, ASAP."

After a capture, the operative left the house within the hour, leaving behind no trace. The house and all of the utilities were registered under a false identity.

"Good work, girl." Kenya gave her a sisterly hug. "Until next time."

"See you then." Olivia smiled, wiped tears out of her eyes, and went downstairs to get Mimi.

Christina Ray had been living in the Los Angeles apartment complex for two weeks when she became aware that the man was watching her.

The man, named Stan Gee, was a convicted rapist who had gotten out of jail after serving only nine months. A travesty of justice.

Christina lived alone with her dog, a Bichon named Mimi . . .

Nostalgia

I saw the house when I was driving home from work late one evening.

I had decided to try a different route from the office to my apartment, because in the five months that I'd been living in Atlanta, I'd been following the same paths to everywhere that I frequented: my job, the Publix supermarket, the barber shop, the bank, the Blockbuster Video store, the bar-and-grill with the cold beer and the hot wings. I felt as though I was already in a rut, like a dog that runs the same dusty trail back and forth across a yard. Five months ago, I had moved here from Illinois to experience something new. But unless I made the effort to see new things, the new would quickly become common-place. Taking a different route home was one small but meaningful way that I demonstrated my commitment to experiencing a fresh perspective.

When I saw the house, however, I was reminded of the life that I had left behind in Illinois.

It was located on a residential street named Common Avenue. Although the road ran parallel with a busy thoroughfare that carried most of the traffic in the area, the abundance of tall, leafy trees that lined the road enveloped the street in a tranquil oasis. Stylish contemporary homes, with trimmed lawns and shiny autos parked in front of two-car garages, sat on each lot. I saw children playing in yards; a young woman power-walking across the sidewalk, her black Labrador trotting beside her; a man in a gray suit climbing out of a sedan, gripping a briefcase in one hand, his other hand unloosening his tie, no doubt relieved to be home after a long day at work. In the middle of this tableau, perhaps halfway down the block, I noticed the house.

As though my foot had a life of its own, I stamped the brakes. I rocked to a halt. I stared.

I could not believe what I saw, but I could not argue with my own eyes.

Unlike the other homes on the avenue, which appeared as though they had been constructed within the past ten years, this house looked to be at least forty years old. It was a Colonial model, painted eggshell white, with red shutters. A two-car garage painted the same colors was attached to the house.

It sat atop a slight hill; a wide, blacktopped driveway extended from the garage to the street. The grass was a bit too long, which was especially noticeable since the surrounding lawns were trimmed. An elm towered on the perimeter of the yard.

In every visible respect, the house was the same as the one in which I had lived for the past eight years: my grandmother's house. I had moved in with Grandma almost immediately after my grandfather had died, charged by my family with the responsibility of doing the "man's work" around the house, and, even more important, keeping Grandma safe.

Grandma would've had a fit if I had let the grass

grow that long, I thought. Grandma had been a stickler for numerous things, but nothing rivaled her zeal for having the grass cut. It was something about her that I'd never understood.

Her voice came to my mind with such clarity she might have been speaking into my ear: *Lord have mercy, we got the worst-looking yard on the block. If you don't cut that grass, Rick, I'm gonna have to pay somebody to do it. You know I ain't got the money for that. I know you busy and all, but that grass—*

I shook my head, clearing away those old mental cobwebs. I realized that I had halted the car in the middle of the street. I parked alongside the curb.

I turned back to the house. Although it was half-past seven and my stomach hungered for dinner, I would not be able to leave until I had taken a closer look.

I got out of the car and crossed the street. I stepped onto the sidewalk.

Who lives here? I wondered. Another widowed black grandmother and her grandson? Do Bible studies take place in the basement every Monday night? Is there a Doberman roving around the back-yard, kept mainly because Grandma knows a dog will scare away thugs?

I did not see any people moving around in the house, and I did not hear a dog barking. There were no cars parked in the driveway, either. The only in-dication that someone lived there was a glowing porch light above a storm door that opened into a breezeway.

The light illuminated the numbers on the weath-ered black mailbox: 2118—2118 Common Avenue.

A chill coursed through me. My grandmother's house number was 2118. The name of her street was

George Avenue, which was hardly similar to Common, but the match of numbers was eerie.

Well, so what? I thought. It's a coincidence. I had once heard a theory that every human being in the world had a person, somewhere, who looked exactly like him. Why not a house? There were probably several dozen homes across the country that looked identical to my grandmother's.

But down to the last detail of the landscaping? I wondered. That elm tree looked exactly like the one I used to climb when I was a kid. How could I explain that?

No ready answer came to mind. Slowly, I walked up the asphalt path that led to the front door, searching for a discrepancy, a detail that would differentiate it from Grandma's place.

As a child, I had spent many lazy summer afternoons playing on her walkway, capturing ants in jars, or riding my bike along it as if it was a motorcycle ramp. Other times, Grandma would emerge from the door and holler that it was time to eat, and my cousins and I would scramble up the path, racing one another to the dinner table.

No, it wasn't this walkway, I reminded myself. The one I remembered was in Illinois. But I'd be damned if I didn't see the same slight cracks, lines, and indentations in this pavement underneath me.

I shook my head. This was too incredible. I plodded forward, looking at the ground. I was searching for something. If I found it, I would—

"Oh, shit," I said aloud. I stopped and knelt. Gaped at the sight below.

On the walkway, beside the garage, I saw the imprint of a child's shoe. It was embedded in the concrete, like some little kid's Walk of Fame.

A garage had been added to my grandparents'

house when I was five years old. Shortly after the foundation had been poured, while it was still soft, I had ventured into the area and dabbed my foot in it, ruining my shoe, but strangely proud that I had made my mark. The builders (who were friends of the family) never bothered to smooth over the footprint.

And here, several hundred miles away from that home in Illinois, was an identical footprint, in front of an identical garage, beside an identical house.

Heart pounding, I stood.

I did not understand what was happening, but I was compelled to find answers. I could not drive away and pretend that I had never seen this.

Because two months ago, Grandma's house had burned to the ground. She had been inside, alone. She had died in the blaze. It was a freak accident, caused by her leaving on the gas burner before she went to bed—something that never would have happened if I had still been living there, because I had always checked the range before turning in for the night. It had been one of my self-imposed responsibilities.

And I have not slept well since.

I have nightmares perhaps three, four times a week. It is always the same haunting dream. I am on the sidewalk in front of Grandma's house, hugging her good-bye, because the day has finally arrived: I am moving away from home and to Atlanta, a city in which I have no friends and no family, only the promise of a new job and a new life. Stifling tears, I turn away from Grandma, take a step . . . And I am instantly upon an airplane that is standing on a runway, seconds before takeoff. Except the runway is the street that runs in front of Grandma's house.

I sit in a passenger seat beside the window, and through the glass I see Grandma on the walkway, waving good-bye. Behind her, the house is on fire—flames and black smoke flapping against the pure blue sky. The airplane begins to roll forward, and still Grandma stands there, waving. I press myself to the glass as we rumble ahead, straining to keep Grandma in sight. . . . And the last vision I have of Grandma is her walking into the burning house.

I always explode out of the dream with a cry bursting from my lips.

Shaking away a chill, I looked at the house before me. There was no fire, like there was in my dream. If it was not for that glowing porch light, I would have assumed that the home was vacant.

Someone lived here. I had to find out who.

I stepped toward the front door. A closed wooden door stood behind the storm door, so that you could not enter the breezeway without first getting through both barriers. At night, Grandma would lock every possible entryway. She worried constantly about break-ins. Sometimes, my cousins and I had jokingly called Grandma's house "The Fortress."

I pressed the doorbell.

If someone answered, I did not know what I would tell them. I hadn't bothered to think of a story that would explain my visit. Maybe I would tell them the truth.

Hello. Excuse me, but I had to see who lived here. My grandmother's house in Illinois looked exactly like yours. See, Grandma died in a fire that burned down the whole place, and I had to make sure that, you know, my Grandma wasn't actually alive and well and living here in Georgia.

She never liked the thought of me being far away from her, if you know what I mean.

In spite of myself, I almost laughed out loud.

After a few seconds, no one had answered. I took a few steps back and gazed at the front windows, to see if anyone might be looking outdoors. I didn't see anyone peering through the curtains. I did, however, notice bright purple petunias blooming in the long flower box beneath the window. The same kind of flowers that Grandma had tended devoutly.

There was coincidence, and then, on a higher level than coincidence, there was Strange Stuff. No doubt, this was Strange Stuff—something that utterly eluded a rational explanation.

I stepped to the doorway again, pressed the bell once more. No response.

I slid my hand to the door handle. Pulled. It was locked.

What would I have done if the door had opened, anyway? I thought. Walked inside? No matter how much this looked like Grandma's house, it was private property. Was I crazy?

Asking myself those questions brought my senses back to me. I didn't know these people who lived here. Whether they were home or not, what would they think of a stranger snooping around their yard? And what about the neighbors? I had probably already invited their suspicion. People tended to pay attention to unfamiliar men who stopped and approached houses in their neighborhood.

My curiosity was not satisfied, but it was time to leave.

I returned to the car.

Before I pulled away, I glanced at the front windows of the house. I saw a gap in the curtains, as though someone was gazing through the glass.

I blinked, trying to see more clearly.

The curtains quickly fell back into place.

I frowned. Had I actually seen them parted, or had I been fooled by the summer twilight?

I peered at the windows again. No one was there.

I rubbed my eyes. They felt grainy. I had been staring at a computer monitor for over eight hours, and after such a long day, I couldn't rely upon my vision to discern everything clearly, especially as night approached. Most likely, I had imagined the movement in the windows.

Nevertheless, as I drove home, I had the nagging feeling that I would be coming back to 2118 Common Avenue. Soon.

I had always been close to my mother. In the few months that I had been away from home, thanks to daily phone calls, my mother and I had grown closer than ever. I told her about virtually everything in my new life. Seeing the strangely familiar house on Common Avenue was no exception.

I was also counting on Mom to give me some insight. The house fell into the category of Strange Stuff, and Mom had become a self-taught expert on such things: ESP, psychic predictions, astrology, tarot cards, guardian angels, ghosts, haunted houses. She learned what she knew from books, the Internet, and most of all, she insisted, personal experience. Her deep interest in the occult seemed odd to me, but harmless. My own interest was limited to horror flicks and the occasional Stephen King novel.

"Hey, Rick," Mom said, her voice perky as usual whenever I called. "How're you doing?"

"To be honest, I'm confused," I said. "I saw something on the way home that I can't explain."

A thoughtful pause. Then: "What was it?"

I told her everything about the house. Being able to relate the story to someone else relaxed me.

"Oh, yes, that's very strange," Mom said when I had finished. "Disturbing, too."

"How so?" I asked.

"Don't play dumb, Rick," she said. "You know what I mean."

I did know what she meant. But I had been unwilling to raise the subject.

"I don't like to talk about what happened to Grandma," I said. "And I don't see how it has anything to do with what I saw today."

"The connection between the houses is obvious," she said. "But you're denying it."

"You've lost me," I said. "You've gone way deep into this, and I'm still paddling around the surface. Enlighten me."

"Do you believe in ghosts, Rick?"

"I've never seen a ghost."

"But do you believe in them?"

"You think I saw a ghost, Mom? I saw a *house.* Ghosts haunt houses. Houses aren't ghosts, and houses don't haunt people."

"A ghost can be anything," she said. "A house, a car, a person. It depends upon why the ghost is conjured."

I sighed. "Where do you get this stuff from?"

"Maybe a ghost is summoned because its spirit needs to be released. Or maybe the ghost is conjured by a living person, who needs to release something from within himself. A person can invoke a ghost with his own subconscious feelings."

"You think I called up this house from the spirit world?" I asked.

"You spent some of the most important years of your life in that house," she said. "You practically grew up there. And your Grandma was like your second mother. The house and the people who lived there are special to you."

"It's the same for you," I said. "But you haven't mentioned seeing the house appear again, out of nowhere, have you?"

"I'm not the one who moved away from home, honey."

"I don't think something like this happens to everyone who moves away from home."

"Not everyone's grandmother dies in a fire two months after they move away from home. Admit it. There are unique circumstances here."

"I still don't know what you're trying to say," I said, knowing that I was lying, knowing that Mom would sense my lie, but knowing that I had to lie because to be honest was too upsetting.

Every day after I moved to Atlanta, I tried to tell myself that I had not done anything wrong. I called Grandma at least twice a week, to check on her and make sure she was doing okay. It wasn't as if I had just moved away and forgotten about her. I tried to use that argument to console myself, but it didn't help. Mom understood the true source of the problem.

She went on: "You blame yourself for what happened to Grandma, but you shouldn't. It was an accident. You couldn't be there to save her from everything. You have the right to move away, to go out on your own, and build your own life. That's what being an adult is all about. No one blames you. You should stop blaming yourself."

"What does blaming myself—and yeah, maybe sometimes I do—have to do with me seeing this house today?"

"You're going to have to make that connection yourself. I think you already understand. You only have to accept it."

"I hear what you're saying," I said. "But I don't buy it. Anyone who would conjure his own ghost—as if that's possible, anyway—belongs in an institution. That's like talking to the walls or something."

Mom chuckled. That was one thing I loved about her. She had strong beliefs, but she didn't take herself too seriously.

"Just think about it," she said. "Be honest with yourself. Don't walk away until you've faced the truth."

"There's no way I could walk away from this yet," I said. "Even though it's probably coincidence, I'm just too curious to lay it to rest."

"That's how it always starts," she said, with satisfaction, as though, in spite of my resistance to accepting her theory, I had proved an important point.

I hung up.

Although Mom thought I had witnessed a ghost, my take on the mystery was more straightforward. Yes, the house did have amazing—even incredible— similarities to the house I remembered. But once you got down to it, it had to be a regular house, with a flesh-and-blood person living there. All I needed to do was to find out the resident's identity, and I would be on my way to solving the puzzle.

I grabbed the Yellow Pages.

* * *

I'd decided to call the Cobb County Tax Assessor's Office. The identity of a property owner was a matter of public record. Within minutes, I should be able to learn who owned the residence at 2118 Common Avenue. Then, armed with a name, I could plunge into a more detailed investigation, if I so desired. I just needed to know, more than anything, that a real, living person owned the house.

I punched in the phone number. After the third ring, a recorded voice came on: "Thank you for calling the Cobb County Tax Assessor's Office. Our offices are now closed. Normal business hours are—"

Cursing softly, I hung up. Of course, the office was closed. It was past eight o'clock in the evening.

I'll call them tomorrow morning, I thought. It's not a big deal, anyway. I only want to satisfy my curiosity.

Then I asked myself: Why should I bother to inquire about the house at all? Did it really matter? I didn't live there. I lived in this apartment, and Grandma, of course, didn't live anywhere on this Earth any more. Why stir up painful memories for the sake of satisfying my curiosity?

My stomach growled. Glad to be distracted from my thoughts about the strange house, I went into the kitchen and grabbed a pizza from the freezer.

While the pizza baked in the oven, I unwrapped that day's newspaper and sat at the dinette table to read. But the paper might as well have been written in Sanskrit. I could not concentrate.

In my mind's eye, I kept seeing the front windows of that house, curtains parted, and someone watching me through the gap.

No, I imagined that. It was getting dark, and I couldn't see clearly. It's all in my head.

I desperately wanted to believe the voice of doubt.

I wanted to chalk up the entire experience—the spectacle in the window, the house itself—to imagination. But another part of me, maybe my conscience, that part of me that compels me to be truthful, would not let me swallow those self-comforting lies. The truth was a big, throat-choking pill, and I was going to have to swallow it.

Someone was in the window watching me. But who? A ghost?

Could the entire house be a ghost, as Mom believed? Summoned by some mysterious power, for some equally mysterious purpose?

Was I going nuts?

Suddenly, the phone rang.

On the second ring, I picked it up.

"Hello?" I answered.

No response. Soft static crackled from the handset, as if it was a long-distance call with a bad connection.

"Hello?" I repeated. "Is anyone there?"

Amidst the static, I detected a voice; it was barely more than a whisper, too soft for me to identify the caller by name or gender.

"Hello?"

The static ceased. Silence as thick as syrup seeped from the phone.

"Is anyone there?" I asked. By then, in a normal situation, I would have hung up. But so much weird stuff had been happening that it was easy to believe a simple phone call might be another piece of this unfolding mystery.

Another noise. Struggling to hear, I pressed the handset to my ear so tightly that the plastic felt fused to my eardrum.

I heard voices in the background, faintly. There was something familiar about them . . .

I closed my eyes. Listened.

The voices grew louder. When I recognized the identities of the people speaking, my eyes snapped open.

I heard myself. And Grandma. Having a conversation we'd had only a week before I moved away from home.

It was impossible, but I was not imagining this, and I was not dreaming. It was as real as any discussion I'd ever overheard on a telephone.

The ghostly voices floated from the handset:

I don't understand why you gotta leave home, Rick. Your family is here, all your friends are here. You go down to Atlanta, and you're gonna be all alone.

I'm sick of living here, Grandma. I don't want to be like everyone else. Born here, live here, die here. I want to experience something new.

That's what vacations are for. Travel somewhere new for a little while, then come home. You don't have to move.

Yes, I do have to move. There's nothing here for me anymore.

Your family is here. I'm here. Ain't that enough?

That's what vacations are for. After I move to Atlanta, I'm going to come back to visit sometimes, Grandma. And I'll call.

You're gonna get down there and forget all about us.

Come on. You know I won't do that.

Atlanta ain't a perfect place, Rick. Don't go there thinking everything is gonna be perfect.

I don't expect it to be perfect. No city is perfect. But I'll enjoy it.

You're deserting me. What am I gonna do without you?

You've got the rest of the family here. You won't be alone.

Do you know that I've never lived by myself?

Yeah, I know.
I can't live in this big house all alone.
Maybe you'll find someone to move in with you.
Oh sure, maybe I should get married again, right?
(A chuckle.) If you want to, Grandma.
I'm just kidding, boy. Any man I'd marry at my age is likely to die before I do.
Well, you know that women usually live longer than men.
I've never lived alone. What if something happens to me?
Nothing is going to happen to you, Grandma. Everyone in the family's going to be here for you. You'll be fine . . .

The voices faded into silence. Static crackled over the line again. Then, the connection was broken.

I blinked. My vision was blurry with tears. I wiped my eyes furiously.

What in the hell was happening? Had I really unleashed something in the spirit world, just to haunt myself? To torture myself with guilt?

I slammed the phone onto the table.

"Nothing is going to happen to you, Grandma," I said aloud, mimicking myself. "You'll be fine."

Regardless of her theories about ghosts, Mom was right about one thing: I was in denial. The truth was, I did blame myself for the fire that had consumed Grandma. If I hadn't been so stubborn, so goddamn set on living my own life and moving a thousand miles away from home, if I had just stayed home with her, the fire never would have happened, she would still be alive. It was my fault.

I might as well have twisted on the gas burner myself.

I cradled my head in my arms. My skull pounded like a giant bass drum.

My eyes were closed, but I kept seeing the images from my nightmare, in brilliant color: Grandma waving at me, then turning to walk into the blazing house.

Nothing is going to happen to you, Grandma. You'll be fine.

Before I realized what I was doing, I bolted upright, grabbed my car keys, and rushed out of the apartment. Raced to my car. Gunned the engine. Zoomed out of the parking lot.

Halfway there, I admitted to myself where I was going.

I was going back to that house on Common Avenue.

Going home.

I pulled into the driveway of the residence at 2118 Common Avenue. I parked in front of the garage.

I'm home. No matter how far away I move, this will always be home.

A fuzzy sense of unreality held sway over me. I remembered an incident when I had been playing football with some kids in the neighborhood: I had been running through the grass with the ball, and practically the whole team tackled me and piled on top of me. Mashed the breath out of me, cut off the oxygen flow to my brain for a bit. Mr. Jackson, who lived next door to Grandma, came and untangled us, and I had walked around in a daze for at least an hour, my body on autopilot.

I felt like that right now. My body was on cruise control. I was simply along for the ride.

I climbed out of the car.

Night had fallen over the city. Porch lights shone outside most of the surrounding houses, and warm, golden light suffused their windows.

This time, the storm door that led to the breeze-way was unlocked. I pulled it open.

The breezeway was dimly lit. A short flight of wooden stairs led to the house. Another door led to the backyard; that door yawned open, barred only with a screen door. I looked through it and saw our dog, Cleo, a Doberman, watching me. Her nubby tail wagged, her sable eyes glimmering in the darkness.

"Hey, girl, how're you doing?" I asked.

She leaped and placed her forepaws on the screen. She whined to be patted.

I waved at her. I climbed the steps to the inner door.

This door would be locked. Grandma always kept this lock engaged.

I found the familiar, shiny gold key in my pocket.

I turned the key in the lock. I pushed open the door.

When I stepped through the doorway and into the kitchen, smoke engulfed me.

Acrid, black smoke seared my nostrils and eyes, snapping me out of my nostalgic daze and into alertness. Coughing, I dropped to the floor and covered my mouth.

The stove stood in front of me, barely visible in the twisting haze. I glimpsed a cast-iron skillet sitting on a sputtering burner, a skillet that Grandma had used for thirty years. Flames and smoke poured from the pan as if it were the opening to Hell.

The fire. This is the fire that killed Grandma. And I'm in it. Oh, shit!

I didn't think about running out of the house.

Grandma was in here. This was my chance to save her. To redeem myself.

Finally, everything made sense.

The blaze had started in the skillet, but I didn't know how to fight it. You couldn't throw water on a grease fire; it would only feed the flames, and even if it could work, the fire had grown too powerful for that approach to be effective.

My only choice was to get Grandma out of the house. I had time. The fire had not yet advanced past the kitchen.

On all fours, keeping close to the floor, I scrambled out of the kitchen and into the carpeted hallway. Thick waves of smoke rolled into the hall and into the living room ahead of me, but nothing in there had caught fire.

Heart hammering, I dashed down the hall to Grandma's bedroom. The door was closed. I rammed it open with my elbow and exploded into the room.

In the warm darkness, I saw Grandma, nestled under her bedsheets. Pungent fumes laced the air.

"Grandma, wake up!" I ran to the bed. "Wake up! There's a fire!"

"Huh?" Her voice was groggy; the bedsprings creaked as she rolled over. "What you say, boy?"

"The house is on fire!" I clutched her arm. "We've gotta get out of here!"

She coughed—a sharp, body-wracking cough that I could feel in my own bones. For perhaps the past five years, Grandma had been plagued by coughs that seemed to flare up as soon as the sun went down. I had grown so accustomed to hearing them as I dozed off to sleep that they had become as commonplace as a cricket's nocturnal whine.

But the quickly spreading smoke spurred these coughs. My own lungs had begun to burn. I dropped to my knees. Grandma and I were face-to-face.

"Oh, Lord," she said. "Fire. The smoke. Oh, Lord, help us."

"We're going to make it out of here." The smoke had brought tears to my eyes; I wiped my eyes with my shirt. "Come on. We're running out of time."

She coughed. "Can't breathe . . . can't walk." Hacking coughs punished her body.

I grabbed her arm and slung it over my shoulder. She slid out of the bed, much of her weight upon me. Under ordinary circumstances, my knees would have buckled, but adrenaline had endowed me with more strength.

With my free hand, I snatched the bedsheet off the mattress and covered our heads with it, hoping it would give us some protection from the deadly fumes.

We shambled toward the bedroom door. In spite of the sheet, smoke scoured my eyes, nose, and throat. I began to feel light-headed. As if from a distance, I heard Grandma coughing.

The smoke's gonna kill us, I thought. I dropped to the floor, pulling her down with me. We crawled out of the bedroom and into the hallway. I lifted the sheet higher to see what was ahead of us.

The flames had spread to the living room and the end of the hall. Furniture that I had grown up with— sofas, chairs, end tables, lamps—blackened like roasted marshmallows in the all-consuming fire. A rancid stench filled the air, and the heat squeezed every ounce of sweat out of me.

We could not go any farther down the hallway without risking our lives. We had to find another way.

Beside me, Grandma whispered. I glanced at her.

Her face was tortured, and her lips moved ceaselessly. I realized that she was praying.

"We're going to make it out alive," I said to her, perhaps attempting to convince myself. "We're not gonna die in here, we'll find another way out."

She continued her prayers, whispering with such intensity that I doubted she had heard me.

A dancing wall of flames slowly advanced toward us. Behind the fiery blockade, objects crashed, sputtered, exploded.

"Let's go back to the bedroom!" I said. "We can climb out through the window!"

Grandma shook her head.

I tried to pull her backward, toward the bedroom. She would not move.

"Let's go!" I said. "To the bedroom! Come on!"

"You go, Rick," she said. She gasped, coughed. "Leave me here."

"What? No!"

"You can't save me, baby," she said, her voice paper-thin. "You've been good to me, a fine man, like a son. But you've got to go on now. My time has come. Please, leave me here."

I shook my head fervently. "But I'm supposed to save you."

"No, no, sugar," she said. "You're supposed to leave me here and go on with your life."

Like a swift bird, the meaning of the words that she had spoken flitted through my thoughts, but, distracted by my growing fear of a fiery doom, I could not focus upon her message.

"No way," I said. "You're coming with me, even if I have to carry you." I reached to get a better hold on her.

As if by spontaneous combustion, Grandma burst

into flames. Her face split open like some kind of bizarre, fiery flower, skin charring, lips peeling back to reveal disintegrating teeth, eyes sinking into her blackening skull. Her arm that I had clutched ignited like a piece of dry wood, fingers curling up, shriveling, bones popping.

I screamed, and let her go. Then reached for her. But there was nothing left of her to grab. Hungry flames devoured her body as if she had been made of straw.

I howled. I had been given a second chance to save her. And I had failed.

The bedsheet on top of us had caught fire, too. Frantic, I cast it off into the fire that had devoured Grandma.

Those flames that attacked Grandma had erupted from nowhere, I thought vaguely. As if she was destined to die here. As if I was meant to learn that nothing I could have done would have saved her.

The meaning of everything that I had witnessed hit me like a jackhammer. Anguished by the hard truth, I felt a sudden urge to throw myself into the inferno, to give up and perish with Grandma and this house that held so many memories. But I couldn't. An invisible force seemed to hold me back and drive me to save myself.

I scrambled into the nearest room. My old bedroom. A double bed, a dresser, a nightstand, not much else. I didn't stop to examine anything. I flung open the only window in the room and stuck my head out through the gap.

It was about a twenty-foot plunge to the grass below. The height of the drop mattered little. I would have taken my chances with a fifty-foot fall rather than accept dying in the blaze.

I climbed onto the windowsill, focused my gaze on a soft-looking spot on the lawn, and drew a deep breath.

Then, I jumped.

I wasn't sure how long I was unconscious. When I awoke, I was lying on grass. Night still reigned.

I looked around. I saw that I was on the front lawn of the residence at 2118 Common Avenue; my car was parked in the driveway. But something was different.

It was not Grandma's house.

The address above the mailbox read 2118, but it was a completely different house. It was a beige, two-story, contemporary-style home that fit in well with the rest of the neighborhood. A FOR SALE sign stood in the yard, creaking softly in the night breeze.

Staring, I got to my feet.

The house was dark, silent . . . and clearly vacant.

I took note of my clothes. They should have reeked of smoke. But they smelled as if they had been laundered yesterday, which, in fact, they had. I did not find any stains, or rips in the fabric.

Countless questions spun through my thoughts. But it was futile to ponder them, because few of the questions had answers. I knew only one thing for sure: I could not change the past. I could only accept it and move on. A tough and unsparing—but, ultimately—liberating truth.

Sighing, I walked to my car. I slid my hand into my pocket.

I pulled out the car keys—and found a shiny gold key that was unattached to the key ring. I recognized the key. For years, I had used it to unlock the door to Grandma's house. Before I had moved away, I had given it back to her.

Now, it had been given back to me.

"Thank you," I said. I pressed the key against my lips, softly. I dropped it into my pocket.

I would keep the key with me for the rest of my life, just as I would keep all my memories of Grandma—with no more guilt to plague my dreams.

I got in the car and drove away.

A Walk Through Darkness

Lee Wright's car broke down one night when he was driving through Tennessee. A late-model Chevy Impala that he'd bought only two months ago, the car coughed, sputtered, and died while he was on the highway, snaking through the Appalachian Mountains.

Rolling with the little momentum he had remaining, Lee steered to the shoulder of the road and slowed to a stop.

"Shit." He mashed his fist against the steering wheel. "Ain't this a bitch?"

It was a few minutes past two o'clock in the morning. A helluva time to get stranded in the rural South. Especially for a black man.

Lee tried to restart the car. The engine made a pathetic clicking noise; it was nowhere near turning over.

He smacked the steering wheel again, popped the hood, and got out of the car.

It was a warm, clear June night. The moon was full, casting a pale glow that made the Chevy's red paint shimmer like fresh blood. Winding through the mountains like a ribbon of black oil, the road was deserted at that hour. Lee's only company were the night creatures, singing their timeless, forlorn songs.

He lifted the hood. Scratching his head, he looked at the mess of cables and boxes and other stuff he couldn't name. This was no good. He didn't know a damn thing about cars other than how to put gas in them and change a tire, and wondered why he'd bothered to raise the hood. Cars weren't his thing. He'd taken an automotive shop class in high school, but that had been years ago—and he'd been too busy chasing girls to pay much attention to his studies, anyway.

Lee decided to call help: Roadside Assistance, a 24/7 emergency service bundled with new cars these days. The toll-free number was printed on a sticker on a window. Peering at the number, he unclipped his cell phone from his belt holster and turned it on.

The phone searched for a carrier signal, the tiny digital dot pulsing . . . and finally declared: NO SERVICE.

"Hell, no," Lee said. He turned off the phone, and then turned it on again.

NO SERVICE.

"Come on, man, shit." He tried it a few more times, with the same result, and though it infuriated him, he was not surprised: he was in the boonies of Tennessee, after all, in one of those infamous, cellular dead zones. For all the wonders of modern technology, the cell phone providers had an uncanny ability to let you down just when you needed them the most.

He holstered the phone in his belt like a useless gun. He tried to start the car again. No luck.

He was stuck out here.

He stared through the windshield at the hulking

mountains and the desolate road ahead. He deserved this, didn't he? Karma was a bitch.

Shit like this happened to you after you'd murdered someone.

Lee had never planned on committing murder. But like so many incidents in his life, shit happened.

In this case, the shit that happened was named Anita Butler.

Lee met Anita on the Internet, on Blackplanet.com. She was in her midthirties, his age, and if the photos she posted on her Web page could be believed, she looked like Toni Braxton. She had no children, lived in a Chicago suburb—and was married.

But Lee had known from the start that she was looking to fool around. Why else would a married woman offer a provocative picture of herself wearing a thong, for the whole world to see, and then name peaches and cream as one of her favorite dishes?

Lee lived in Atlanta, which crawled with sistas hungry for men, but he liked to broaden his horizons and go out of state, too, when it was worth it.

He believed Anita was worth it. He sent her an e-mail.

Three weeks later, he drove to Illinois, and they went on their first date at Chicago's Navy Pier. Anita didn't look exactly like Toni Braxton—everyone knew those stars got cosmetic surgery anyway—but she was still a cutie, with big brown eyes, luscious lips, and a shapely, petite figure. You could never be too sure about a woman you met online. Lee had been burned before by women who posted high school graduation photos, yet had graduated ten years—and fifty pounds lighter—ago. But Anita was the real deal.

Her husband, Gary, was a salesman and was

constantly out of town on business, she said. But Lee and Anita spent that first weekend together at a downtown hotel.

And the next weekend.

And the one after that.

Then, after three months, they got careless and started hanging out at Anita's house. Lee never knew what they had done that tipped off the husband that they were messing around. But when Lee and Anita came back to her place from a jazz club late one Saturday night, hubby was waiting for them in the living room, stroking the barrel of a 12 gauge shotgun like a favorite pet.

"Enjoy your night on the town?" Gary asked. A crazed grin twisted his face, and Lee, whose bowels had seemed to liquefy, caught a whiff of scotch.

His eyes red and feral, Gary swiveled the gun toward Lee. "How long have you been fucking my wife?"

Lee didn't respond. He ran.

He ran down the hall, burst through a door, and stumbled into a dark, dank garage. He almost smashed his balls against the corner of a car, staggered away, and crashed into a tool bench, his hands scrabbling for purchase. One of his hands touched a tire iron. He held on to it for dear life. It was a weapon, his only hope.

Lee hid behind the door and caught Gary with a savage blow to the cranium when the guy stepped through the doorway. Gary emitted a strangled scream and crumpled to the floor, but he held on to the shotgun. Through a mouthful of smashed teeth, he cursed Lee and fumbled to raise the gun.

He was a tough bastard. The fight wasn't over yet.

Panic overwhelmed Lee. He started swinging the tire iron, wildly, thrashing the man on the floor, warm blood spattering his face as hard iron connected with soft flesh.

He might have gone on beating the man if he had not spotted Anita. She stood in the doorway, fist in her mouth, biting down so hard on one knuckle that blood streamed down her finger.

"Shit," Lee said. He looked at all of the blood around him as if seeing it for the first time. "What the fuck did I do?"

"You killed him," Anita whispered.

Lee looked at Gary's pulverized body. He promptly vomited the undigested remains of the Fettuccine Alfredo he'd eaten that night.

Anita put her hand on Lee's shoulder. Her touch was like ice, and her eyes were cold, too.

"You aren't going to jail," she said, in a steady voice. She glanced at Gary's corpse. "We've got to get rid of the body."

"H-h-how?" Lee asked.

"Listen to me," she said. "I've got a plan . . ."

I could use a plan right now, Lee thought, gazing out the windshield at the darkness. He couldn't sit here like this and wait for someone to rescue him, or wait for his car to magically turn on, or wait for the cell phone company to spin a satellite his way. He had to act.

He thought of hitchhiking, and nixed the idea, for three reasons. Firstly, there were hardly any cars out here—he hadn't seen one pass since he'd pulled over. Secondly, few drivers would be willing to pick up a six foot three black man who looked like a linebacker for the Atlanta Falcons. Thirdly, any driver who would pick up him could very well be a racist redneck that'd shoot him and drag him from the rear bumper like a soda can on a string. Hadn't something like that happened to a brother in Texas?

Sitting in the car was equally unthinkable. No one was going to help him out here. The days of Good Samaritans who'd go out of their way to aid you were long past.

There was only one thing to do: he had to walk through the darkness to find a gas station. Simple as that.

He opened the glove compartment and removed the .38 revolver. It was fully loaded. Black bears roamed the wilderness in this part of the state. It was good to be prepared.

Holstering the gun, he climbed out of the car and locked the doors.

The night had fallen silent, as if a deadly wind had swept through the land and obliterated every living creature. A ragged cloud passed across the moon, and during that minute or so when the moonlight was gone, Lee encountered the deepest night he had ever known. It was like being abandoned in a bottomless pit. His insides shrank.

Thankfully, the cloud moved, and the moon smiled on him again.

"Fuck this," he said. He opened the trunk, and found a utility flashlight sitting in a red metal toolbox. He'd gone to his mom's house last week to install a drainage system in her basement—although he didn't know jack shit about cars, he was handy around the house—and he'd forgotten about the tools and left them in the trunk. Lucky for him.

Holding the flashlight, Lee began to walk along the gravel shoulder of the road.

He'd driven this route several times when traveling back home after visiting Anita in Chicago. He tried to remember where the next rest area or gas station was. But most times when he was driving, he put on a CD of his favorite smooth jazz songs and cruised, paying little attention to road markers unless he needed to get gas or grab a bite to eat.

He might pay for his ignorance tonight. The closest gas station could be ten miles ahead, for all he knew.

There might be houses, up in the hills. But he didn't dare approach one and ask to use a telephone. Would a redneck respond positively to a black man banging on his door at two o'clock in the morning? Lee would probably catch a load of buckshot the instant he stepped on the front porch.

Ain't this a bitch?

He kicked pebbles ahead of him. In the moonlight, the rocks looked like loose teeth knocked out of a dead man's mouth.

He turned on his cell phone again, as if having walked a few hundred feet would make a difference. It didn't. The infuriating NO SERVICE message blinked back at him.

Cursing, he clicked off the phone.

That was when he looked up in the mountains and saw someone following him.

"We'll drive to Wisconsin," Anita said. "We'll make it look like someone robbed him and dump the car in a lake."

Anita had lit a Newport. Leaning against the car—Gary's Jaguar XK8—smoking, she regarded Gary's bloody corpse with no visible emotion. She'd offered Lee a cigarette, and though he never smoked—

other than weed every now and then—he was puffing away.

"You sure about this?" he asked. "I don't know."

"You want to go to prison, Lee?" she asked. "You know what happens to brothers in prison, don't you? You'll be somebody's bitch."

"Fuck that," Lee said, summoning some bravado. "I ain't doing time."

"Then get with the program," she said. "Let's do this. Grab his legs and I'll pop the trunk."

Lee bent to snag the dead man by the ankles. He stopped, peered at Anita.

"One question," he said. "Did you ever love this dude?"

She shrugged. "I married him for his money. A woman's gotta do what a woman's gotta do."

As Lee bent to work, he thought about what she'd just said. She was looking out for number one. That meant she would sell him out in a heartbeat if the heat came down.

As he lugged the dead body to the trunk, he started to think that if he was left with no choice and his neck was on the line, he might also have to kill Anita.

When Lee looked at the mountains and spotted someone following him, his first thought was that the interplay of moonlight and darkness had fooled him. There couldn't possibly be anyone up there, at this hour of the night. He'd most likely seen a tree or large shrub quivering in the wind, and his imagination had turned it into something threatening.

Except that trees were not shaped like men, and they didn't travel on two legs.

Lee stopped walking. He put his hand on the butt of the gun and stared up into the hills.

At that moment, a cloud cloaked the moon, dipping the mountains in darkness. The blackness was so complete that Lee could barely see his own hand in front of his face.

He switched on the flashlight. He played the beam across the rocky outcroppings and trees and bushes. He saw nothing to alarm him, but the vegetation was thick, and the flashlight didn't do a good job of illuminating the mountainside from this distance. There could be something hidden in those trees.

He sure *felt* as if something was lurking up there. Watching him from the darkness.

Lee lowered the flashlight and began walking—briskly.

He was thinking about black bears. He'd once taken a trip to Gatlinburg, Tennessee, with another woman he'd met on the Internet, and when they toured the Smoky Mountains, they had spotted a bear. The animal was six feet tall and must have weighed four hundred pounds. When it stood on its hind legs, it looked like something out of a fright film.

The bears supposedly were not interested in people . . . But there had been cases of attacks. Maulings. Killings.

He quickened his pace. As he pumped his legs, he tried to remain peripherally aware of the surrounding mountains. He didn't sense any movement. But he still had the uncanny feeling that something was keeping pace with him, following his every footstep.

Finally, he halted, and whirled, bringing up the flashlight like a weapon.

He didn't see anything. But he felt it.

"Who's up there?" he shouted.

A cool wind whistled through the mountains, rattling the underbrush.

"Come on out, motherfucker!" Lee said.

Something clattered down the mountainside. Something small. Lee chased it with the flashlight, but it was too tiny for him to make out what it was. A rock, maybe?

The thing skipped down the shelf of the mountains and bounced onto the shoulder of the road. Lee stepped forward, panning the light beam across the ground.

When he found the object, a gasp escaped him.

It was a gold hoop earring, covered in fresh blood.

They pulled off Anita's plan without a hitch. Late that night, they found a lake at a secluded park, south of Milwaukee. They emptied Gary's pockets, and ripped the stereo out of the Jaguar for good measure. Then they took the car to a knoll overlooking the lake, shifted into NEUTRAL, and sent the car rolling down the hillside, over the shore, and into the water.

Several minutes later, the car had sunk into the murky depths, out of sight.

"Later tonight, I'll call the police and give them an anonymous tip about seeing someone robbed here," Anita said. "It'll be fine."

"You've got to promise me you'll never talk about this," Lee said. "This is some serious shit. Both of us could go to jail."

Anita looked at him as if he was crazy. "Why would I do that when I plan to file for the life insurance money?"

"Huh? How much insurance?"

"One million dollars. I took out the policy on him years ago."

Lee licked his lips. The engine in his mind was revving. "Can you share some of that with me?"

"What?" She gave him a bug-eyed look.

"I helped you do this, didn't I? I deserve a cut."

"Hell to the naw. I was married to him for eight years. That money is mine."

She started to walk away from him, heading back to the car. He grabbed her arm and spun her around.

"Look, bitch—"

That was when she pulled a gun out of her purse. He recognized it as a .32.

"Get your hands off me," she said.

"Okay, okay, be cool." He released her and stuck his hands in the air. "Put that thing away, girl." He forced a laugh. "You don't need that on me."

"Go back to ATL," she said. "I don't wanna talk to you again."

"Are you crazy—"

"This night never happened," she said. "You say anything about what went down here, I'm going to the police and saying I saw *you*. I got your fingerprints all over the tire iron, baby."

"You can't do that." He stepped forward. "That's bullshit!"

She cocked the trigger and aimed it at his chest.

"Don't try me," she said. She smiled sweetly. "'Bye, 'bye."

She went to her Mercedes coupe and drove away, leaving him out there, alone. Fortunately, a gas station was only a mile away.

By the time he'd reached the gas station, he'd decided that he would have to kill Anita. He couldn't trust her not to turn him in, and he deserved a portion of that million-dollar insurance payout. If he couldn't have it, she wasn't going to get it, either.

He'd never considered himself a murderer. But she had left him with no choice. He had to protect his ass.

He returned to Atlanta, to make plans and prepare.

Two weeks later, he broke into her house in the middle of night.

But Anita was already dead.

She lay in bed, her face bloody and bruised and smashed . . . as if by a tire iron. It looked like she'd been dead for several hours.

Lee didn't hesitate. He holstered his .38, wiped down the doorknob with a handkerchief, and got the hell out of there. He hit the highway and started driving back to Atlanta.

He didn't know who had murdered Anita, and he didn't want to know. He wanted to forget all about her and her husband and his own crime.

He was swearing off online dating for good.

But shortly after two o'clock in the morning, as he was driving through Tennessee, his car broke down.

Lee's heart knocked. Kneeling, he used the flashlight to flip over the hoop earring in the gravel.

There was no doubt. The earring had belonged to Anita.

It was probably covered in her blood, too.

He pulled out his .38 and directed the flashlight into the hills above.

"Who are you?" he shouted. "What do you want?"

His voice echoed hollowly through the stillness. No one answered him.

But someone was up there, and it was not a bear

or an animal of any kind. It was a human being. The person who had butchered Anita.

Now, whoever he was, he was stalking Lee.

Lee tried to think of anyone he knew who might be motivated by revenge. He could think of only one person: Anita's husband, Gary.

But he'd killed Gary.

He remembered the grisly sight of the man's battered face, eyes drooping from their sockets, nose mashed like a piece of misshapen clay . . .

"I've got a gun," Lee said, to the darkness above. "I'll bust a cap in your ass!"

Once the echoes of his voice faded, quiet claimed the night.

A gritty, metallic taste—the taste of fear—lay thick on his tongue. The person hunting him was cunning. That much was clear. He was toying with Lee, using the darkness and the mountains to his advantage.

Lee crossed to the other side of the road. He started walking quickly.

Then, he started running.

He hadn't run in years—making runs to the liquor store didn't qualify—and within a couple of minutes, a painful stitch had developed along his side. He ignored the pain and kept pushing, sucking in great deep breaths. He kept his attention focused straight ahead. He was afraid that if he looked behind him, he would see his pursuer, and it would be the ghastly face of Death himself.

He raced around a bend in the road.

There was a service station about a quarter of a mile ahead. Moonlight glimmered on the windows.

Lee lowered his head and willed all of his remaining stamina into his leg muscles.

He ran across the gas station parking lot, his feet

swishing through the weeds sprouting from the cracked asphalt. As he neared the building, he saw that slabs of plywood covered the front door and many of the windows. The gas pumps looked as if they hadn't dispensed gasoline since 1970.

The station was closed, and probably had been for years.

"Shit!" he shouted. Pain wormed through his stomach, and he bent double, gasping. He wanted nothing more than to lie on the ground and catch his breath.

But fear kept him on his feet.

He swung around, to see if anyone had followed him. But he saw nothing, only the hulking mountains and the silent road.

A pay phone stood at the edge of the parking lot. Lee went to it, holding his aching belly. He lifted the handset off the cradle.

The phone was dead.

"Dammit, ain't this a bitch?" He slammed the phone back onto the cradle.

What next? Only one answer: keep walking.

He heard the hum of an approaching car. His heart skipped with excitement.

Then he spotted a pair of headlights, weaving around the curve in the road.

He'd been afraid of hitchhiking before, but he'd take his chances. Nothing could be worse than walking out here in the dead of night being stalked by Anita's unknown killer.

He sprinted to the shoulder of the road, waving his arms.

"Hey!" he yelled. "Hey, I need a ride!"

The car—it appeared to be a black sedan—began to slow.

"Hallelujah, thank you, Jesus!" Lee cried. He loathed church, but he swore that he was going next Sunday and would drop a hefty offering into the collection plate.

Lee pulled his shirt over his belt, to hide the gun. No sense frightening his rescuer. He wiped his face with a handkerchief, removed his cap, and ran his fingers through his short hair, to make himself presentable.

The car drew to a stop.

In the process of walking closer, Lee stopped, too.

It was a Mercedes. With Illinois license plates. The plates read: ASMUV1.

It was Anita's car.

The passenger door swung open.

And in the backsplash of the interior light, Lee saw Anita. She sat behind the steering wheel, face bashed in and crusted with blood, ruptured eyes rolling in their sockets, like a Halloween mask.

Anita's busted lips twisted in a grin. Something— a loose tooth—rolled out of her ruined mouth.

It's a mask, makeup, this is a joke, this isn't real . . .

Gagging on his own fear, Lee stumbled backward. He fumbled for the gun in his waistband, though a rational part of his mind—the only rational part left—asked him why bother using a gun against someone who was already dead?

He backed into something solid. The old gas pumps. Then a putrid stench filled his nostrils. He turned, hands trembling on the revolver.

Gary stepped around the corner of the island.

He looked as battered and dead as Lee had left him when he'd pushed the car into the lake.

Lee couldn't speak, couldn't move. He felt something warm streaming down his leg, and realized, vaguely, that he'd pissed on himself.

"I got to that bitch before you did," Gary said, in a water-choked baritone. "Got her behaving like a proper wife again. But you didn't think I'd forget about you, did you, Lee?"

Gary gripped a tire iron. He raised it.

Lee regained his motor functions again. He aimed the gun at Gary and squeezed the trigger.

A bullet drilled into Gary's forehead. Dark watery fluid poured from the wound.

But Gary kept coming.

"My turn," Gary said.

Lee spun, and ran.

He got maybe fifteen feet when Anita drove after him. The Mercedes smashed into his legs. He fell to the pavement, screaming. He tried to get up, but his legs wouldn't obey.

Gary shuffled toward him. Malice shone in his yellow dead eyes.

"Please," Lee said. "I'm sorry, man, I never meant to kill you. Oh, God, please, don't kill me!"

Gary swung the tire iron at Lee's head.

Lee blacked out.

Lee awoke sometime later.

How much later, he was not sure. But it was dawn— a sunrise crested the ridge of the mountains. Looking at the sunshine made his head hurt. He felt a knot throbbing on his skull.

He lay on the ground, on a bed of thick grass. His hands were bound behind him, and ropes bound his legs, too. He had been stripped down to his boxer shorts.

Something sticky and warm had been smeared on his chest, arms, and thighs. It smelled like honey. A cloud of insects buzzed around him, alighting on his honey-smothered flesh.

What the hell was this? Where was he? How had he wound up here?

He rolled onto his side, and saw a bloodstained tire iron.

Jesus, that was all real? I thought it was a nightmare . . .

In the distance—but not too far away—something grunted. Something big.

What would make a grunt like that, in the Tennessee mountains?

He didn't want to think about it.

A minute later, he didn't have to. Branches crackled and weeds crunched, and an enormous black bear emerged through the maples.

Lee began to laugh. It was the braying cackle of a man who had lost his mind.

"Ain't this a bitch?" he asked. "I'm left up in some mountains by a dead man to get eaten by a bear! Come on over here, Smoky! You ever tasted dark meat?"

Grumbling, the bear lumbered toward him. Drool dripped from its large, yellow teeth and spattered like warm butter on Lee's stomach.

"I'm dipped in honey!" Lee cried. "Eat up, motherfucker!"

The bear roared.

The Monster

It was half-past two o'clock in the morning, and what frightened Jared more than anything in the world was having to get out of his bed in the middle of the night and go to the bathroom. Most times, he'd rather pee on himself. But he was ten and couldn't pee on himself any more. Mom would get upset, and Dad would . . . well, he didn't want to think about what Dad would do to him.

But the thought of getting out of bed was actually worse than thinking of what Dad would do to him if he peed on himself. See, there was a monster under his bed.

Jared lay under the covers, his bladder throbbing. It was way too dark in the room; the curtains were closed and Dad wouldn't let him sleep with a night-light. The only light came from the clock on the nightstand. The clock digits gave off a ghostly, greenish glow.

He rose, his eyes slowly adjusting to the darkness. He held his breath. Listened.

He heard the monster, breathing softly. It might be asleep. Did monsters sleep? He didn't know. He had never even seen the monster, really. But it was real. It crawled under the bed only at night, and he always heard it breathing, shifting around, or whispering in a strange language that he didn't understand.

The monster had begun living under his bed a few months ago. He remembered when the monster first arrived. It had been the night that Mom and Dad had gotten into the worst fight they'd ever had (until then). Crouched under his bed covers, Jared had heard every turn of his parents' battle: the shouts, the breaking dishes, the cries, and the scary sound of flesh smacking flesh. Jared had wanted to do something to help Mom, but he was afraid. Later that night, Dad had left the house, and that was when Jared realized that he hated his father—well, stepfather, really. Mom taught him that it was wrong to hate people, but Jared couldn't help the way he felt. Sometimes he was sure that Mom hated Dad, too.

And in the middle of that unforgettable night, unable to sleep, Jared suddenly became aware of deep breathing beneath his bed, as if a big dog had crawled under there and fallen asleep. Summoning his courage, he peeked underneath the bed. He saw the faint glimmer of a pair of bluish eyes.

The sight had sent him to his parents' room, screaming. Mom thought he was upset about the big fight and let him sleep in the bed with her. Ordinarily, he never would've wanted to sleep in Mom's bed because that was for babies, but he was too scared to go back to his room. He didn't tell Mom about the monster. She would never believe him. Adults never believed anything that kids his age talked about—especially when the subject was a monster.

When morning finally came, he crept into his

room and checked under the bed. Nothing was there. He wondered if he had dreamed up everything.

That was, until the monster returned a few nights later, when Mom and Dad had another fight.

There was one thing Jared knew for sure about the monster: it came around only in the late night hours, after his parents had fought.

He began to believe that the monster was there to keep him company. The monster scared him, but in a strange way, he sort of felt safe when it arrived. Kind of like Mario Jenkins, the biggest, baddest bully at his school, who seemed to like him for a reason he didn't understand. Mario frightened Jared and he was careful not to upset him, but he felt that whenever Mario was around, he was protected. It was weird.

Mom and Dad had been fighting again that night, so the monster was there. But Dad hadn't left the house. Jared thought Dad was sleeping on the couch downstairs. During the fight, Jared heard Mom run upstairs and lock herself in the bedroom, and Dad had been crashing around downstairs, making so much noise Jared was sure the police would come. But they never did. After a while, Dad finally got quiet and probably fell asleep in front of the TV like he usually did.

Jared looked at the bedroom door, which was open just a crack. The white door seemed to be far away, like the other end of a whole basketball court. But things were always like that at night, in the dark. His senses got screwy.

His stomach was starting to hurt, he needed to pee so badly.

Slowly, he pulled away the covers. Cool air wrapped around his legs. Dad always kept it so cold in the house that Jared sometimes slept with socks on. He didn't have socks on then. He wished that he did, to protect his feet in case the monster grabbed a foot.

He would have to be fast.

He got an idea. Instead of swinging his legs over the side of the bed, and risk getting snared by the monster's tentacles (he figured the monster had to have long, ropy tentacles, like an octopus), he stood on the mattress; it creaked a little beneath him. Quietly, he walked to the end of the bed. He checked the surrounding carpet to make sure that nothing waited to trip him.

Then he leaped off the mattress.

He landed on the floor with a soft thump.

He looked behind him. Nothing rushed out at him from under the bed. He didn't see a tentacle, or glowing blue eyes. Everything looked normal.

But he heard the monster breathing. Its breaths were not as slow and deep as before; it drew shorter breaths, as if it was awake. Alert.

Maybe it planned to catch him when he returned to the bed. If that was what it really wanted to do. He didn't know. He hadn't even begun to plan how he would manage to climb under the covers. He couldn't think about it yet. His bladder was aching.

He flung open the door and rushed down the hall-way to the bathroom. He could barely get his paja-mas down fast enough to keep from leaking all over himself. Nasty.

It seemed like he peed forever. He'd drunk a lot of Pepsi before he went to bed. Mom had ordered a pepperoni-and-cheese pizza for dinner and a twelve-pack of Pepsi, and soon after the pizza got there, she and Dad had gotten into the argument. Jared had taken the cola to his room and sipped it nervously while he listened to them battle. He must've drunk four cans' worth. Mom would've been upset if she had known.

Jared had just finished relieving himself and was washing his hands when he heard Dad's heavy footsteps on the stairs.

Jared frantically dried his hands on a towel. He reached to switch off the bathroom light . . .

"Jared, what the hell are you doing up?" Dad asked.

Jared froze, hand poised over the light switch. Dad emerged like a giant from the darkness of the hallway, entering the arc of light that spilled from the bathroom. He wore his normal sleeping gear: white underwear. That was all. Dad had been living with him and Mom for three years, and Jared had never gotten used to the sight of the man strolling around in his underwear. There was something disgusting about it.

Dad carried his black leather belt loosely in his hand; it resembled a dormant snake. Both Mom and Jared knew the belt very well.

"Speak up, boy," Dad said. Leaning against the wall, he dug his hand into his crotch and scratched. "Damn, why you always act like you can't talk?"

"Umm, I was just using the bathroom," Jared said. "I'm going back to bed."

"Slow down, little man." Dad raised his hand. Jared smelled whiskey and funk rolling like hot steam from Dad's body; he coughed into his hand. "You know what me and your Mama were tangling about tonight?"

Jared shrugged. He chastised himself for not escaping back to his room before Dad appeared.

"Don't act dumb, Jared. It was about your sorry-assed daddy. I don't want him calling my house. I don't care if he's only calling for you. This is my crib and he's disrespecting me." Dad suddenly farted loudly, and the nauseating sound was like an exclamation point. Jared grimaced.

"The next time he calls here, you hang up on him," Dad said. "You don't say a word to him, and you don't tell your mother. Clear?"

"But . . ."

Dad sprang from the wall. "But what?"

Jared chewed his lip. "But . . . he's my father. You aren't." The words slipped out of him, and the instant they did, he knew he'd made a mistake.

Although Dad had been drinking, he moved toward Jared with startling speed. The next thing Jared knew, Dad had seized him by his shoulders, hefted him in the air, and pinned him against the wall. Terror ran like hot oil through his veins, and he felt himself needing to pee again.

Dad's face, twisted by fury, floated like a death mask in front of him. Spittle sprayed from Dad's lips as he spoke.

"You listen to me, you little bastard. I'm your daddy. That nigga that you think is your daddy—forget him. He ain't here. I pay the bills and take care of you and your Mama. If I ever hear you disrespect me like that again, I'm gonna break my belt over your ass. Clear?"

Jared could barely breathe. When he tried to speak only a thin whistle of air came out.

Dad shook him, making Jared's head knock against the wall. He felt dizzy.

"Hear me? Is that clear?"

Tears leaked from Jared's eyes. His throat was too tight for him to say anything, heart pounding so hard he felt like he was going to choke. He felt warm pee streaming down his leg, and the shame that burned through him made him cry harder.

"Put my baby down right now!"

Mom's enraged voice cut through the haze in Jared's mind. His mouth flew open, and all he cried out was, "Mama, help!"

Dad dropped him, and Jared hit the floor on numbed legs. He stumbled, tears blurring his vision, but not even his tears kept him from seeing Mom in her nightgown, coming at Dad with a hammer.

Bust his head wide open, Mama, bust it open like a watermelon, he wanted to shout at her. But she was so tiny compared with Dad. Even with a weapon, she couldn't beat Dad. He was just too big, too strong.

As Mom swung the hammer at Dad, he snagged her arm in midair. He backhanded her across the mouth. She cried out, spun around and struck the wall.

"I'm the king of this house, goddammit!" Dad said. He took the hammer and smashed it against the wall, paint chips crashing to the floor. He whipped the hammer around in another wild arc, clobbered another wall. Jared was sure he was going to hit Mom. Mom cowered under Dad, holding her lip.

Jared couldn't stand back and act helpless anymore. He just couldn't. He had to help Mom.

He fled to his bedroom.

Dad whirled. "That's it, run, you little bastard. This is all your fault anyway, you know that? Everything would be fine if you hadn't been born!"

Jared made it inside his room. Had to get his hands on something that could keep Dad away from Mom. He could get his baseball bat. Mom had bought him a nice Louisville Slugger for Christmas last year.

He looked back and forth across his room. He didn't see the bat. Where was it . . . ?

He remembered that he'd left it under the bed.

He'd put the bat under the bed months ago, in anticipation of something just like this happening. But that was before the monster had arrived.

There was no way he was going to reach under the bed with the monster there. No way.

Outside in the hallway, he heard leather snapping against flesh, Dad cursing, and Mom crying softly. She endured Dad's belt whippings quietly.

He felt sick. He wanted to cover his ears and crawl back under the covers, like he always did. But he couldn't. He just couldn't take this anymore. Bat or no bat.

He rushed to the doorway. Dad's back to him; Mom was sprawled underneath Dad, her delicate body trembling as Dad popped the belt against her legs and arms in smooth, rhythmic strokes.

"Get away from her, you crazy motherfucker," Jared said. It was the first time he'd ever used the "F" word, and it felt strange coming from his lips. "Get away from her right now."

"What?" Dad looked at him. "What did you say, boy?"

"I . . ." Jared couldn't finish his sentence. He couldn't believe what he'd just said. Oh, was he in for it now.

Dad charged after him. Jared backpedaled into his room, fists balled at his side.

He wanted to hide, but there was nowhere to go. The only escape was through the doorway.

And now Dad was there.

Dad chuckled, winding the belt around his hand like a whip. "You think you're a big man now, huh? I'm gonna beat the black off your ass. This is my house, dammit."

Jared backed all the way up against the wall. Cold sweat had glued his fingers together. He couldn't have held a baseball bat if he'd had one.

"Leave him alone," Mom said from the hallway, but her voice sounded frail, beaten. There would be no rescue this time, Jared realized. He would endure this beating like a man. No more crying.

"Trying to be brave, little man?" Dad asked. "We'll see how brave you act when I start popping this belt."

Jared breathed so hard and fast he was light-headed. He felt like he could be dreaming. He wished he was dreaming and he would wake up and everything would be okay in the morning, and it would be only him and Mom in the house (they'd lived there before Dad, though Dad always called it "my house"), and Dad was gone forever. But that was only a dream. He wasn't dreaming. This was real, and Dad was going to get him.

Dad stalked forward, belt swinging, fingers flexing.

Jared always closed his eyes when he was getting a whipping. But he wouldn't close them this time. He'd suffer the beating with his eyes wide open.

If he had closed his eyes, he would've missed what happened.

As Dad stomped past the foot of the bed, a thick, purple-black tentacle launched from under the bed and wrapped around Dad's ankle with a wet, slapping sound.

"What the . . . ?" Dad started to say, staring at the rope of flesh around his ankle, and his voice was suddenly drowned out by an inhuman roar that exploded from beneath the bed, as if a lion was under there. Jared's eyes grew large enough to pop out of his head.

It's the monster, the monster, the monster . . .

The creature yanked Dad's ankle, and Dad hit the floor on his back, yelling in a high-pitched voice: "Oh, shit! What the hell? Help me, help me!" But Jared's feet seemed to be nailed to the carpet; he couldn't have moved if he'd wanted to. He was mesmerized, terrified.

Another dark tentacle shot out and twisted around Dad's other leg.

"Help me!" Dad was hollering now. He reminded Jared of an old woman.

The monster bellowed, a sound that made the walls tremble and the bed quake.

Jared didn't move. He imagined the creature beneath his bed as something that looked like an alligator but with lots of tentacles, and even more teeth . . . uh-uh, he wasn't moving.

The beast began to pull Dad toward the bed. Dad's arms flailed wildly. His hand snagged the leg of Jared's desk, slowing his progress toward the darkness underneath the bed.

Jared ran forward, raised his foot, and stomped on Dad's fingers. His hand fell away from the desk leg, and he slid closer to the bed.

"You bastard, I'm gonna get you. . . ." Dad groped for Jared's leg, but Jared moved out of his reach.

The monster thundered louder than before— and the bed itself was flung upward as if it was the lid of a hole. It hovered at almost a ninety-degree angle, suspended by an invisible force.

Beneath, there was the monster.

It resembled an alligator, like Jared had imagined . . . but not really. It had maybe a dozen muscular tentacles, like an octopus . . . But it didn't look like an octopus either, really. Its eyes glowed a gas-jet blue.

And it had teeth . . . rows and rows of long, sharp teeth.

How did this thing fit under my bed? The question flitted around the back of Jared's mind. How did I ever sleep with something like that right under me?

A shimmering pool of blackness surrounded the monster, like a dark ocean. Jared thought that the monster was much bigger than he'd figured; most of its body was concealed in the dark, watery aura.

Dad screamed.

The monster reeled Dad in, its enormous, toothy mouth wide open, Dad shrieking the entire way.

Jared wanted to turn away. He didn't want to watch. He had seen enough. But he could not stop staring.

The monster swallowed Dad whole, like pythons gulp down their prey, except the monster did it so quickly that one instant Jared saw Dad . . . and the next instant the only thing left of Dad was his worn leather belt, dangling like a spaghetti noodle from the creature's lips. Then the creature sucked in the belt, too.

Jared stared at the monster's glowing blue eyes. He waited for a tentacle to come out and grab him, too.

But the monster did not attack. Perhaps it was only his imagination, but it seemed to wink at him.

The bed, which had been suspended in the air the whole time, banged back to the floor.

Jared exhaled. His chest hurt.

He turned and saw Mom watching from the doorway. "Did you see that?" he asked.

Mom nodded. Her eyes were wide. "All of it."

Jared cautiously went to the bed. He didn't hear the monster breathing. He nudged the bed sideways a few feet.

Underneath, there was only the carpet, a few forgotten socks, and his Louisville Slugger baseball bat. No sign of the monster. No otherworldly pool of darkness.

No sign of Dad.

Mom came forward and put her arm around his shoulders.

"I don't think it'll ever come back," Jared said. "I guess it got what it wanted."

"That's right—the monster," Mom said, and they walked out of the bedroom together.

Death Notice

Ever since her husband's death eight years ago, Mrs. Mary Pryor could never wait for morning to arrive.

Every evening, she went to bed no later than nine o'clock, and woke up at six AM. She was usually just in time to shuffle outside in her house robe and slippers and pick up *The Harbor News* from her driveway even while the delivery van was still in sight, trundling down the street.

Standing at the kitchen table, Mary would carefully unfurl the paper with her spindly copper-brown fingers. She'd flip past the front-page news, sports, business, and lifestyle sections, to peel open the most important part of the paper: the Metro section.

It contained the obituaries.

No matter the day, the obituaries were always there. Someone had always died. And more often than not, Mary knew one of the deceased.

Pencil in hand, bifocals balanced on her hawk nose, she would scan the death notices, making check marks near the names of those she certainly had known, those she thought she or someone of her acquaintance might have known, and those she wanted to learn more about—to confirm whether she had ever known them or not.

After marking off the obits of interest, she would extract them with a pair of scissors as carefully as a surgeon removing an organ from a living body, and spread them on the kitchen table. She would then brew a weak cup of Folgers.

When the clock struck seven, she would start making phone calls.

She worked the phone like a telemarketer on a deadline, telling family and friends who had died, skillfully probing for connections. It was a small world—six degrees of separation and all that—but in Mary's experience, in a small town like Spring Harbor, it was more like two degrees of separation.

Sometimes, she had to dig deep to discover the connections. For instance, there was the time last year when she'd told her daughter, Denise, that an elderly gentleman who had died used to be the stepfather of the mother of the boy who'd had a crush on her in high school thirty years ago, before he went to Vietnam and got killed. Her daughter had been amazed at Mary's research.

Mary took seriously the task of unraveling the obits. Too seriously, her daughter told her. But that was fine. Her daughter was only fifty—a long ways away from Mary's wizened seventy-six—and the promise of Death wasn't near enough to her for her to understand how critical Mary's role was.

People needed to know. It was her duty to tell them.

But Friday morning, things were different.

That morning, Mary shuffled outside at dawn to pick up the newspaper, and when she brought it to the kitchen table and unrolled it, she discovered something that almost made her scream.

The obituaries were missing.

Pages four and five, which always contained the obits, featured only advertisements for cars and furniture. There were no death notices.

Mary flipped through the rest of the section, and could not find them. She searched through the entire newspaper. There were no obits, anywhere.

Had the folks at the paper forgotten to include them? In nearly a decade of her plying her trade, that had never happened. It seemed like a sick joke.

Maybe she'd gotten a defective paper.

She grabbed the phone and punched in the speed dial number for the newspaper, to demand redelivery. She was no good with gadgets; her daughter had programmed the number in for her, since Mary often called the office to complain when the paper arrived more than thirty minutes late.

A prerecorded message greeted her:

"THANK YOU FOR CALLING *THE HARBOR NEWS* CUSTOMER SERVICE DEPARTMENT. OUR BUSINESS HOURS ARE MONDAY THROUGH FRIDAY, EIGHT AM TO——"

She hung up. In her anger, she'd forgotten that the paper didn't open its offices until eight o'clock, two hours from now. She couldn't bear waiting that long to read the obits.

The telephone rang.

She glanced at the wall clock—6:05. Who would be calling her this early?

Maybe someone's died, she thought. A strange glee coursed through her.

She snatched up the phone. "Hello?"

Crackling static filled the phone. Underneath the static, she heard, faintly, voices, as if a television was playing in the background. But she couldn't understand what was being said.

"Who's this?" she asked.

Static. Low, garbled voices.

She hung up. The phone didn't ring again. It must've been a wrong number.

Back to her problem.

She parted the drapes at the front window. She spotted a paper, bundled in blue plastic, lying at the mouth of Mrs. Johnson's driveway across the street. Mrs. Johnson, the insufferably proud owner of the lush lawn that resembled the greens on a golf course.

Problem solved.

Gathering her house robe around her, Mary crept across the street. She felt like a thief, and perhaps she was doing something wrong by stealing her neighbor's paper, but it was in the service of a noble cause, she believed.

She snagged Mrs. Johnson's paper and hurried back across the road, nearly tripping over the curb in her haste to get back to her yard.

She couldn't wait until she reached the kitchen to look. Once she reached her walkway, she ripped the paper out of the wrapper and dug through it, sections falling to the pavement and skipping away in the cool morning breeze.

"No," she said.

The obits were missing from Mrs. Johnson's paper, too.

Eyes narrowed, Mary looked up and down the block. Many of her other neighbors subscribed to

The Harbor News, but what if theirs were defective, too? Stealing all of their papers would be foolish and risky.

But her need to know who had died was like a hunger pain.

Her watch read a quarter after six. Her daughter would be up; she had to be at work by seven thirty. If Mary left now, she could catch Denise while she was still home. Denise subscribed to the paper, and she lived on the other side of town, where perhaps this awful mistake had not been perpetrated.

She could have called Denise first, but she knew her daughter would refuse to look up the obits for her. She didn't understand how important they were.

The Harbor News was sold at local convenience stores, too, but that meant Mary would have to pay fifty cents, and she'd already paid for her own subscription. She lived on a fixed income and couldn't afford to waste even a half dollar.

She dressed quickly in gray sweatpants and a shirt— her exercise clothes—and got in her old Cadillac DeVille to drive to her daughter's house.

"Morning, Mama," Denise said, opening the door. She wore a house robe, and red rollers were in her hair. "You look upset. Is everything okay?"

"Did you get the paper?" Mary asked, brushing past Denise as she came inside the house, her head swiveling about like a vulture's seeking a tasty morsel.

"Huh?" Denise frowned. "Yeah, I—"

"Where is it?"

"In the kitchen, I was reading it like I always do before I go to work. What's this all about, Mama?"

But Mary had already set off down the hallway. She hurried into the kitchen.

Terrell, her twelve-year-old grandson, sat at the table. He was eating Froot Loops and reading the comics page. His eyes widened in surprise when he saw her.

"Hey, Grandma. Why you here so early?"

"I need that." She snatched the newspaper away from him. Hands trembling, she searched through it.

But her search was in vain. The obits weren't in there.

She gnashed her teeth. This was just crazy.

Denise came into the room. "Mama, what's this all about?"

"I'm looking for my obits, but they ain't in there." She tossed the paper onto the floor. "They ain't in none of the papers. It don't make any damn sense!"

"Ah, those obituaries." Denise nodded, comprehension coming into her eyes. She smiled. "Well, if they aren't in there, maybe no one's died lately. Isn't that a good thing?"

"Someone's always died. I need to know who." Mary wrung her hands.

"I've never understood it, Mama. Why are these obituaries such a big deal to you?"

"People need to know who's passed on," Mary said. "Not everyone gets the paper like I do. I got to tell folks."

Although Mary tried to explain herself as clearly as possible to her daughter, she could see from Denise's puzzled expression that her daughter didn't understand. Her daughter thought she was some loony old woman. That was one of the things Mary hated about growing older; younger folk thought you were losing your mind whenever you did something they didn't understand.

But Denise would learn better once she reached Mary's age, when Death loomed like a rising sun on the horizon of your life. She'd learn the importance of informing the living who had passed on. Because we all had to go someday. It seemed like common sense to Mary that the deceased would want everyone who'd ever known them to be told that they were no longer dwelling in this world and had moved on to a better place.

Terrell watched her, too, with the same look of puzzlement. But of course, he was only a child. Mary didn't expect him to know any better. He'd never even been to a funeral, poor baby.

"If you say so," Denise said. "But it seems kinda morbid to me."

"It's part of life. I hope that when I pass on someone makes sure my obit runs."

"Please don't talk like that, Mama." Denise frowned.

Mary laughed harshly. "You learn to get comfortable with dying when you reach my age, girl. Anyway, can you look up the obits on the computer?"

"I've got to get ready for work," Denise said. "Terrell can go on the Web and look for you."

"Mom!" Terrell said, and groaned. "I gotta go to school."

Mary hooked her long fingers around Terrell's wrist, like talons. "Come on, boy. It ain't gonna take that long. Let's go to that computer."

Terrell had a computer in his bedroom. It amazed Mary how younger people were so comfortable with these machines. Using her microwave and a remote control for her TV was about as technologically inclined as she got.

While her grandson sat at the desk and tapped confidently on the keyboard, Mary waited behind him and watched the screen.

"Found 'em, Grandma," Terrell said. He pulled up a screen filled with black text.

Mary pushed up her bifocals on her nose and leaned forward. She studied the obituaries.

"Those ain't it," she said. "Those is yesterday's obits. I done seen them already."

"But that's all they have on here."

"Look again."

"Grandma, I gotta get ready for school!"

"Then go get ready. Lemme look myself."

"But you don't know how to use a computer."

"Don't tell me what I don't know how to do, boy! Get up out that chair and go get dressed."

"Yes, ma'am." Terrell shrugged, slid out of the chair. "It's all yours."

"Hmmph." Mary settled in front of the computer. Squinting, she studied the keyboard and the screen. She'd used a typewriter before, when she'd worked as an admin at the VA; this was just like that, sort of. Except for that little gadget on the side they called a rat, or whatever. Terrell had been using that rat-thing to move the arrow across the screen, and he'd click it when he wanted to do something.

She placed her hand on the rat and moved it around the foam pad. She clicked the little button on there.

The screen flickered—and then went black.

"Uh-oh," she said, looking around. "I done broke this thing."

She clicked the button again. Nothing happened. She plucked some keys on the keyboard. Still, the blackness remained on the screen.

What could she have done wrong?

As she was about to call her grandson back in to check it out, she heard static sputter from the computer's small speakers, both of which were mounted like ears on either side of the monitor.

Lord, she had *really* broken this thing.

Then, she heard something mingled with the static. Strangled voices, difficult to understand. It was as if the computer was broadcasting a weak radio signal.

She leaned closer.

The static-obscured voices grew louder. It was like a crowd of people talking all at once. What were they saying? Had someone just said her name?

"Mary . . . want to talk to you . . . tell you . . ."

They had said her name. Clearly.

What in the name of Jesus was this?

"Mary . . . Mary . . . need you . . ."

The blackness on the screen appeared to be shifting, congealing into . . . something. Murky images flashed on the display, and ghostly lights flickered, too.

"Mary . . . listen . . ."

Terror poured through her veins.

Shaking, she bent, snagged the power cord, and ripped it out of the socket.

The voices fell silent, and the screen became a featureless black.

She exhaled.

"Grandma, why'd you unplug the computer?" Terrell asked. He came inside, holding a dripping toothbrush. "Did you find any of those obittiaries?"

"No," she said, not bothering to correct his mis-pronunciation of her prized obits. She wanted to run out of the room, but that would only scare her grandson, so she calmly pushed away from the desk and walked away. "I've gotta go now, baby. You finish getting ready for school, you hear?"

She didn't look back at the computer on her way out. She didn't want to think about what she'd seen and heard.

Because she didn't know what it had been.

Mary left her daughter's house and began driving home, a frown carved deep in the furrows of her face.

Her only recourse, she realized, was to wait until eight o'clock, when she could call the newspaper, complain about the missing obits, and demand re-delivery of a correct paper. She would not consider Denise's comment—*maybe no one had died*—because someone had always died.

As she drove, she noticed a familiar figure walking on the opposite side of the road, coming her way. It was a slender black woman with silver, shoulder-length hair, dressed in a powder blue jogging suit. It was Lillie Mae, a longtime friend. They used to work at the VA together.

Mary hadn't talked to or seen Lillie Mae in at least two weeks. The last she'd heard, Lillie Mae had been sick with pneumonia. What was she doing out this morning, strutting like a spring chicken?

Mary tapped the horn. Lillie Mae saw her, waved, and smiled.

There was something odd about her smile, Mary thought. Something secretive about it. As if she'd caught Lillie Mae daydreaming about something naughty.

Mary frowned. Lowering her window, she slowed the car.

"Hey, girl," Mary said. "What you doing out here walking? I heard you was sick."

"I *was* sick, Mary." Lillie Mae approached the car. "But I feel much, much better now, praise God."

"Praise Him," Mary said, automatically. She eyed Lillie Mae closer. She couldn't put her finger on exactly what it was, but there was something different about Lillie Mae, and it wasn't only the mysterious smile that her friend wore.

"You seen the obits today?" Mary asked.

Lillie Mae shook her head, slowly, as if she was in a daze. Her eyes, Mary noticed, appeared to be unfocused, too.

Lillie Mae gave another enigmatic smile. "Let the living tend to the dead. It's their duty."

"Amen," Mary said, and nodded sagely, but she didn't know what in the world Lillie Mae was talking about. She wondered if Lillie Mae had a fever and had gotten out of bed and started walking without her family knowing her whereabouts. She was tempted to place her palm against Lillie Mae's forehead and check her for a temperature—but the idea of touching her friend was . . . well, creepy. And Mary couldn't figure out why.

A draft seemed to have slipped inside the car and wrapped its cold arms around her.

Lillie Mae was still smiling.

"You sure you're okay, Lillie Mae?" Mary asked. "Maybe I should give you a ride back home."

"I gotta finish my walk," Lillie Mae said.

Secretly, Mary was relieved. Although she'd made

the offer to take Lillie Mae home, the idea of the woman riding next to her in the car made her skin tighten.

"When I die, Mary, I want you to make sure folks know," Lillie Mae said. "Will you do that for me?"

"Don't talk like that now, girl," Mary said. "The way you up and walking 'round you got plenty of time left."

"Remember what I said." Lillie Mae wagged her finger, and began to walk away.

The old girl was sick, Mary thought. Sick, and she didn't even know it. She wasn't making any kind of sense.

She began to drive again. She glanced in her rear-view mirror, to see if Lillie Mae was walking okay. But the woman was gone.

Still thinking about her weird encounter with Lillie Mae, Mary arrived home.

She'd hoped, a bit naively, that a new, revised paper would have been delivered and would be waiting in her driveway. But there was nothing.

The clock read seven thirty. A half hour until the newspaper office opened. She decided to pass the time by reviewing yesterday's obituaries, for which some follow-up was still needed. The background of Mr. Taylor, one of the deceased, eluded her. She was pretty sure he was the gentleman who used to drive through the neighborhood in a battered Chevy pickup, collecting soda cans to redeem for money, but she'd been unable to confirm her suspicions, and it frustrated her. She would eventually figure it out. She always did.

At eight o'clock sharp, she reached for the telephone. But it rang first.

"Hello," she said.

Heavy static answered her.

Static had never frightened her, but this time, it brought to mind what had happened while she was using her grandson's computer. A chill rushed along her spine.

Underneath the static, she thought she heard voices. A chorus of them.

They were calling her name.

"Mary . . . Mary . . . have to tell you about . . ."

Mary's knuckles, wrapped around the handset, turned pale.

". . . need you to let people . . ."

Shrieking, she tore the phone away from her ear, slammed it onto the cradle, but missed it. The phone landed on its side on the table, the tinny voices crackling from the earpiece.

"Help me . . . Mary . . ."

Trembling, she replaced the phone on the cradle.

"Lord Jesus," she whispered. She touched her chest, felt the frenzied pounding of her heart. She was convinced that she was going to suffer a heart attack.

A glass of water stood on the table. She grabbed it, drank all of it.

The clock read three minutes past eight. The newspaper office was open. But she wasn't interested in calling. The phone, previously a reliable tool for trading in gossip and information, had become an instrument of terror. She would not touch it.

The only thing she was interested in touching right now was her Bible. She would read a word from the Lord, for comfort, and then figure out what to do regarding the obits.

Her thick, tattered Bible—the book had outlived

two husbands and seen her birth three children—
lay on a small oak table in the living room, beside
her recliner. She liked to study Scripture in the afternoons, in between watching the court programs
on TV.

She picked up the Bible. The familiar feel of the
worn leather binding slowed her racing heart. She
settled into the recliner and pushed up her bifocals
on her nose, preparing to read.

The television switched on. A blizzard of electric
snow filled the screen.

Mary hadn't moved her hand within a foot of the
remote control. The TV had powered up of its own
accord.

She stared at the screen, disbelieving, as if denying what had happened would somehow make it go
away.

The TV set's volume rose several decibels; it was
so high that the static storm hurt her ears.

She grabbed the remote control on the table and
mashed the POWER button.

The television remained on.

She pressed the VOLUME button, trying to lower it.
But it didn't work.

And then, mingled with the static, she heard voices.
The same voices she'd heard on her grandson's
computer; the same ones she'd heard on her telephone minutes ago.

They were speaking her name again.

"Mary . . . we need you . . . to tell them . . ."

Mary crossed herself, pressed her Bible close to her
bosom.

Take them away, Lord, she prayed. *Whoever they are,
take them away. Deliver me, Jesus.*

But the voices did not go away. The electric snow

began to metamorphose into images. Visions of faces, the color washed out of them, as if they were behind a veil.

She could make out the face of Lillie Mae.

"Help me, Mary . . . let them know . . . you promised . . ."

A scream struggled at the base of Mary's throat, threatening to explode from her lips.

Lillie Mae's ghostly eyes fixated on Mary.

"Tell them, Mary . . . I was born September 15, 1929 . . . to Clarence Lee and Thelma Johnson . . . I lived a full and passionate life . . ."

The scream dissolved in Mary's throat.

Understanding, at last, drew her to her feet.

". . . I loved cooking, gardening . . . spending time with my family . . ."

Mary went to the kitchen table. She picked up a legal pad and a pencil.

". . . I was a member of Trinity Baptist Church and sang in the choir . . . I worked at the VA . . ."

Mary pulled a chair up close to the television and balanced the pad and pencil on her lap with sure hands.

". . . On May 19, 2006, I was called home to rest with my Heavenly Father . . ."

And Mary began to write what her departed friend was telling her, composing an obituary.

People needed to know. It was her duty to tell them.

The Woman Next Door

Late on a Saturday morning in June, Eric Richards was in the front yard, pulling weeds, when she arrived.

The Ford Expedition cruised down the street and turned into the driveway of the house next door. Eric snapped out of his daydream of being a lottery winner—one of his favorite fantasies—and watched the visitors.

"Wonder if those are the new neighbors," he muttered. He straightened, grasping a tuft of weeds in one hand. His back throbbed—a sign that, even though he was only thirty, his body was no longer a finely honed machine—and he massaged the ache with his free hand.

The Expedition's passenger door faced Eric. The door opened, and a lovely, bronze female leg, capped with a sandal, poked out.

Eric drew in a breath.

The woman who climbed out of the Ford very well might have stepped out of his daydreams and into the world of flesh and blood, because she was his dream woman, in every visible sense. Although at least thirty feet separated them, her beauty was as vivid and arresting as if he stood only inches away from her.

She was about five-six, with a shapely body that was alluringly showcased in a bright red sundress. Her lustrous dark hair fell to her shoulders in silky waves. She half-turned in his direction, and the profile of her face—large, doe-eyes, full lips, pert nose, sculpted cheekbones—snatched the remaining breath out of his lungs.

I don't believe this, he thought feverishly, like a starving man who suddenly found himself at a dinner banquet. *She's too beautiful to even be real.*

She smiled, and he swore that he saw her white teeth sparkle. She waved at him.

Startled, Eric lifted his hand and returned the gesture—involuntarily releasing the fistful of weeds. They scattered in his face, and he hastily brushed them out of his eyes.

But not before he saw the gold wedding band winking on her finger.

She's married, he thought, and felt a strange sense of disappointment. Strange because he was married, too. What was wrong with him, getting so caught up in this woman? A twinge of guilt screwed through his stomach.

The woman laughed, lightly, as if accustomed to causing men to lose their bearings. She turned to face a tall, skinny black man who walked around the front of the SUV. The couple spoke in hushed tones. He wore a wedding ring, too. He was her husband. Of course.

The man saw Eric, but he did not wave. Lowering his head, almost like a servant obeying a queen, he shuffled to the back of the Expedition, popped open the cargo door, and began to unload boxes.

The woman didn't assist her spouse. She whirled and strutted to the house's front door, hips swaying gently. Even her walk was graceful, feline, and irresistibly sensual.

She disappeared inside the house, and Eric released a pent-up sigh. He bent down and began searching for more weeds to yank.

But instead of crabgrass, he kept seeing the woman's swaying hips, statuesque legs, and diamond-bright smile.

What would your wife think? he asked himself, *if she knew you were thinking like this about another woman— a woman who is now your neighbor?*

Shame flushed his face. He had been with Tina for four years, married for three, and had never been unfaithful. Had never really been tempted to stray. His marriage was far from perfect, yet he took pride in his devotion to his wife.

But he'd never seen a woman like the one next door, either. Someone so beautiful—and so close by.

Although he knew it was wrong, he was already looking forward to meeting her.

A half hour later, feeling uncharacteristically antsy, Eric went inside his house to get a drink of water and relax for a short while.

Inside, Tina was busy doing the two things she seemed to love most: cooking and talking on the phone.

"Yeah, girl, would you believe she did that?" Tina asked, speaking into the telephone headset that she wore so often it might have been a piece of garish jewelry. Undoubtedly, she was talking to one of her girlfriends. "And then she had the nerve to come back and tell me . . ."

Eric tuned her out, a survival tactic he'd learned in his first few months of marriage. He grabbed a bottle of water out of the refrigerator and leaned against the kitchen counter, sipping and watching his wife.

Tina, in her own world, didn't notice him standing there—or didn't care. Her hands were a frenzy of activity as she whipped up yet another chocolate cake. She wore baggy Levi's, a drab blue T-shirt, and worn-out house shoes. Her brittle hair was wrapped in a scarf, and a smudge of cake frosting marred her chin.

This woman had changed so much since he had married her. When they had been dating, she had loved outdoor activities, aerobics, and healthful eating. She'd been a size five, and got her nails and hair done almost weekly. She'd been a stylish dresser who favored bold colors and formfitting outfits. And she loved to have sex.

But the woman who shuffled around the kitchen in front of him might have been Tina's ugly duckling, ice-maiden sister.

In three years of marriage, she'd ballooned up to a size eighteen. She visited her hair stylist only a couple of times a year, and hadn't gotten her nails done in months. She preferred to dress in baggy, grungy clothes, like a tomboy. During weekends, when she didn't have to work, she avoided going outdoors unless it was to go to the mall, a grocery store, or church, as if she was agoraphobic. She binged on junk food and sweets. And she had lost all desire for sex.

His marriage had suddenly become the prison that he'd always feared it would be. He was chained to a wife who bore little resemblance to the woman he'd fallen in love with.

If only I'd waited, he thought sometimes. *If only I'd held out a little longer, for the woman that I knew, beyond all doubt, was Ms. Right.*

If only he'd waited, he might've met the woman next door.

Tina finished her call. Eric spoke up before she dialed the next friend on her call list.

"We have new neighbors," he said. "I just saw them moving in this morning."

"Do we?" she asked absently. She didn't bother to look at him, intent on her baking. "We'll have to go meet them sometime."

He knew that she had no interest in meeting the neighbors. It would take her outside of her house, away from her friends and baking.

"It's a nice day," he said. "I think I'm going to go walking this evening. Want to join me?"

Her face puckered sourly. "You know I hate walking outside, Eric. The pavement's bad on my knees."

"But it's good exercise."

"I'd rather use the treadmill."

He almost laughed. The treadmill that she referred to sat in their bedroom, serving more as Tina's makeshift clothes hanger than as an exercise machine. She hadn't used the thing since he'd bought it for her birthday two years ago.

"I wish you'd get off this physical fitness kick," she added. "I married you because I wanted a husband, not a personal trainer."

"But—"

"In sickness, and in health," she went on. "You married me for my spirit, not my body."

"Right," he said.

"You act like I'm a slob. I've put on a few pounds, I admit, but I still look good, to me. I'm happy with myself, so you should be happy, too."

"That's cool, but, Tina . . ."

The phone chirped. Tina pressed the button to answer it, with the practiced swiftness of a switchboard operator. She squealed with delight when she heard who was on the phone. One of her girlfriends who lived out of town.

Although Eric wanted to continue their conversation, he knew it was pointless. Tina had tuned him out, caught up in the drama of her friend's life.

He trudged out of the kitchen and returned to the front yard.

Maybe I should learn to be content with my marriage, he thought. After all, it could've been worse. Tina kept a clean house, and cooked for them virtually every day. She was employed full time and made good money as a paralegal. She was a devout, church-going woman who believed in honesty, decency, and loyalty. She was a good woman, and would likely make a wonderful mother to their children. He was fortunate to have her.

But he just wasn't attracted to her anymore. The thought was painful and oddly liberating at the same time.

He looked longingly at the house next door, hoping to see the woman. She didn't reappear. The house was quiet. He would've expected to see a moving truck, but evidently, they would be bringing in their belongings later. Maybe he would see her again then. And then, perhaps he would meet her.

As it turned out, a week passed before he finally met the woman.

* * *

The morning of the following Saturday, Eric was outdoors, mowing grass, when the garage door of the house next door lumbered upward. The Ford Expedition rumbled out.

The passenger seat was empty, but the husband was driving.

Eric's heart leapt. Could the woman be in the house, alone?

The SUV rolled out of the driveway, down the street, and out of sight.

He quit pushing the lawn mower. The blades thumped into silence.

Since last weekend, the woman had dominated Eric's thoughts. In his mind, she had become—impossibly—even more beautiful and desirable. He longed to see her again, and had watched the house every day, waiting for a treasured glimpse of her, an opportunity to make her acquaintance.

Now, with her husband gone, he had his chance.

Chance to do what? he asked himself, as he walked briskly toward the house. *Remember, Eric, nothing can happen. Both of us are married. I'll get a friendly conversation out of this, that's all.*

Tina was in the house, talking on the phone. She would never notice that he was gone. But he felt like a kid sneaking away to steal a cookie.

His heart hammered.

He rang the doorbell. Within just a few seconds, the door swung open—as if she had been waiting for him.

When he saw what the woman was wearing, his mouth slipped open.

She wore an orange tank top that revealed deep, lush cleavage, high-cut denim shorts (Daisy Dukes,

Eric thought vaguely), and that was all. She looked like a chocolate goddess.

He pulled his gaze away from her body, and spoke. "Hi, my name's Eric. I live next door. I wanted to introduce myself and welcome you to the neighborhood."

"Pleased to meet you, Eric. I'm Diana." She had a mellow, throaty voice—just the kind he liked. Smiling broadly, she offered her hand.

Was it just his imagination, or did a current of delicious energy pass through him when he grasped her warm, soft hand?

He didn't know. He felt slightly dizzy. She was even more beautiful up close than he had hoped. He could sink in her eyes, and her glossy red lipstick looked so good on her luscious lips that he wanted to draw them in his mouth and nibble on them, like plump fruit.

"Diana, huh? That's a nice name." Although he had waited days for this opportunity, he couldn't think of anything witty and charming to say. "Like Diana Ross."

"Or the goddess Diana," she said.

"Well, you could be a goddess," he said. The words tumbled out before he realized what he'd said, and he wanted to kick himself. This was supposed to be an innocent, friendly chat, not a pickup attempt. What was wrong with him?

But he didn't apologize, and Diana didn't frown disapprovingly.

"I've noticed that you spend a lot of time outdoors working on your lawn," she said. Her voice lowered. "Do you put as much energy into everything you do?"

"If I love doing it, yes." Damn, this woman is flirting with me!

She chuckled softly, and glanced at his wedding ring. "I'm sure your wife appreciates that."

"She used to," he said.

He was edging into dangerous, uncharted territory. But he couldn't stop.

"Aww, shame on her." Diana shook her head. "Strong black men are hard to find."

"That's what they say. But it looks like you found one. Your husband."

"We've been married for only a few weeks," Diana said. "He works long hours, leaving little old me here, all alone."

"That's not very wise of him—especially with another strong black man so close by."

He could not believe the things he was saying. He didn't even sound like himself. Where was this stuff coming from?

But God, it felt so good to flirt with a beautiful woman who seemed just as interested in him.

Diana leaned closer, across the threshold. The sweet, spicy scent of her perfume enveloped him, like a mist.

He leaned closer to her. Their faces were only a few inches apart.

"I'd invite you in for a drink, but my husband will be back soon," she said. "Besides, your wife might get jealous."

"Maybe that's what she needs," he said.

She raised one long, elegant finger, pressed it against her lips, and then pushed it gently against his bottom lip, smearing blood-red lipstick across his skin.

"In time, Eric," she said in a whisper. "We're neighbors, lucky for us. You'll see me again, very soon."

As he was about to reply that he could hardly wait, he heard a vehicle roll into the driveway behind him.

Her husband had returned.

Frantically—but discreetly—trying to wipe the lipstick off his bottom lip, Eric backed away from the door. Smiling secretively, Diana mouthed the words, "'Bye, Eric," and vanished into the house.

Eric didn't want to meet her husband, worried that guilt would be evident on his face, but it was the only sensible thing to do, seeing as he was standing on the guy's property. Eric approached the man when he got out of the vehicle.

"Hi, my name's Eric. I live next door. I was just introducing myself to your wife."

The guy grunted. "I saw that." Hefting a paper grocery bag in one hand, he shuffled toward the house.

Eric stuck out his hand to be shook. Mumbling, "Name's Ted," and not meeting Eric's eyes, the man quickly shook Eric's hand. He had a weak grip.

In fact, Eric noted, the man looked fragile in general. Although he was about six-two, a couple of inches taller than Eric, he was very thin, no more than one hundred fifty pounds, and he didn't look healthy. His brown skin was sallow, his face drawn and sunken. His eyes were tinged with red. He had a long, unkempt Afro that was speckled with dandruff, and he badly needed to shave.

What did Diana see in this man? He didn't seem to be her type at all.

"Take care, be safe around here," Ted muttered, and brushed past Eric on his way to the front door. He walked with a slow, dragging gait, as if each footstep drained him. Eric had walked like that once himself—it had been when he was in the hospital, walking for the first time after having an appendectomy.

Ted was obviously ill. He didn't need to be out running errands, or working. He needed to be in the bed, being nursed back to health.

And what did he mean by that comment, ". . . be safe around here"? It wasn't as though they lived in a war zone. They resided in a comfortable, middle-class community.

Ted went in the house. Frowning, Eric walked back to his yard and restarted the lawn mower.

And promptly forgot about Ted and began daydreaming about Diana. She liked him; he liked her. What was going to happen next?

He shook his head, as if awakening from a dream.

"Nothing is going to happen next," he sternly told himself. "You're married, Eric. Remember? Forget about her, man."

But she was all he thought about for the rest of the day.

The next morning, at church, the pastor preached on a popular topic: resisting the sinful temptations of the flesh.

Eric sank lower in the pew, as if to avoid the minister's alert gaze—or anyone else in the congregation who might look at him and detect the immoral desires that burned in his heart. Although their church had over two thousand members, Eric was half-convinced that the preacher's sermon was intended solely for him.

He practically ran out of the church after service.

At home, he changed out of his suit and went into the study upstairs, to surf the Web. Tina, predictably, pursued her favorite postchurch activity: napping.

He was sitting at his computer, playing an online game, when he happened to glance out of the window beside his desk. What he saw made his mouth go dry.

The window provided a view of the house next door, and that house also had a second-floor window. Diana stood revealed in the glass, arms raised, evidently hanging blinds.

She was completely topless.

Even from a distance, the perfection of her body was obvious. Her breasts were round, full, and firm, the dark nipples like chocolate-covered cherries.

A huge, pulsating erection fought against Eric's shorts.

Close the blinds, Eric, he ordered himself. *You don't need to be watching this. What if Tina sees you?*

But he didn't move.

In fact, he wondered where he had placed his binoculars. They were somewhere in the house, maybe in the garage. He was afraid to go look for them. He didn't want to miss one second of this voyeuristic treat.

You're going to burn in hell for this.

So what? It would be worth it, she's so beautiful . . .

Suddenly, Diana spotted him watching her. He froze like a possum caught in car headlights.

She waved at him cheerfully. Then she dropped down the newly hung blinds, covering the window.

He blew out a chestful of air.

She knew I was watching her all along. She's teasing me. And it's working.

He wondered if she walked around the house in the nude. The thought was almost painfully arousing.

Forehead filmed with sweat, he closed the blinds on his window, too. But that didn't solve his most urgent problem: a throbbing hard-on that wasn't going to leave anytime soon.

He went to the bedroom. His wife slumbered on her side. She wore a baggy T-shirt and sagging sweat-pants, and her hair stuck up in wild strands.

She was hardly an attractive sight, he hated to admit, but he ached for release, and she was his wife. He stretched out beside her and pressed his stiff dick against her wide butt, rubbed insistently.

"Uh-uh, honey," she mumbled groggily. She reached back and swatted him as if he was an annoying fly. "I'm sleeping . . ."

"Come on, baby." He reached to caress one of her breasts.

"Later," she muttered, and flopped over onto her stomach, taking her hips and breasts away from him.

Eric wanted to scream. He lay there staring at the ceiling fan, images of Diana's breasts lodged in his head. His eager dick ached.

Outside of sexual activity, there was only one sure way to beat down lust—exercise. He laced his Nike running shoes, then set about running on the road that weaved through their subdivision.

When he was a few blocks away from the house, jogging along the side of the road, a vehicle roared behind him. Alarmed, he looked over his shoulder. A Ford Expedition thundered his way.

Shouting curses, he leapt onto the grass, out of the SUV's path. He stumbled over his feet and fell.

The Ford rocked to a stop. Ted, his neighbor, climbed out.

Eric got up, brushing grass off his skinned knees. "What the hell is wrong with you, man? You were gonna hit me!"

Coming around the front of the truck, Ted looked sicker than ever. Dark circles ringed his eyes. He'd lost more weight. His hair and beard grew wildly, as if he was a mountain man.

Ted pointed at Eric with a shaky finger.

"Do I have your attention now, brother?" He'd obviously meant to shout, but his voice came out soft. "Stay away from her! You don't know what you're getting into."

"Look, I don't know what you're talking about."

Ted rushed forward with unexpected quickness, snagged Eric by his shirt, and shook him.

"I'm talking about *her*!" he shouted hoarsely, spittle spraying Eric's face. "I'm warning you, if you know what's good for you, you'll keep away from her."

"Get off me, man." Eric pushed the guy away from him.

Ted staggered, and he once again appeared frail and sickly.

"I tried," Ted mumbled, shaking his head sadly. "Guy's thinking with the wrong head."

"Are you sick or something?" Eric asked.

Ted raised his head, and there was no mistaking the emotion in his watery eyes: fear.

What was this guy so afraid of?

"Just stay away from her," Ted said, in a lifeless tone. Hitching his jeans over his sunken hips, he shuffled around the truck, got in, and drove away.

"He's a nutcase," Eric decided. "And a jealous one at that."

Diana had probably said something about him to Ted—something innocent—and Ted, being a jealous husband, had gotten pissed off. The crazy dude had come out here trying to throw a scare into him. Ted's look of fear likely stemmed from his worry that Eric would steal his wife.

Couldn't say I blame him for that, Eric thought. *If she was mine, I'd be paranoid that some guy would take her from me, too.*

Still, he wondered if he was right. Something about Ted's voice bothered him. There didn't seem to be a personal threat in Ted's words. Ted's warning, in fact, seemed to be genuinely goodwilled, as if he saw Eric unknowingly walking into a lion's den and wanted to save him.

But that would mean that Diana herself was dangerous. And that, of course, was ridiculous. She wasn't a monster. She was a beautiful woman—who happened to be attracted to him.

Thinking about seeing her in the window made him start running again.

That night, Eric and his wife went to bed without making love. Eric did a mental tabulation: this marked the thirtieth day that he'd gone without sex.

A whole month without sex, and he was married, for God's sake. That was ridiculous.

Earlier that evening, he'd tried again to initiate lovemaking with Tina, and again, she spurned him. He wasn't surprised, really. She'd always had the strange idea that there was something sinful about having sex on Sunday.

So he fell asleep fantasizing about the woman next door. Those breasts . . .

When he awoke in the middle of the night from

an erotic dream, he sensed that there was someone in the room with him and his wife.

He blinked, his eyes slowly adjusting to the darkness. A slim figure stood at the foot of the bed. A sweet fragrance teased his nostrils.

It was Diana.

His heart clutched.

Diana raised her finger to her lips. She spoke in a whisper. "Hush, Eric. Don't say a word, or I'll leave."

He pressed his lips together tightly. It took a mighty effort to suppress the words he wanted to say, such as: *How did you get in my house?*

On the wall beside the bedroom door, a red light glowed on the security system control panel. The system was engaged. There was no way someone could get in without tripping the alarm. It was impossible.

But she was there.

He kept silent, nevertheless, his eagerness to see what she was going to do more powerful than his desire to ask any questions.

Beside him, Tina slumbered deeply. Nothing short of a nuclear blast could ever wake her.

Diana was nude; it was dark, but he could see her nakedness. As if a switch had been clicked in his body, his dick immediately grew stiff and ready.

In front of him, she knelt, lifted the bedspread. She burrowed underneath.

What is she going to do to me?

He felt her warm fingers tracing circles across his thighs. It was a sensual, tickling sensation. A thrill of pleasure ran through him.

The shape of her head slid closer, to the juncture between his legs.

Oh, God. I don't believe this.

Her fingers loosened his dick from his boxer shorts. She stroked him, gently, insistently.

He moaned.

Her pliant lips kissed the insides of his thighs. Soft, teasing kisses.

He squeezed his eyes shut.

Then she slid her warm, moist lips over the head of his dick. She flicked her tongue across the tip.

He grabbed fistfuls of the bedsheet in his sweaty hands.

She pleasured him with feather-light flutterings of her tongue. Then she took him all the way into her mouth. She worked him in and out—expertly, lovingly.

I don't believe this, this is the best blowjob I've ever had in my life, oh, Jesus . . .

Underneath the sheet, her head bobbed rhythmically.

As he rushed toward what would certainly be an explosive climax, she suddenly withdrew her mouth.

No! He nearly shouted the word. He teetered on the edge of an orgasm.

But she slithered from underneath the bedsheet, and rose.

"You can't do this to me," he said in a choked whisper.

Diana blew him a kiss. She quickly left the room.

He stumbled out of the bed on wobbly knees. His wet member jutted in front of him like a pole.

He searched the house for the woman. But she was gone, and all of the doors were locked.

How the hell had she gotten inside in the first place? Why was she doing this to him? This was torture.

He looked out a window, at the house next door.

He caught, briefly, a flicker of strange, greenish

light coming from a second-floor window. Then the house grew dark.

I'm warning you, if you know what's good for you, you'll keep away from her.

But Ted's warning, whatever its true meaning, was useless. Right now, he could no more keep away from her than he could keep from drawing breath. He had to have the woman.

He had to have her, no matter what.

And he began to hatch a plan to do it.

The next morning, Monday, Eric played sick. He lay in bed and spluttered out fake coughs.

"I'm sorry you aren't feeling well, honey," Tina said, dressed for work in a blue pantsuit. She lay her palm against his forehead, checking his temperature. "You want me to stay here for a little while? I can go to the office late."

"I'll be all right, you go ahead to work," he said, in the raspiest voice he could manage. He coughed. "I'm just going to pop Tylenol and stay in bed all day."

"Okay, baby. I'll call and check on you at lunchtime." She kissed him on the forehead, and left.

He felt guilty as he watched his wife leave. Tina loved him, trusted him, and he was lying to her. In spite of her faults and her inability to please him, she was a good woman. A genuine wave of sickness passed through him.

The ill feeling faded when he thought about Diana's soft lips kissing his dick last night.

Ted's right, I'm thinking with the wrong head—which gets brothers in trouble all the time, he thought. *But I'll be damned if I can help it.*

He lay in bed until he heard Tina's car drive away. Then he threw off the bedsheet.

He called in sick to work, dressed in a T-shirt and shorts, made some coffee, and hunkered down on the sofa near the window that faced Diana's house. And waited, and watched.

At precisely 8:05, Ted drove out of the garage in the Expedition and pulled away. Diana wasn't with him. She didn't have a car, and she didn't work. At first, Eric had thought that was odd, since they didn't have any children. Now, he thought it was the perfect situation for what he wanted to do.

Within three minutes, he was at Diana's front door, ringing the doorbell.

No answer. But she had to be in there.

He knocked. When knocking brought no response, he put his hand on the doorknob, and turned. The door opened.

You're about to walk into another woman's arms, his conscience told him. *You're going to cheat on Tina. Is it worth it? Think about the consequences.*

He was a man who always did the right, responsible things. Treated his wife with respect and love, worked with integrity, carried himself with dignity. His being here, standing at the door of a gorgeous woman who he wanted to fuck so badly it hurt, was like an episode out of a sinful fantasy. Eric Richards didn't do stuff like this in real life.

But he was there on the threshold, and though his conscience shouted at him to run away, his body hungered for the woman.

Hunger won out.

He stepped inside. He called out, "Diana? Are you here?"

Silence. He walked deeper into the house. A sweet, spicy scent hung in the air.

Diana's scent, he thought, and felt his loins stir.

But the weird thing was that the house had no furniture. No sofas, tables, chairs. No televisions or radios.

He looked in the refrigerator. It was packed with cases of bottled water—dozens of bottles in all. That was it. There was no food in the freezer, either.

Puzzled, he went upstairs. "Diana? It's Eric. Where are you?"

Still no answer. He wandered into the master bedroom.

A large, circular bed lay on the floor. It reminded him of those low, padded beds that dogs slept on, except it was large enough to accommodate two adults. Red-stained sheets lay crumpled across the cushions. Blood?

As he was bending closer to examine them, he saw movement outside the window that overlooked the backyard.

It was Diana. She was walking into the woods behind their property. He got a glimpse of her backside. She was nude.

His mouth grew watery. Forgetting about the stained sheets, he ran out of the house to follow her.

A fine morning mist covered the forest. The woods stretched on for at least half a mile, Eric remembered, from his initial tour of the housing community. Anything could happen back there . . . and no one would know.

He raced through the underbrush, searching for Diana. After several minutes of running without seeing a sign of her, he reached a clearing, and stopped to regain his breath.

Where had she gone? She hadn't been that far ahead of him—

Someone shoved him from behind.

He stuck his arms out just in time to cushion his fall.

Behind him, Diana laughed. "Gotcha, Eric."

She was completely nude. The dark, crispy hairs of her sex glimmered in the morning light.

He had several questions he wanted to ask her. How had she gotten in the house last night? Why wasn't there any furniture in their house, and only water in the refrigerator? And what was the deal with that weird bed?

But he didn't ask a single question. It didn't seem to matter, right then.

"You led me on a hell of a chase," he said. He started to get to his feet.

Diana put her foot against his chest and pushed him back down.

"Stay. Lie there and take off your clothes."

He obeyed. Stripping out of his T-shirt and shorts took only half a minute. His dick strained against his boxers.

"Boxers, too," Diana ordered.

Okay, now this is getting freaky, Eric thought. But he did as she asked. The air was cool against his skin. His dick stood up like an exclamation point.

"Very good," she said. "Now, spread your arms and legs."

"What are you going to do?"

"Shut up and do it."

He obeyed again, grass brushing against his skin.

One of his secret fantasies, that he'd never shared with anyone, was for a woman to dominate him.

In fact, it was another of his fantasies to have sex in the woods. And it was another to—*damn, how does she know this*? he thought, as he watched what she was doing—be tied up.

Loops of rope encircled the surrounding trees; she had planned in advance for this, it seemed. Using them, Diana bound his ankles, then his wrists. She drew the ropes tight—not painfully so—but taut enough to immobilize him.

Spread-eagled on the forest floor, he was under her control. His breaths came in short, excited gasps.

Diana stood over him, a smile curved across her radiant face.

"How do you know so much about my fantasies?" he asked. "It's like you're reading my mind."

"Maybe I am."

Then she slid on top of him, his dick pressed against the damp hairs of her sex, yet not penetrating her. She lay against him and rubbed her body against his, her breasts sliding across his chest. She kissed him, and her tongue was like warm liquid.

He groaned. His erection throbbed almost painfully.

Diana reached down between them, dipped her fingers into her juices, and then wrapped her slick hand around his dick. She stroked it.

"I want this," she said. "Can I have it?"

"It's all yours."

She smiled. "Can I have you?"

"I'm all yours, too."

Closing her eyes, she leaned back, her hand guiding him inside her. It was a miracle that he didn't explode right then. She was so warm and so tight, wrapping around him like a wet, second skin. She began to rock, with nearly excruciating slowness.

He closed his eyes and allowed ecstasy to overtake him.

A distant part of his mind thought: *I'm lying here in the forest, tied up, getting my brains fucked out by the most beautiful woman in the world. I can die after this, because nothing will ever feel this good . . .*

He heard a soft hissing coming from somewhere nearby. Lulled into a sexual stupor, he opened his eyes lazily.

The hissing came from Diana.

Or rather, the creature that used to be Diana.

It was the same size as the woman, but the similarities ended there. It was a reptilian thing, with green-purple scales, a large, egg-shaped head, and glowing, alien yellow eyes. Sibilant hisses issued from the creature's fang-filled mouth.

Eric screamed. He struggled to break away.

But the ropes had trapped him in place.

Oblivious to his terror, the beast continued to move on top of him. Its muscles squeezed his dick insistently, as if it was milking him, and in spite of his revulsion, he felt his body thundering toward a soul-quaking orgasm.

Oh, God, help me, please help me, God . . .

When the orgasm came, it was like being turned inside out. He howled, emptying himself into the creature's womb, and the creature shrieked, too, and he simultaneously felt a warm fluid saturating his pumping dick. Daring to look, he saw a greenish substance pooling across his groin. It burned, like rubbing alcohol seeping into an open wound. Tears filled his vision.

I'm infected, shit, this thing's infected me with something . . .

He prayed that he would pass out. But he didn't. He closed his eyes, as if this was only a nightmare that he would wake from when he opened his eyes.

When he opened his eyes, the woman was back. She leaned over him, smiling.

She was so gorgeous that he wondered whether he had imagined the monster.

"You saw me as I truly am," she said, dashing his hopes that his imagination had run away with him. "I've never been able to keep up my disguise when I get that turned on."

His stomach roiled. But he had the presence of mind to ask, "What . . . What are you?"

"Ever heard of a succubus?"

He vaguely remembered what the word meant— something about a female demon that seduced men—but he couldn't think clearly enough to trust his memory.

Her brown eyes gleamed, like a cat's that had trapped a mouse under its paw.

"You're mine now," she said. "You'll come when I call you. Be ready."

She bent to kiss him. Repulsed, he tried to turn away. She only laughed. She kissed the corner of his mouth.

"Good-bye, baby. For now."

Climbing off him, she strutted away and vanished into the woods.

You're mine now.

He couldn't accept what he had seen and heard. Wouldn't accept it. It was too crazy to believe.

Frantically, he worked to free himself from the ropes. The ropes loosened after a few strong tugs. He freed his wrists, then his ankles.

As he dressed, he noticed that his pubic area was red and sore. The green fluid . . .

It didn't happen, he told himself. *Don't think about it.*

But he was starting to feel feverish and weak.

Somehow, he made it out of the forest and back to his house. He didn't even look at the neighbor's house. He stumbled inside and collapsed on the sofa.

When Tina called at lunch to check on him, he wasn't lying this time when he told her that he felt awful.

Eric was bedridden for two days. He faded in and out of nightmares in which he lay on a bed, and a serpentlike creature curled up against him, attached its tentacles to tender parts of his body, and steadily sucked his blood.

The evening of the second day, Tina came into the bedroom with a bowl of chicken-and-noodle soup on a tray.

"Dinner," she said.

"Thank you, honey." He scooted up into a sitting position. His strength was beginning to return.

Tina placed the tray on his lap, and then sat on the side of the bed. Although she wore her usual T-shirt and baggy sweatpants, she had never looked more beautiful to him.

That's what guilt does to you, he thought. *Makes you appreciate the things you have.*

He ate with gusto.

"You know, about an hour ago, an ambulance was at the house next door," Tina said.

He nearly dropped his spoon. "It was?"

"The paramedics carried out a man on a stretcher. From the looks of it, he had died. What a shame.

Those folks moved in only a couple of weeks ago. I never got the chance to meet them . . ."

With a shaky hand, Eric pushed away the soup. "I'm full."

"You sure? You seemed hungry."

"I'm fine. I'm going to go back to sleep."

Her brow was furrowed with worry. "Let me check your temperature—"

"Later, Tina. Please, just let me get some rest."

When she left, he lay there, heart racing.

Ted was dead. He'd looked unhealthy since Eric had first met him. As if he was just wasting away.

Dread sat in his stomach, like a ball of ice. He didn't understand where it came from, but it was there.

Something terrible was going to happen to him, he knew.

It happened at midnight.

Eric lay in bed beside his wife, trying unsuccessfully to relax and slip back into sleep, when the voice rang in his mind like a clear bell.

Come to me, Eric. It's time.

As if he was a puppet manipulated by strings, he bolted upright. He climbed out of bed and left the house.

As he walked, he ordered his body to disobey the call, turn around, and go back to bed. But it was impossible to resist the command. His body was no longer his own.

It was hers.

She was waiting for him at the front door of the house next door. Although she looked like a woman, her eyes glowed faintly with that yellowish light.

Terror made his heart pound wildly, but he was powerless to run away.

She embraced him tightly, her hand pressed against his buttocks. He felt a sharp pain in the flesh of his left hip and then blood being siphoned out of his body.

Even if he'd had the ability to control his body, he would've been too scared to look over his shoulder and see how she was doing this to him.

"I hope you'll sustain me longer than Ted did," she whispered. "Maintaining this wonderful female body demands a great deal of hot male blood."

Everything finally came together for Eric. Diana, truly, was not a woman at all. She was some kind of creature—that fed on men. It explained why Ted had looked so sickly. It explained why Ted had warned him to stay away from her.

But he'd been too drunk with lust to listen.

"We're leaving for a new home tonight," she said to him. "I don't like to stay in one place for too long. Humans are too nosy."

He hoped he would see his wife again, but suddenly he realized it was never going to happen. Diana was never going to let him go.

"Go upstairs and pack our bed," Diana ordered.

Dutifully, he lowered his head and shuffled to the stairs.

His life was over. She was going to use him, like she'd used Ted, and then pick her next victim.

He only hoped that he could convince the next man to stay away from her, before it was too late.

Flight 463

As soon as the Boeing 757 started roaring down the runway for takeoff, Mya, Sean's wife of barely more than forty-eight hours, reached into his lap, grasped one of his hands, squeezed her eyes shut, and started praying.

Sean, always embarrassed at public prayer anywhere outside of church walls, looked around to see who might be watching them. They were seated on the right-hand side of the plane, and had the three seats to themselves. On the other side of the aisle, a teenage girl listened to an iPod, bobbing her head to the beat, and a businessman perused *The Wall Street Journal*. No one paid attention to Sean and his wife.

The aircraft began to ascend into the morning sky.

Mya bowed her head, her long black hair falling over her cinnamon face. "Lord, as we embark on this honeymoon to celebrate our marriage, we ask that you grant us safe passage to and from our destination in Hawaii. Send one of your guardian angels to watch over us, dear Lord, and keep us from harm. We put our abiding faith in you, Lord; our welfare is in your unchanging hands. In Christ Jesus' name we pray, Amen."

Sean moved his lips to say, "Amen," but didn't voice the word. The same way that he lip-synched hymns in church.

Unaware, as always, of his deception, Mya glanced out the porthole—she'd insisted on having the window seat—and looked back at him. She smiled tightly.

"I love you," she said. "My hubby."

"Love you, too." He kissed her forehead. "Wifey."

The airplane steadily climbed. Atlanta's skyline began to recede in the hazy distance.

"I wish we were already in Maui," Mya said. "This is going to be a long trip."

"No kidding. Five hours to LA, then five more to Kahalui—we're gonna be beat when we finally get to the hotel." He admired her figure; petite and shapely, Mya wore khaki shorts and a pink halter top. Sean sighed with regret. "I doubt we'll be consummating our marriage tonight."

"We'll have plenty of time for that." She grinned.

They were booked for six nights at the Westin in Maui. The honeymoon would cost them a small fortune—and since Sean was an elementary school teacher and Mya was a nurse, they weren't exactly the Rockefellers—but it was, Sean hoped, the first and only time he'd ever *go* on a honeymoon. Mya was the love of his life, and he'd resolved that they would splurge on occasions that mattered to them. Their honeymoon mattered.

"I wish your grandma had been there," Mya said, admiring the sea of clouds outside the airplane. "It wasn't the same without her."

"She was there in spirit," Sean said.

He had to believe that, or else he would go insane.

They'd had a small but elegant wedding at New Life Baptist, Mya's family church, and a reception afterward in the fellowship hall. Only forty family and friends had attended. Although it had been a beautiful, joyous affair, it had also been melancholy, as the person who had been a major part of Sean's life was missing: his grandmother, who'd raised him by herself since he was a baby. Grandma had died six months ago, and every day Sean felt her absence, poignantly.

And bitterly, he thought. A stroke had felled Grandma, turning the woman who had once been the epitome of a strong black woman into an adult-sized child unable to speak without saliva dripping from her mouth, unable to feed herself, unable to take care of her own bodily functions, and worst of all, barely able to remember who he was. She'd spent the last two years of her life in a nursing home, gazing vacantly at ugly wallpaper for hours at a time and silently enduring her humiliating condition, seeming to care only about the old, thick Bible that she kept in her lap—like a child clutching her favorite blanket.

Her attachment to the Good Book struck Sean as ironic. What had happened to Grandma was God's fault. Grandma had been a devout Baptist, in church three times a week, always ready to feed the hungry and clothe the homeless. She'd spent her life serving God, but God had deserted her in her hour of need. Did a loving, compassionate God allow his children to suffer?

Sean had decided that the answer was: No. God was neither loving nor compassionate. God didn't give a damn. You might as well worship the sun or the moon. At least you could see them.

Mya pulled Sean's hand close to her heart.

"I hope we enjoy a long life together," she said. "Full of kids, grandkids . . . great-grandkids. I want us to share all of those things, sweetie."

"We will."

"You sound so sure. I wish I had your confidence. I worry too much sometimes. Like about this flight . . ."

"Hush now," he said. "It'll be fine. You said a prayer, remember? Have faith."

"Do you have faith?" She looked at him, full on.

"Of course I do. Why would you ask me that?"

She shrugged. "Sometimes I wonder, that's all."

He felt the heat of guilt warming his face. Mya knew the truth. He hadn't fooled her.

But he said only, "I have challenges every now and then, like everyone else. Does that make me an atheist?"

"I didn't say you were an atheist. Why are you so defensive?"

Why the hell are you asking me about my faith? he almost snapped. But he checked himself. They were on their honeymoon. This wasn't the time for an argument.

"I'm sorry," he said. "I guess I'm tired, a little irritable."

"I'm tired, too." She yawned. She'd taken a Dramamine before they boarded, and the effects were probably kicking in. "I'm gonna take a nap for a little while."

"Sounds like a plan."

But as he watched her close her eyes, her question rebounded in his thoughts. *Do you have faith?*

He had faith, of a certain kind. He had faith that God was heartless and cold and would abandon you when you cried out His name. He had loads of faith in that.

But he could never be bluntly honest with his

wife. He put on an act, for her benefit, because she *wanted* to believe, and it would be cruel to tell her the truth about God. She would learn, in due time, on her own.

Yawning, Sean picked up the in-flight magazine. He started to read.

Several minutes later, the captain announced that they had reached a cruising altitude of thirty-three thousand feet, and switched off the seatbelt sign and gave them permission to move around the cabin. Sean rose from his seat and walked down the aisle, toward the lavatory.

Halfway there, the aircraft hit a stomach-tossing patch of turbulence. Sean pitched forward and braced himself against a seat, breaking what would have been an embarrassing fall.

When he looked up, he found himself staring at the occupant of a seat a couple of rows ahead. An elderly black woman.

She looked exactly like his dead grandmother.

Staring at the woman, Sean's spine went as rigid as a steel pole.

This can't be Grandma. Your mind is playing tricks on you, Sean. You're thinking about Grandma because of what Mya said and you're imagining that this old lady is her.

But the resemblance was uncanny. The woman had smooth walnut-toned skin, hair as white as cotton, a generous mouth, full lips, and large copper-colored eyes. She wore a navy blue dress. Her large hands—Grandma had strong hands because she'd spent her youth picking cotton in Mississippi—gripped a giant, tattered Bible. It was just like the Bible that Grandma had owned.

But Grandma's been dead for six months. This isn't her.

"Excuse me, sir," came a woman's voice from behind him. "Are you going to the lavatory?"

"Uh, yeah, sorry." Sean gave an apologetic glance to the woman, a flight attendant. He forced himself to walk forward. It felt as though his shoes were cast in concrete.

The old black woman stared straight ahead. Sean braced himself to walk past her.

If I hear her talk and she sounds like Grandma, I'm going to lose it.

But as he brushed past, taking extra care not to touch her, she didn't say a word, and she didn't look at him. She slipped on a pair of bifocals that lay on her bosom, opened her Bible, and began to read.

Sean got into the lavatory and used the toilet. He splashed cold, purifying water on his face.

"Get a grip," he said to his reflection in the mirror. "It's coincidence. Everyone has a twin, remember."

He'd heard the theory many times before, had actually advanced it himself when someone that he was meeting for the first time said that he reminded them of someone they knew. "Well, everyone has a twin, you know?" he would say. "There's five billion people on the planet. Chances are, a few of us look a lot alike."

But there was a major difference between a strong resemblance and a *replica*.

He loathed walking down the aisle again and passing the woman. But obviously it was the only way back to his seat.

He left the lavatory. Ahead, he spotted the top of the woman's snow-white cap of hair. His heart hammered.

He marched forward.

As he passed the woman's seat, she spoke.

"Hey, mister. Hold on."

She sounded like Grandma: a soft, raspy voice with a thick Mississippi Delta accent. No one could imitate that voice.

He clamped his teeth against a scream. Slowly, he turned.

The woman was studying him. She smiled. Her teeth were large, and very white. Dentures.

"Yes?" he asked, his voice cracking on the word.

"I was sitting here thinking," she said. "You look like my grandbaby. Called him Sonny Boy. Raised him myself 'cause his mama died giving birth to him."

Sean couldn't speak.

Sonny Boy was Grandma's nickname for him. His mother had died in childbirth.

Coincidence! his mind shrieked.

The woman's brow creased. "I'm kinda worried about Sonny Boy. He done lost his way, blaming God for things that was just meant to happen. Saying he don't need God and all that mess. When we do that, you know, sometimes God'll let you see what it's like when He ain't around. Leave you out there all alone in the darkness. . . . And you know who dwells in the darkness, don't you?"

Sean began to move away. His knees shook, and he had to grip the seats to keep from falling.

"You's all alone, Sonny Boy," she said. She grinned. "God ain't around to hear them phony prayers of yours no mo'."

Sean spun around, in his haste nearly knocking over a man, and raced back to his seat.

His frantic return awakened Mya.

"What's wrong?" she asked. "You look like you've seen a ghost."

You've no idea, he thought. A wave of demented laughter bubbled at the back of his throat, and he

clamped his mouth shut, worried that if he allowed
the laughter to escape, it would never stop.

*Who did I see sitting back there? It wasn't Grandma.
Could it have been . . . ?*

"Sean?" Mya touched his hand.

"I'm okay," Sean said. Greasy sweat streamed down
his face. He lifted the edge of his shirt and mopped
away the perspiration.

Mya watched him with a skeptical gaze.

"Want a Dramamine?" she asked.

"No." The last thing he wanted was to become
drowsy, not with that

(devil)

person sitting a few rows behind him. He couldn't
afford to be anything less than one hundred percent
alert.

"You don't look good," she said. "Are you going
to be okay?"

He was about to tell her to stop asking him questions and shut the fuck up. But he kept his mouth
shut. She was only concerned about him, as a wife
should be. He had to get his shit together.

The first step in doing that was proving that his
grandmother—or something impersonating her—
was not sitting on the plane. He wanted to prove that
he was hallucinating. Although such an intense,
disturbing hallucination would open an entirely
different Pandora's box.

"Can you do me a favor?" he asked Mya.

"Sure, honey."

"Walk to the back, to the lavatory. Let me know if
you see anyone familiar sitting around row fourteen or so."

"Who?" She frowned.

My dead grandmother . . .

"I'm not sure who it is," he lied. "But it's someone we've seen before, I think. The person's name slips my tongue. . . . You know how I am with names."

"Don't I know it. You barely remembered my sister's name at the wedding."

He forced himself to smile, indulgently.

"And they're sitting in row fourteen?" she asked.

"Yeah, around there."

"I'll be right back."

She rose out of her seat and clambered over him. If he was in his normal, playful mood, he would have groped at her breasts as she passed by. Now, he kept his sweaty hands knotted together in his lap.

Mya walked down the aisle. He waited. Wondering whom Mya would see sitting back there.

You know who dwells in the darkness, don't you?

Coldness spread from his spine through every point of his body. He snatched the blanket from the seat next to him and covered himself with it. Still, gooseflesh rose on his arms.

Mya came back. "You must be imagining things, Sean. There's no one back there that I know."

"Who was in row fourteen?"

"No one." She slid into her seat and buckled her seatbelt. "The entire row was empty."

"That can't be."

"Check again for yourself." She looked at him, intently. "Who'd you see back there that you recognized, anyway?"

He faltered. He was too shaken to conjure a plausible lie.

"Forget about it," he finally said. "I must've been mistaken."

She looked at him for a beat, and then shrugged, placed a pillow between the window and her head, and closed her eyes. Clearly, as far as Mya was concerned, the matter was forgotten.

But he couldn't forget.

He sat there, gripping the armrests, gnawing his bottom lip.

Then, on impulse, he threw off the blanket, grabbed the back of the seat in front of him, and pulled himself upright. He staggered into the aisle. He walked toward row fourteen.

The row was vacant, like Mya had said. No black woman occupied any of the seats around, either.

I'm losing my mind, he thought. He was, in fact, not feeling quite like himself. He was hungry; he'd eaten only a granola bar before they'd left the house for the airport, and he hadn't yet sipped his usual morning cup of java.

Perhaps one of the side effects of caffeine withdrawal was hallucinations, he thought, a bit crazily.

But why would he have imagined his grandmother, of all people? Why would he have imagined that she would say such awful things to him?

Scratching his head, he turned to go back to his seat. As he neared it, he glimpsed that familiar cap of frosty white hair.

In his row.

Lead-footed, Sean shuffled back to his seat.

His grandmother—or whoever she was—sat in the seat closest to the aisle. The middle seat, his, was empty. Mya was in the window seat, fast asleep.

His grandmother looked up at him. Grinned.

He noticed bits of a black substance stuck between her teeth, as if she had been chewing on coals.

"Take a load off, Sonny Boy." She patted the seat next to her. "Ain't nowhere else to go. Long way to go to Hawaii."

Standing there, gawking at this woman, Sean came up with a completely reasonable explanation for what was happening.

He was dreaming.

He was as unconscious as Mya, perhaps had ingested a capsule of Dramamine himself. He was asleep, and caught in this nightmare.

But what a vivid dream. The smell of hot coffee drifting to him from the food-and-beverage cart ahead. The humming of the aircraft's engine. The faint taste of the granola bar still on his tongue.

No matter how real it seems, it's still a dream. There's no other answer.

Sean moved to his seat, being careful to avoid touching her.

She touched his hand. Her skin was cold and clammy. "Now we can talk."

"About what?" He pulled his hand away.

"Why I'm here," she said. "What I got to offer you."

"Offer me?"

She folded her hands together, over the huge Bible. Glancing at the worn black-leather cover, he noticed a strange detail. The gold cross underneath the words Holy Bible was upside down.

Fear simmered in his chest. Years ago, he'd seen something on television about Satanists. One of the cult's prized figures was the inverted cross, signifying a mockery of Christianity's most hallowed symbol.

As he looked at the woman's hands, he saw dirt caked underneath her nails, too. Grandma was the cleanest woman he'd ever known, would wash her hands several times a day. This could not possibly be her, and since his imagination had engineered this perversion of her for a dream, he needed serious counseling. He'd obviously lost his grip on his sanity.

"Lemme make you an offer," the woman said, in a voice that was still a dead ringer for Grandma's. "An offer you can't refuse, like Marlon Brando said in *The Godfather*. Wanna hear it, Sonny Boy?"

"No, but I don't guess that I have a choice."

She cackled.

"God gave you free will, didn't he?" she asked. "Ain't that what you used to believe?"

"I don't want to talk about that."

Smirking, she motioned above. "Look."

From the ceiling, a flat screen levered down from a compartment. The flight crew used the monitors to show safety instructions and in-flight movies. But Sean had an unsettling feeling about what he would see this time.

Electric snow filled the screen . . . and then faded to reveal a TV newsman seated at a desk. The guy was talking, and his words were as audible as if they were being broadcast over the captain's intercom. But in the illogical fashion of dreams, only Sean and the old woman paid any attention to the screen and seemed to hear the newsman.

". . . Flight 463, en route from Atlanta to Los Angeles, crashed as it was flying over the Arizona desert. There were only a handful of survivors . . ."

Sean almost bolted out of his seat, forgetting his belief that he was dreaming. "What the hell is that? This plane is gonna crash?"

"As surely as the sun is gonna set," the woman said. "Got some kinda engine problem. By the time they figure it out, be too late for y'all."

Footage of the wreckage flashed on the screen. Paramedics loaded bodies wrapped in black bags into ambulances. Corpses of the victims.

"There were a hundred and sixteen passengers," the newsman continued. "Fewer than ten survived . . ."

"A hundred people dead?" Sean asked. Numb, he looked around. All of the passengers were oblivious to what he was watching and hearing. He glanced at Mya, afraid to ask his next question, but he had to: "What about us?"

The woman cracked her gnarled knuckles. "Ah, now that's what our bidness is about. You and your bride. I got an offer; you gots a choice."

Remember, it's only a dream, Sean thought. But the increasingly grave tone of this conversation had begun to sap his confidence. The horrific images on the screen had jammed up his brain. *Was it true that if you died in a dream, you died in real life . . . ?*

"What choice?" he asked.

"Serve me," she said. "Sign over your soul. Do that, and you and your sugar pie will be some of them survivors."

He blinked. "You're kidding. You want me to sign my name in blood or something, like in one of those stupid horror movies?"

But the woman didn't smile. She opened the Bible. Except it was no longer a Bible; the facing page, instead of being full of Scriptures, had only a few lines of text, and a long, blank signature line at the bottom.

"Don't need your name in blood." She extended a fountain pen toward him. "This'll do just fine."

He didn't accept the pen. "Who the hell are you?"

"Stop foolin', sugar. You know the answer to that, don't you?"

You know who dwells in the darkness.

Sean swallowed. His Adam's apple felt stuck at the base of his throat, as if he'd swallowed a golf ball.

"Hurry up now," she said. "I got places to go, thangs to do."

"This is bullshit," Sean said, the logical side of his brain struggling to reassert itself. "I don't believe in the Devil. That's a bunch of religious nonsense."

The woman tapped the pen against her lips. "You believe in God?"

"I don't have faith—"

"I ain't asking whether you have faith in a kind, loving God," she said. "I'm asking if you believe He exists."

"Of course I do."

"Thought so. You believe in Him, even though you and Him been having issues lately." She smirked. "Right?"

"Yeah. So?"

"So there ain't no light without dark, Sonny Boy. No hot without cold. Got joy—got pain. Everything's got an opposite. God, too."

Following the logic, Sean had begun to nod.

"Even if you exist," he said. "I'm not gonna believe a word you say. The Bible says you're the Father of Lies."

"Ain't you got some nerve?" the woman asked, rearing back. "Since when you start quoting Scripture? You—who can't even humble hisself enough to say 'Amen'? Who'd look dead in his wife's face and tell *her* to have faith?"

Sean lowered his head. His gaze slid over the book in the woman's lap. The contract. "In return for the survival of himself and his wife on Flight 463, Signee pledges to assign care of his soul to Me . . ."

"No," Sean said. "The answer to your offer is no. Get away from me. Or I'll—"

"Ask God for help?" She smiled, but it was a

terrible, cold expression, the way a snake might smile. "You're lost, sugar. All confused, don't know what to believe anymore. Well, believe in this."

She placed her hand on top of his. When she had touched him before, her skin had been cold as a dead trout.

Now, it was scorching hot. His flesh sizzled and smoked.

"Believe in this!"

Sean screamed.

Sean awoke with a shriek exploding from the back of his throat. He clamped his mouth shut in time to keep from howling—the scream came out as a violent gasp.

He was sitting in his seat on the airplane. The in-flight magazine lay on his lap.

Mya sat beside him, asleep. Beyond the porthole, he saw that the aircraft tilled a field of clouds.

Above him, the flat screens had lowered from the ceiling. A Jim Carrey comedy, *Bruce Almighty*, was in progress. Passengers around him were giggling.

All a dream, he thought. *Just a nightmare.*

But his left hand ached.

Don't you dare look at it. If you do, you'll regret it for the rest of your life.

Heart throbbing, he slid his hands from underneath the magazine.

A red burn pulsated on his left hand, between the base of his knuckles and his wrist.

It looked as if someone with scalding-hot fingers had touched him.

* * *

For the remainder of the flight to Los Angeles, Sean was wide-awake. He requested two extra cups of coffee from the flight attendants, and drank them greedily.

In the event of a crash, he had to be alert.

When Mya awoke, it required all of his self-restraint for him to resist telling her what he'd dreamt. His head felt as though it would burst from the pressure of the dream images and the old woman's prediction of doom. But he kept his mouth shut.

Mya, after all, thought he had faith in God's goodness.

The only thing he couldn't hide was the burn mark. While Mya was asleep, he'd asked a flight attendant for ointment and a bandage and dressed the wound. When Mya asked about it, he told her he'd spilled coffee on himself.

As they continued to fly, Sean listened for a mechanical malfunction, any unfamiliar, *wrong*-sounding noise. He heard only the engine's constant drone. But when the captain announced that they were nearing the Grand Canyon, and they hit a ripple of turbulence, Sean nearly leapt out of his seat and screamed.

They passed over the canyon, and the rest of the Arizona desert, without incident.

It was all a lie, he realized. The plane wasn't going to crash; he and Mya weren't going to perish in fiery wreckage. It was a lie, intended to fool him into signing his soul away.

Relief washed over him.

"You okay?" Mya asked. She lowered the novel that she was reading and looked at him. "You were looking kinda tense."

"I'm fine," he said. "Never felt better."

They landed at LAX, and boarded the connecting flight to Kahalui, arriving there late in the afternoon.

*   *   *

Later that evening, at the Westin Maui Resort, Sean was in the bathroom applying a fresh coat of ointment to his burn when Mya called him into the bedroom.

He stuck his head out of the bathroom. Mya knelt beside the bed. She wore her nightgown, her dark hair spilling across her shoulders. Beyond the large window, surf crashed against the shore.

"Yes?" Sean asked. But he knew what she wanted, had been dreading this.

"I'm about to say my prayers," she said. "Want to join me?"

You—who can't even humble hisself enough to say 'Amen'?

"You go ahead," he said. "I'll say mine after I'm done in here."

Nodding, Mya turned away and bowed her head. She began to pray in a soft, fervent voice. She said Sean's name, asking God to help him develop stronger faith.

He stepped back into the bathroom and shut the door.

Help Sean's faith, Lord.

Sean looked at his reflection in the mirror.

Her prayer had failed, because he saw a man full of doubt.

Saturday evening, a week later, they arrived back home in Atlanta. Mya arose early the next morning to attend church. She sang a gospel hymn as she dressed. Tangled in sheets, Sean watched her from the bed with one eye cocked open.

She saw him looking. "Good morning, Sleepy-head. Coming to church with me?"

"I don't think so. I'm wiped out. Jetlag."

"Humph." She pursed her lips with disapproval. "I think you need to go. It'll help you."

What'll help me is you getting the hell out of here so I can go back to sleep. I don't want to go to any damn church. Don't you get it?

"I'm really tired, Mya," he said.

"Fine." She zipped up her red dress, and placed a big red hat on her head. "But I hope our marriage isn't going to be like this, with you sleeping in every Sunday morning missing church."

He didn't respond to that jab. He rolled over and feigned sleep.

He heard her moving around in the bedroom, sighing loudly, to let him know that she was annoyed. After a few minutes, she left.

But Sean was unable to drift back to sleep. The sunlight streaming through the windows—she had opened the blinds to give them sun rays at full blast, a ploy to keep him awake—spotlighted the burn mark on his hand. It had faded in the past week, but it was still there. An uncomfortable reminder of his crisis of faith.

Giving up hope for sleep, he rose out of bed and dressed. He left the house in his Nissan Sentra.

He picked up a bouquet of fresh flowers at a local Kroger grocery store. Then he drove to Magnolia Grove Cemetery.

Grandma was buried there.

Since her death, he hadn't visited her grave once. His emotional wounds were too tender. A visit to her grave would reawaken his anguish and plunge him into another despairing fit of grief.

But this morning, for reasons that he couldn't explain, he felt compelled to go.

He parked in the cemetery, at the crest of the gravel path. Although the graveyard was home to several hundred decedents, he found Grandma's plot quickly. A leafy maple offered a shady respite against the bright morning sun.

Grief stung Sean as he knelt in front of the headstone.

Marlene Robinson
1924–2005
A daughter of God. A servant of God.

A daughter of God? Well, God treated his children like shit.

Tears scalded Sean's eyes. He carefully placed the flowers in the vase.

He dipped his head. He felt as though he should pray—for Grandma's joy in the afterlife, perhaps for the care of his own soul. But his lips felt glued together.

He absently rubbed the burn mark.

Now that I'm here, I don't know what the hell to do. Is this what paying your respects is all about?

"I had a feeling you'd come here," a familiar voice said.

Startled, Sean looked up. Mya moved from behind the nearby maple tree, wearing a sky blue dress. At that moment, she was so beautiful to him she might have been an angel come to comfort him in his grief.

He wiped his eyes. "What are you doing here? I thought you went to church."

"I did," she said. "But then something told me you

would be coming here, and I wanted to be here with you."

He never would have thought of asking Mya to accompany him to his grandmother's grave. He'd thought it was something he'd prefer to do in solitude. But he was glad that she was there.

She came to him and took his hand. She squeezed it, reassuringly.

"Thanks for being here." He looked at the headstone. "I don't really know why I came here, to be honest."

"You're looking for answers. You want to know why God took Grandma—after letting her suffer so terribly—when she was a woman of such strong faith. You don't think God cares about people."

She had read his mind, as she was apt to do sometimes. He nodded, solemnly.

"You've been angry at Him ever since Grandma passed," she said.

"Furious," he said. "Grandma deserved better. Why should anyone spend their life praying and going to church and serving God just so He can abandon you when you need Him the most?"

"Good questions," she said. "But how do you know that God abandoned your grandmother?"

Sean pulled his hand away. "Come on, Mya. You saw how Grandma suffered."

"Sometimes, God uses suffering to teach us lessons. What if God had been preparing your grandmother to pass on?"

"Preparing her by letting her sit senile in a nursing home, drooling like a baby and pissing on herself? That doesn't sound like a loving God to me."

"It is harsh." Mya took his hand again and kissed it softly, which left a tingling sensation on his skin. "But not all lessons are easy, baby."

Her words reverberated in his thoughts. He knelt to the headstone again. He ran his fingers across the inscription.

"I'll leave you alone for now," Mya said. "See you at home."

"Okay," he mumbled.

Alone again, he contemplated the headstone for a while.

God uses suffering to teach us lessons.

He had to admit, he didn't understand God, not one bit. But he was willing to concede that maybe the relationship between his grandmother and God was personal, and none of his business.

. . . not all lessons are easy, baby.

He remained at the gravesite for another fifteen minutes, then he walked back to his car and drove home.

The house was quiet. Mya must have returned to church after she'd left the cemetery. The service she attended usually ended at ten thirty. He had about a half hour before she arrived home, so he set about preparing breakfast for them.

When Mya entered the house, he embraced her.

"Thanks for being there with me at the cemetery," he said. "I fixed breakfast for us."

"What're you talking about?" Her face crinkled into a frown.

"You met me at my grandma's grave this morning, said some stuff that's had me thinking. I was just thanking you for that."

"Baby, I never went to the cemetery. I've been at church the whole time."

He opened his mouth to disagree—and then he noticed her clothes. She wore a red dress, which she'd been wearing when she'd left the house for church; when he saw her at the cemetery, she was wearing blue.

His world tilted, and began to spin. He stumbled to a chair.

"You okay?" she asked. She knelt in front of him, took his hands in hers.

He looked at his hand. At the cemetery, Mya—or whoever it had been—had kissed it.

The burn mark was gone.

Presumed Dead

Everyone thought Michael Benson was dead.

On a chilly October night eight years ago, he'd reportedly plunged his Mustang into the frigid waters of Lake Michigan. When the police discovered the vehicle a week later, they found clothes, a collection of hip-hop CDs, a fifth of Jack Daniel's, and a suicide note preserved in a Ziploc bag. *My life is hell, and I can't take it anymore.*

Although the cops never found a corpse, Michael Benson was presumed dead. A small cluster of friends and relatives attended the funeral, mourning over a blown-up photo of him, in lieu of a body.

But while they grieved, Michael was alive and enjoying his freedom.

He'd always been fascinated by the thought of his own death, had wondered who would attend his funeral, and what would happen there. Who would cry? Who would eulogize him? What would they say?

But when it actually went down, he'd already left town. He couldn't take any chances of being seen anywhere in Zion.

Not while Big Daddy Jay was still around.

If Big Daddy Jay knew Michael was alive, he would arrange another death for him—and that one would be real.

Afterward, Michael moved to Atlanta.

Atlanta was the place to be for a young, single, upwardly mobile black man like him. A man like him could accomplish big things in A-Town.

He changed his name to Ricky; Richard was his middle name, and his mother, who'd passed when he was a teenager, used to call him Ricky. He changed his last name to Jordan, because he'd been a longtime fan of the great basketball player. He used an underground connection to get a new Social Security Number, too.

Carrying twenty-five thousand dollars—his life savings—in a briefcase, he moved to a one-bedroom apartment in College Park, a city on the Southside, and got a job barbering at a local barbershop. He'd learned to cut hair during a two-year stint in prison (he'd landed there due to a trumped-up burglary beef). His skills with clippers came in handy as he set up his new life.

In no time, he'd built up a list of reliable clients, and was earning good money. He met a woman, named Kisha, a thick Georgia Peach sister, and she moved in with him. She was a fabulous cook and even better in bed. Life was good.

But his old life called to him, like a sweet, forbidden lover.

Cards.

The cards had gotten him into trouble back home. The cards had made him decide to plan his death. He owed big debts to Big Daddy Jay because of those cards. Debts he couldn't repay if he lived to be two hundred.

It took all of his self-discipline to avoid the cards' powerful pull. But he did. He knew that if he gave in to the urge to play, he would eventually find himself in the same bind there in Atlanta. And then he might blow his cover. He couldn't risk blowing his cover, not ever.

Big Daddy Jay's reach extended far outside of Illinois, after all.

So he stayed away from the cards. But he satisfied his thirst to stay abreast of happenings in his hometown by studying the local metro newspaper, *The News Sun,* on the Internet. He missed home terribly. But he could never return for a visit, not while Big Daddy Jay was alive.

Therefore, he paid special attention to the obituaries.

Eight years later, when he was up late one night cruising the newspaper online, he read the obituary that he'd dreamt so long of finding.

Big Daddy Jay had died, of natural causes, at the age of eighty-seven. Owner of Jay's Meats & Foods, a mom-and-pop business (which was no more than a legit front for his illegal activities), the paper included a recent photo of the great man. He wore a Kangol cocked on his bald head, his snow-white mustache trimmed to perfection. His face lean and grave, he bore a strong resemblance to the actor Lou Gossett Jr. He used to joke that people would approach the actor and ask him if he was Big Daddy Jay—not the other way around.

Big Daddy Jay was that kind of man.

When Michael read the obituary, he let out a

whoop of joy so loud that Kisha awoke and came to ask him what was going on.

"It's nothing," Michael said. "I thought my Power-ball numbers had hit. I was wrong."

Frowning, she returned to bed.

But Michael stayed up for a while longer. This was almost as good as winning the lottery.

Finally, he thought. *Finally, I can go home.*

Two weeks later, he did.

"This looks like a nice little town, Ricky," Kisha said, as he steered the Jeep along Sheridan Road, the town's primary drag. "Has it changed much since the last time you was here?"

"It's changed a lot," he said. "That Applebee's we just passed—that wasn't here when I moved away. And they didn't have that Comfort Inn or a Wal-Mart, either."

"No Wal-Mart?" Kisha's eyes widened, as if the thought of a town without a Wal-Mart was as unthink-able as a house without plumbing. "Dang, where did y'all go, then?"

We went to Big Daddy Jay's, Michael wanted to tell her, but kept his mouth shut. *There, you could get everything you needed—and then some.*

They were nearing the old, two-story brick build-ing that Big Daddy Jay had owned for as long as Michael could remember. A big, faded red and white sign announcing JAY'S MEATS & FOODS hung out front. Just like Michael remembered.

Passing by the store, he slowed.

"That was y'alls grocery store?" Kisha clucked her tongue. "Ain't they got a Publix or something here?"

Michael shook his head absently. He was staring at the building.

It was a few minutes past ten o'clock in the evening, and the grocery store closed at nine. The CLOSED sign hung on the front door.

But he wasn't looking at the store. He was looking at the second-floor, which housed Big Daddy Jay's office.

The blinds were closed but could not hide the light burning inside.

The infamous poker games always took place up there. In that same room, after a long night of horrifyingly bad luck, Michael had decided that the only way to stay alive was for him to convince Big Daddy Jay that he was dead—and escape town.

What was going on in there? Were the games still in progress, even after the great man's death?

Chilled, and not quite sure why, he kept driving.

They had booked a room at a Best Western in Waukegan, a city fifteen minutes south of town. As Kisha dressed for bed, Michael grabbed his car keys.

"Where you going, baby?" she asked. Wearing a silk negligee, she lay on the bed atop the comforter. One of her hands touched her large, round breasts, lingered on a nipple.

Ordinarily the sight of Kisha, dressed provocatively and eager for sex, would've kept him inside even if a tornado had been bearing down on them. But he only looked at her, shrugged.

"I need to go somewhere," he said. "Alone. I won't be gone long, an hour or so."

"You're leaving me here?" Her voice bordered on a whine.

"I'll be back soon."

He kissed her quickly and went to the Jeep. Driving, he marveled at how easily he remembered his way around. While a lot had changed, some things never do, he thought.

The same thought occurred to him when he arrived in the small parking lot behind Big Daddy Jay's store. A collection of cars—an Oldsmobile, a Dodge Ram, a Chevy sedan, a Buick—occupied the lot. Cars that belonged to the players, for sure.

But a gleaming white Cadillac sedan was parked in the corner, beside the door. Big Daddy Jay's car. The man drove Cadillacs, exclusively, and used to joke that he'd be buried in his Coup DeVille.

Obviously, since the old man had died, no one had bothered to touch his car. Maybe out of respect. But it surprised Michael. He had assumed that Big Daddy Jay's son, Tommy Boy, had assumed full control of the business. Ever since he'd been a teenager, Tommy Boy had done most of the work at the market, anyway (the legal work, that is). Why leave the car sitting there like that?

Michael's gaze traveled upward, to the shuttered windows, behind which lights still shone.

And why continue the card games?

Someone tapped on Michael's window.

Michael stifled a scream. He'd been so entranced with thoughts of what was happening up there that he hadn't seen anyone approach.

A lean, rangy black man waited beside the Jeep. Dressed in a dark suit with a loosely knotted tie, the guy smoked a cigarette, puffing wispy rings into the night air. In his other hand, he held a brown paper bag that, in the timeless manner of drunks, undoubtedly concealed a flask of whisky.

But his black beady eyes focused intently on Michael.

Michael didn't lower the window. Although it was dark out and he couldn't see every detail of the guy's face, he knew this man—people around town called him "Peanut." Peanut, a veteran gambler, had lost a few grand to Michael, back in the day.

Peanut bent and peered closer.

"Don't I know you, brother?" He spoke in a ragged, smoker's voice.

"Uh, no. I don't think so. I'm not from here."

"I never forget a man's eyes." Rising, Peanut took a swig of whisky. "You got eyes just like a brother I used to know. Name was Mike B."

After faking his death, Michael had drastically changed his appearance. He'd lost thirty pounds. (It was easy to lose weight when your life, literally, depended on it.) He'd grown a goatee, wearing facial hair for the first time. He wore contact lenses, instead of glasses. He'd cut his hair short, ditching the wild, Michael Evans-from-*Good Times* Afro. He didn't look like the same person.

But Michael knew—and Peanut knew—that you never forget someone you played cards with; especially if you'd lost money to the man. You remembered the eyes. The eyes never changed.

Big Daddy Jay's eyes haunted Michael's dreams.

"You've mistaken me for someone else," Michael said. He slid his hand to the gearshift. It was time to get out of here.

Michael's gaze flicked across the upper window of the building. A tall, broad silhouette had moved to the glass.

Michael's heartbeat accelerated.

"No, I ain't mistaken you for someone else,"

Peanut said. His lips curled in a smile, and it registered with Michael that something was *wrong* with Peanut's face; it seemed bloodless, like dead skin.

"Naw," Peanut continued. "You know better, Mike B."

Michael couldn't afford to stay around here another minute. He slammed the gears into DRIVE. He mashed the gas pedal and ripped across the gravel.

Behind him, Peanut shouted: "Wait till Big Daddy finds out!"

Big Daddy Jay's dead, Michael thought, as cold sweat ran down his back.

But as he drove back to the hotel, he couldn't get the image of that tall, broad silhouette out of his mind.

Kisha was awake, watching Jay Leno, when Michael returned to the hotel room.

"Where was you?" She sat up. "I almost fell asleep waiting on your butt."

"I wanted to do a little sightseeing."

"This late?"

He stood at the foot of the king-size bed. Kisha had pulled up the bedsheets to cover herself. He yanked the sheets away; she was nude underneath, and the sight of her voluptuous body sent desire crackling through his muscles.

"I need you," he said. "Badly."

"Then come on, baby. I been waiting."

He stripped out of his clothes and climbed onto the bed.

He made love to Kisha with a fierce—almost desperate—energy that he'd never known. Propped on his arms above her, thrusting wildly, he climaxed, shouting and sweating.

Kisha pulled him down on top of her. She massaged his back.

"Feel better now?" she asked.

"Yeah." His heart still raced from the after effects of the orgasm.

"Something's been heavy on your mind. I see right through you, you know."

He paused. "It'll be okay."

He made the statement to calm Kisha, but he found that he felt more composed, too. More clear-headed. He saw his ridiculous fears that Big Daddy Jay had returned as just that—ridiculous. That shadow he'd spotted in the window had to have been someone else.

Wait till Big Daddy finds out!

And Peanut, his pallor showing that he was clearly ill, had been drunk and talking nonsense. Even when Michael had known him, back in the day, the guy had been prone to chugging whisky like an athlete drinking Gatorade. He'd only been trying to scare Michael with his drunken gibberish.

Big Daddy Jay was dead. For real.

Kisha squeezed his butt, drawing his attention. "Will you take me to Chi-town tomorrow, Ricky?"

How could he turn down a woman who'd just given him a brain-busting orgasm? Besides, he'd like to hang out in Chicago, too. Get away from his shitty hometown and all its ghosts.

"Sure," he said, "that'll be cool."

"I wanna see Navy Pier. And go shopping on Minnesota Avenue."

"That's Michigan Avenue." He yawned. "And yeah, we can check out Navy Pier, too."

"Can I get one of them Chicago-style hot dogs? And some deep-dish pizza?"

"That's a lotta eating, girl . . . don't want you to get too wide . . ."

Kisha continued to prattle on about places she wanted to see, things she wanted to do, food she wanted to eat. Michael eventually tuned her out. He fell asleep.

He awoke at seven fifteen, according to the digital clock on the nightstand. Kisha lay beside him, slumbering quietly.

He rose out of bed and padded to the bathroom to take a piss.

And stopped short of the doorway.

Something lay on the carpet, near the front door, as if it had been slipped underneath.

A playing card. The red back faced up.

Coldness drenched him. He knew what he was going to see before he looked; his gut tightened with a certain, terrible knowledge. Nevertheless, he bent and flipped the card over.

It was a Joker.

That was the moment when he realized two things, irrefutably: Big Daddy Jay was alive. And he was planning to kill Michael.

Michael carried the card into the bathroom. He laid it near the sink. As he did his business at the toilet, his gaze remained riveted to the card.

The Joker's grinning face mocked him.

The wild card had a special meaning for Big Daddy Jay. Michael had once sat in on a poker game with Big Daddy Jay, Peanut, and a handful of other regulars. Peanut, drunk as usual, made a comment that Big Daddy didn't appreciate—something about the man's daughter and how she was so cute. Big Daddy,

who had warned all of them about so much as looking at his daughter, cocked his head and said to
Peanut, "I told you once before never to talk about
my daughter, Peanut. You think I'm a joker?"

Suddenly quite sober, Peanut began to apologize,
stuttering like a schoolboy.

But it was too late. Big Daddy whacked him upside
the head with his pearl-handled cane. Peanut had
required seventeen stitches to repair the gash.

You think I'm a joker?

Big Daddy Jay asked that question only when he
was being deadly serious.

The card was a clear message: he knew Michael was
alive, and he most assuredly was not joking with him
about getting the money Michael owed him from
eight years ago—which, knowing how Big Daddy
operated, would include substantial interest.

Michael could never pay him. He owed the man
a hundred thousand dollars. He hadn't been able
to pay it then, and he sure as hell couldn't pay it now.

He never should have come back home. Big Daddy
Jay was crafty, probably knew that faking his own death
would flush out a lot of his debtors, like a tomcat
retiring to the shadows to fool the mice into coming
out to play. Michael had fallen right into the trap.

Holding the card, he went to the bed. Kisha continued to sleep.

I can run, he thought. *Just clear out of Atlanta and
start over again somewhere else, with a new name, a new
look.*

He looked at Kisha. He thought about the decent
life he was building with her. He'd kept his nose
clean, had left the old life behind. He'd become a
stable, tax-paying citizen.

He didn't want to give that up. He didn't want to run. He'd been running from his past for eight years.

Anyway, now that Big Daddy Jay knew he was alive, running was not a viable option. Big Daddy Jay had connections everywhere. He would find him.

Michael had to settle this business once and for all. Like a man.

He threw on a T-shirt and jeans and went to the Jeep. He kept a small leather case in the cargo hold. He grabbed it and carried it back inside the hotel, opened it.

It contained a loaded 9 mm pistol, and ammunition.

Some things changed. But some things remained the same.

Kisha awoke, brushing her hair out of her eyes. "Why you up so early, baby?"

He quickly closed the case.

"I wanted to get a jump on our day in the city," he said. "Wake up, lazy girl."

She giggled, and tossed a pillow at him.

He laughed, but he was already thinking about paying a visit to Big Daddy Jay's store later that night.

At a quarter to nine that evening, Michael pushed through the front door of Jay's Meats & Foods. He wore a dark Windbreaker that concealed his gun.

He found Tommy Boy behind the counter, running the store alone. Tommy Boy, with the same tall, broad-shouldered build as his father, had to be in his early thirties by now. But he looked exactly as Michael remembered, as if he hadn't aged a day. Michael guessed that that was why they called him Tommy Boy—he had the face of an ageless kid.

Tommy Boy didn't appear to recognize Michael.

"Need any help, mister?" Tommy Boy asked. "We're closing in fifteen minutes, by the way."

Michael placed his hands on the counter, facing the guy directly. "You recognize me?"

"Naw, don't think so." Tommy Boy frowned, scratched his head.

"Cut the bullshit," Michael said. "I'm Mike B. I know Peanut told the whole world that he saw me in the back last night."

"Mike B.?" His eyes grew large. "But you died—"

"Give it up, man. Or does Big Daddy really keep you in the dark like that?"

"I don't know what you're talking about. My daddy passed. And Peanut—"

"Big Daddy isn't dead, and you know it." Michael flung the Joker card onto the counter. "He left this in my hotel room this morning."

Tommy Boy shook his head wildly. "I'm telling you, my daddy died a few weeks ago!"

"He faked his death," Michael said. "I know all about how to do that, man. He faked his death and now he's settling debts."

"You're crazy," Tommy Boy said. He came around the counter. "You say you saw Peanut? Well, he passed like five or six months ago, had lung cancer or something. You're imagining shit."

"I saw him out back last night," Michael said. "There were a bunch of cars parked back there— guys playing cards upstairs."

"No one's been upstairs since Daddy passed," Tommy Boy said. "Now, unless you're gonna buy something, it's time for you to leave."

Michael unveiled his gun.

"Hold on, now." Tommy Boy stuck his hands in the air. He laughed nervously. "You don't need that."

"Big Daddy put you up to this, didn't he?" Michael asked. "Trying to screw with my mind. Well, fuck that." Michael headed toward a door at the back of the store.

Tommy Boy moved in front of him. "Where you going?"

"Upstairs to talk to your daddy. Get outta the way."

"Don't go up there! For . . . For your own good, I'm warning you."

"Your daddy's scared the shit out of you, hasn't he?" Michael asked. "Did he beat you when you were a kid? Maybe with that cane of his?"

"If you were smart, you'd go home. Just get the hell out of here and go back to wherever you were living!"

Michael hesitated. The way the kid behaved was beginning to unnerve him. He talked as though Big Daddy Jay was running a death camp or something.

Tommy Boy touched Michael's arm. "Go. Please."

I might be making the wrong choice, but I'll be damned if I'll punk out again.

"I've gotta do this." Michael shrugged off Tommy Boy's hand. He motioned with the muzzle of the gun. "Step aside."

Tommy Boy's shoulders drooped. Lowering his head, he moved out of the way.

Michael opened the door. A dim yellow light at the top of the landing spilled down the stairwell, illuminating the steps in front of him.

The Stairway to Hell, the old crew had called this flight. Over the years, Michael had walked up those steps hundreds of times on his way to card games, some of which he'd won, many of which he'd lost. Men like him had lost fortunes—and perhaps their lives—traversing these stairs.

Drawing a breath, he checked that his gun was loaded and ready, and climbed the steps.

The landing at the top of the stairs opened into a small seating area. A handful of rickety folding chairs leaned against the wall, like skeletal remains. On the far wall, a scarred door, as red as blood, led to the big man's office.

Michael approached the door.

This is it. The end of the line.

He opened the door.

Peanut stood on the threshold. He flashed a death's-head grin at Michael. Then he hit Michael over the head.

Michael awoke sometime later to weak light and a headache.

He was seated in a chair, in front of a large slab of mahogany that he remembered served as Big Daddy Jay's desk. Big Daddy wasn't there. But Peanut sat on the edge of the desk. He twirled Michael's gun around his fingers.

In the light, Peanut looked something awful. He looked like Death—in the actual sense of the phrase.

His dark brown skin had begun to turn purple. His eyes were yellow, rheumy, clouded. His head was bald, as was his habit, but swollen sores marred his scalp, as if his skull was going soft.

When Peanut opened his mouth, a fetid stench came out that nearly knocked Michael unconscious again.

You say you saw Peanut? Well, he passed like five or six months ago, had lung cancer or something. You're imagining shit . . .

Michael was suddenly convinced that he was dreaming, or imagining shit, as Tommy Boy had said. Dead men didn't walk.

"I tole Big Daddy you was back," Peanut said.

And dead men didn't talk, either.

Peanut took a swig of whisky from the flask in the wrinkled paper bag. Then he coughed—violent spasms that racked his withered body.

Peanut wiped his mouth. "You knew he was gonna get you, didn't you? Old boy got me, too, man. Big Daddy ain't about to let you get away without paying him his money."

"Tommy Boy said you were dead," Michael said.

Peanut grinned, exposing a row of blackened, crumbling teeth.

"Still had to pay my debts," Peanut said. "Dying don't clean the slate, not for Big Daddy Jay, not for the man he work for."

"You know who Big Daddy works for?"

Michael was surprised that he had the clarity of mind to ask, to follow a logical line of questioning. But he'd just asked Peanut one of those questions that had floated around Big Daddy Jay for decades. In spite of his influence and the fear he inspired, Big Daddy supposedly was the front man for someone far more frightening—and even more mysterious. But no one had ever seen this individual, spoken to him, or even learned his name. Amongst the hustlers and gamblers in town, the mystery man had taken on an air of myth, like an urban legend.

Twirling the gun, Peanut only smiled. "If I knew, think I'd tell you?"

"Where's Big Daddy Jay?"

Michael heard a heavy footstep behind him. Then a hollow clop, like a cane striking a floorboard.

Peanut's smile fell away. He straightened.

Michael sat ramrod straight in the chair.

The dragging footsteps and clopping cane grew closer—and so did a noxious smell. Michael squeezed his eyes shut. He didn't want to see. He didn't want to believe this was happening.

Dead men don't walk, dead men don't walk, dead men don't walk . . .

The walking noises ended behind the desk.

"You owe Big Daddy Jay a lotta money, son," a familiar, guttural voice said. "Think you fooled me pulling off that little suicide?"

Michael opened his eyes.

Big Daddy Jay sat in his old leather chair. As dead-looking as a corpse that had been in the grave for a few weeks. Milky eyes. Bloated, greenish-blue skin. Fingers like fat, spoiled sausages.

Big Daddy Jay leaned back in the chair, one fat hand massaging the pearl-handled cane.

"You think I'm a joker?" Big Daddy Jay asked. "That what you think?"

I think you're a dead man who can't be here talking to me.

Michael licked his dry lips. "I . . . I don't know what to say. I can't pay you. I don't have all the money."

"Should've thought about that before you went all in at the table," Big Daddy Jay said. He belched, and a stench steamed forth, making Michael's stomach turn.

"I can't pay you. So I guess you'll just have to kill me."

Peanut started to chuckle. So did Big Daddy Jay, and he was not a man prone to laughter.

"Why would we want to kill you, son?" Big Daddy Jay asked. "When we can own your soul forever?"

Michael looked at Peanut, raised from the dead and looking the worse for it. Peanut, who'd always drunk too much and struggled to cover his bets. Peanut, who, drowning in debts, most likely had signed over his soul to Big Daddy Jay and his enigmatic silent partner.

"That's right," Big Daddy Jay said, reading his thoughts. "Just like Peanut."

Peanut shrugged. He spun the gun on his finger.

Michael leapt out of the chair and wrested the gun out of Peanut's hand. He must have pulled too hard, because Peanut's arm came off with a soft, squishy sound. Peanut wailed as his arm plopped to the floor.

His gut churning with revulsion, Michael stepped away from the desk. He aimed the gun at Big Daddy Jay.

Big Daddy Jay grinned, unconcerned.

Michael shot him in the head.

Dark blood drained like water from the head shot, and Big Daddy Jay's head snapped backward. Then his head bounced forward, as if attached to a coiled spring. He smiled at Michael.

"I ain't no joker," he said. "You ain't getting away this time."

Michael heard shuffling footsteps behind him. He spun.

Five men, all of them dead, their bodies in various stages of decomposition, dragged across the room, toward him. He recognized a couple of them; they were men he'd played cards with, guys who, like him, sometimes won, and often lost.

He wondered if all of them were indebted to Big Daddy Jay.

"Fuck this," he said.

The zombies reached toward him.

Michael barreled through them like a running back breaking a tackle, batting away their groping, dead hands. He threw open the door and rushed to the stairs. He took the steps three at a time, landed on the bottom, banged through the back door, and stumbled into the alley behind the building.

And into the path of a white Cadillac.

The car hit him head-on. He flew in the air, smashed against the windshield, flipped over the roof, and bounced to the gravel in a ragged, broken heap.

Was just about to make a getaway, he thought, dimly. *Big Daddy Jay had someone back here waiting for me, sneaky bastard . . .*

Someone climbed out of the Cadillac. The driver walked toward him, crunching across gravel. He looked down at Michael.

It was Tommy Boy.

"Hey," Michael said, weakly. "Help . . . me."

"I tried to help you, Michael—or should I call you Ricky, the name you've been using in Atlanta?" Tommy Boy gave a small smile. "I warned you to run away. I was hoping you would. It would've been fun to hunt you down."

In spite of his agony, Michael frowned. *What the hell . . . ?*

"Confused, eh? Thought I was merely Big Daddy Jay's obedient little boy, tending shop?" Tommy Boy smirked. "His apparently ageless son? Funny how people in a small town don't question such telling details."

As comprehension settled over Michael, he tried to open his mouth to scream. But his ruined throat emitted only a desperate croak.

Tommy Boy knelt, leaned over him. His eyes danced—they were much darker and deeper than Michael remembered.

"You owe me, Michael," Tommy Boy said, as his face began to pulsate and shift into something evil and utterly inhuman. "Do I look like a joker?"

The Last Train Home

When Tonya's boss popped his head over the wall of her cubicle an hour before she was scheduled to go home, she anticipated what he was going to say. It had happened many times before, too many.

"Hey, Tonya," Roger said. A fortyish white man with a pale moon of a face, he brushed a strand of his stringy hair across his bald spot, an unconscious gesture that many of the customer service reps in her department ridiculed. *Who that man think he foolin?* Benita, Tonya's cube mate, would say. *Brushing his hair across that big fat head of his like he covering up something. Everybody know he going bald . . .*

"Hey, Rog," Tonya said. She turned away from the computer, where she had been typing comments into a call log, and gave him a sweet—and thoroughly fake—smile. "What's up?"

"I hate to ask you this," Roger said, and grinned, proof that he didn't hate asking her at all. "But I need you to stay late tonight."

She'd known he was going to ask her to work late. Roger's facial expressions were as easy to read as her son's picture books.

She held in her breath, stifling her annoyance, and listened to him.

"Our department is ten days behind on our work-flows," Roger continued. "We've got the worst work-flow stats of any department in the region, actually. The Powers That Be want us to take care of that. So . . ."

"How late do you need me to stay?" she asked. Her gaze flicked across the framed photograph of her five-year-old son, Aaron. In the photo, he was posed with Bugs Bunny. She'd taken the picture of him this past summer, at Six Flags Great America. That had been a wonderful day. Looking at the picture reminded her of why she worked so hard at a job that she despised: so she could give her son opportunities to brighten the world with his smile.

"Oh, a few hours," Roger said. He slid his short, hairy arms over the cubicle wall and inadvertently knocked down a sheet of paper that she had pinned to the wall. He didn't apologize. "Till about eight or so. We'll order in, like we always do."

We'll order in. As if the promise of pizza or Chinese takeout was adequate compensation for her losing precious hours of quality time with her son.

There was also the train to consider. She commuted via train from her home in Zion to her job at the insurance company in downtown Chicago. The last northbound train departed at . . . she glanced at the Metra/Union Pacific timetable tacked to the wall . . . eight thirty-five. It wouldn't arrive in Zion until nine fifty.

She hated riding the train at night. It was December, two weeks before Christmas, and already the snow had begun falling and the temperature had dropped into the teens. Her car would be covered with ice. And it would be dark. At night, the Zion station had an aura of complete abandonment that scared her.

But four hours of overtime pay would be a big help in buying Aaron's Christmas presents. Last Christmas had been difficult, what with her getting laid off from her good-paying job at a utility company. She'd vowed that once she started working again, she would do better in providing for her son. She'd been working as a customer service rep for eight months, and she took advantage of overtime whenever it was offered. She couldn't afford to turn it down.

Roger watched her with his small, marble eyes. His gaze skipped, ever so quickly, across her cleavage. That was another reason why the reps—all except one of whom were women—disliked him. He was a voyeur. He was harmless, but it was annoying all the same.

"Okay," she said. "I'll stay until eight."

Nodding, Roger smiled and rapped the top of her cubicle with his knuckles.

"Thanks for being a team player, Tonya. I knew I could count on you."

When he walked away, Tonya rolled her eyes. She studied Aaron's photo.

She would have to call her mother and tell her that she'd be home late. By the time she arrived home, Aaron would already be asleep. She put him to bed at eight thirty on school nights. Aaron didn't like going to bed without her tucking him in, and despite her mother's smooth reassurances, would worry that something had happened to her.

"Sorry, baby," she said to her son's picture. "But Mommy's doing this for you."

* * *

"You working late, huh?" Benita asked. Tonya was at the coffee station, refilling her big plastic Gulp cup with water, when Benita wandered out of the women's restroom and approached her. "I can't stand that asshole Rog."

Benita was a sister, in her late thirties, dark brown and full-figured—and all attitude. She didn't try to hide how much she despised Roger and the company. Benita's venomous comments could often be amusing, but sometimes they had the effect of making Tonya feel worse about an already upsetting situation.

Tonya shrugged. "I need the money. Christmas is coming up. Aaron wrote a wish list as long as my arm."

"Yeah, I hear you," Benita said. She had three children of her own, by three different fathers. "If these motherfuckas paid us more maybe we'd finish the workflows on time, and we wouldn't have to sit our black asses up in here working overtime looking at dumb-ass Rog."

"You've got a point," Tonya said. "Kinda hard to be motivated when you're earning nickels and dimes."

"Nickels and dimes? Shit, girl, pennies. I can't half pay my rent on this salary. If I didn't get my child support I don't know what I'd do."

"Yeah," Tonya said. She gazed at the company flyers on the bulletin board, but she wasn't really seeing them; the mention of child support had further dampened her spirits. Aaron's father, Marcus, was five months behind on his payments. She felt the lack of that money like a hunger pain in her stomach. Marcus was just getting back on his feet after being out of work for a while, and she was trying to be sympathetic to his situation, but she had to raise their child. She would have to take him back to court if he didn't resume his payments soon.

"Hmmm," Benita said. She motioned down the hallway and leaned close to Tonya. "Look at that."

Tonya looked. A tall, broad-shouldered brother was striding toward them. He appeared to be in his late-twenties; he had flawless, chocolate-brown skin and deep-set eyes. He wore a shirt and tie, the knot loosened and his sleeves rolled up to reveal muscular forearms adorned with tattoos.

He was an undeniably attractive man. Tonya had caught a quick glimpse of him a few times before. But when she looked at him now, her first time really seeing him for longer than a second, her gut clenched. It wasn't a good feeling.

"He looks like a model, don't he?" Benita asked. "I think he work in shipping. He can pack me up any day . . ."

"Evening, ladies," the man said in a deep bass voice. Although he addressed both of them, he focused on Tonya. "Working hard, or hardly working?"

"You know the answer to that, honey," Benita said, and laughed loudly.

The man only glanced at Benita, as if she wasn't worth his interest. He gazed at Tonya expectantly.

"I'd better get back to my desk," Tonya said. She laughed nervously. "Gotta make that money."

"See you around, sister," he said. He winked at her, and then headed to the restrooms.

Benita followed Tonya down the hall. "Well, damn, ain't I worth a wink?"

"You can have him," Tonya said, nearing her desk.

"Why you say that?"

The phone rang, saving Tonya from having to respond to Benita's question. She was thankful for the distraction, because she didn't know why the man made her uncomfortable. It was a feeling that she couldn't put into words. A feeling of . . . apprehension.

When she picked up the phone and heard her son's cheerful voice, her troubling feelings immediately departed.

"Hi, Mommy," Aaron said. "What you doing?"

"How are you, sweetheart? Mommy's still working. How was school?"

"School was good. I got a star. And we had taffy apples."

Tonya smiled. It didn't take much to make her son happy. Recognition and a taffy apple, and he was in heaven.

God, she wished she could be home with him tonight.

"Ooh, that sounds good," she said. She heard a cartoon playing in the background. "Are you doing your homework?"

"Yeah," he said. Then he giggled, most likely at something he saw on TV.

"Let me talk to Grandma, sweetie," Tonya said.

"'kay." There was a bumping sound as Aaron fumbled the phone. "Grandma, Mommy wants to talk to you!"

A few seconds later, Tonya's mother answered.

"Hi, Mom. Why is Aaron watching cartoons? He needs to finish his homework first."

"He's watching TV?" Her mother laughed, self-consciously. "These kids are so smart, ain't they? Turn my back and he's got the remote control and flipping channels."

"Right, Mom." Tonya had to smile. Her mother had a soft spot for Aaron, gave in to almost anything the boy wanted. Aaron, thank God, never demanded much, though. He was an easygoing kid.

Tonya heard the television fall silent. Her mother promised Aaron that he could watch cartoons once he finished his homework.

Aaron didn't whine; he said, "Yes, ma'am," and that was that.

"There," Mom said. "Are you working late tonight?"

"I was going to call you about that. Yes, I am. How'd you know?"

"It's a quarter to four and I ain't heard you zipping up your bag yet."

"I won't get off till eight, Mom. Then I have to catch the last train home, so I won't walk in until ten, if I'm lucky."

"I'll put him to bed at eight thirty," Mom said. "You want me to leave a plate for you? I'm fixing chicken and rice."

"Would you please? That sounds good." Her mom's cooking was far more appealing than any takeout food her company would order.

"Be careful on that train, Tonya. You know how I feel about you riding those trains at night. There's too many crazy folk out there, and they see a young, pretty woman like you riding home alone—"

"I'll be fine, Mom. I've done it before."

Tonya was twenty-nine years old and had lived on her own, raising her son, for five years, yet sometimes her mother treated her as if she was thirteen. And ever since Tonya had moved back home earlier in the year, to get her bearings after losing her job, Mom had worried more than ever before. She worked Tonya's nerves, but Tonya reminded herself that her mother did it only out of love and concern.

Besides, her mom's worries had a basis in reality.

It *was* a dangerous world for a young woman. Every night, the media ran stories of women abducted, raped, beaten, murdered. You could never be too careful.

"You got your phone?" Mom asked.

"Of course I do. I'll keep it on."

"All right," Mom said. Then she added again: "Be careful."

"Okay." Tonya sighed. "Can I talk to Aaron again, please?"

Her son came on the phone. "You working late, Mommy?"

Aaron sounded depressed. Her heart twisted.

"I am, baby," she said. "But I want you to know that I love you."

"You aren't gonna tuck me in?"

"Not tonight, sweetie. Grandma will tuck you in tonight."

"I want you to tuck me in, Mommy."

Normally, Aaron was not whiny like this. Where was this coming from?

She struggled for words that would reassure him. "I want to tuck you in, too. But I have to work late tonight, baby. You'll be asleep before I get home. That's why Grandma will tuck you in."

"Can I stay up till you get home?"

Why was he acting like this? He never talked like this before. She felt like the world's most neglectful mother.

Aaron started to cry.

"Baby, don't cry." Tonya wanted to scream in frustration. "Please don't cry. Be . . . Be a big boy for Mommy, okay?"

But he wouldn't stop. His cries grew louder.

Her mother got on the phone again. "What's going on, Tonya?"

"He's upset because I'm working late." She felt on the verge of tears herself. "He wants me to be there to tuck him in."

"He'll be okay," Mom said, softly. "He just misses you, that's all. You've been working a lot lately."

"Let him stay up until I get home," Tonya said.

"But you won't get in until past his bedtime."

"I know that, Mom. But letting him stay up later, this one time, won't hurt him. It's more important that he sees me tonight."

"All right, then," Mom said. "But he might fall asleep before you get here."

"Maybe so. Let me talk to him again, please."

Sniffling, Aaron came on the phone. "You coming home, Mommy?"

"Mommy will be there to tuck you in tonight," she said. "That's a promise, okay, sweetheart?"

He immediately stopped sniffling. "'kay."

"I love you, Aaron."

"Love you, too."

Then her son spoke three words that echoed in Tonya's thoughts for hours afterward:

"Be careful, Mommy."

Tonya was hard at work for the next few hours. Benita refused to work overtime—she claimed she had a date that night, which was probably a lie—so Tonya was able to labor without distraction. When the pizzas arrived, Roger strolling around magnanimously, announcing their arrival as if he was treating them to filet mignon and lobster, Tonya declined and kept working. She was determined to get out of there at eight o'clock and be home to tuck in her son at ten. Children took promises seriously, and if she failed to come through for Aaron, he would remember it for a long time and resent her for it.

"Working late?" a familiar deep voice from above her suddenly asked.

Tonya was so shocked to hear a voice that she almost screamed. She'd been working in solitude for over an hour.

The brother from the shipping department leaned against the cubicle wall, peering down at her. He smiled.

He had a nice smile. His teeth were straight and white. But that clench in her gut returned.

"You scared the mess out of me," she said.

"My bad," he said. He juggled a tube of glue in one hand. "I was on my way downstairs and saw you typing away . . . thought I'd drop by to introduce myself. My name is Jamal. It's nice to meet you, Tonya Washington."

"How do you know my name?"

"It's right there." Capturing the glue in midair, he pointed at the nameplate affixed to the outer wall of her cubicle. "Tonya Washington. Sounds like the name of an actress."

"Oh, well, yeah." She laughed, ran her fingers through her hair. Why did this man make her so uncomfortable?

Jamal fixed her with a steady gaze. She knew, then, why he bothered her. It was the look in his eyes. He was intense, overly so. She liked serious brothers, didn't go for the comedian type, but Jamal's piercing stare was disconcerting. It was as though he was trying to peel away the vital layers of her—body, mind, and soul—with his eyes.

She squirmed in her chair. She wished he would walk away.

"How long have you been working here?" he asked.

Maybe if she acted busy, he would get the hint.

She swiveled to her computer and started typing. "About eight months."

"That right?" He sounded conversational, not at all ready to leave. "How do you like it?"

She continued to type. "Hmmm?"

"How do you like working here?"

"Oh. It's okay."

"Yeah, I've been here about three weeks. I've seen you around a few times. Finally got the nerve tonight to come up to you and chat."

He wasn't making it easy for her. It had to be obvious to him that she wasn't interested in talking. But he seemed to be one of those persistent men who didn't readily take no for an answer.

"Well, I'm pretty busy here, Jamal," she finally said. She softened her words with a brief smile. If you were too rude to men like him they were liable to go off on you—call you a bitch and cause a nasty scene. She couldn't afford to let that happen here.

"I'm supposed to be working, too," he said. He grinned, as if they were involved in a conspiracy together. "So you take the train home to . . . Zion?"

"Excuse me?" She stopped typing. "How'd you know that?"

He shrugged. "There's a train schedule on your wall there. I saw that you'd circled the Zion arrival times and figured that was where you laid your head."

Had this man been studying her desk while she was away? She didn't like this at all.

"That's because I used to live in Zion," she said,

and wondered why she was lying. "I recently moved to the city."

"Yeah? Whereabouts?"

"Southside."

His eyes brightened. "I grew up on the South-side, Evergreen Park. Where you livin'?"

Shit, why did I have to say that? He's going to know I'm lying if I can't tell him which neighborhood.

As she was trying to think of a credible answer, Roger approached her desk.

"Hey, Tonya. We're having a quick powwow in the conference room down the hall. Please sit in."

"Okay, Roger. Be right there." She wanted to kiss Roger for saving her.

She looked at Jamal. "Sorry, gotta go."

"Take care, sister. We'll talk again soon."

I hope not, Tonya thought.

She felt his unwavering gaze on her as she walked away down the corridor. Blessed with a shapely, sista-girl booty, and a hip-swinging stroll that men liked—her ex told her that she walked like a runway model—she downplayed her walk to a slow shuffle, to minimize her assets. She didn't want Jamal to think she was flirting with him.

When she reached the conference room doorway, she glanced over her shoulder.

Jamal was still watching her.

When the team meeting ended fifteen minutes later, Tonya was relieved to see that Jamal had left. Worried that he was going to hang around her desk until she returned, she'd barely heard a word exchanged during the department discussion.

She found a Post-it note attached to her keyboard.

She read it; the message was written in tightly packed cursive.

"Hyde Park would have been a good answer."

There was a smiley face sketched underneath the sentence.

Jamal had written the note, she realized. And it was clear: he had known that she was lying about living in Chicago.

Okay, so what? She thought. *I don't know him. I don't have to tell him where I live. It's none of his damn business.*

But the cautious part of her replayed her mother's warning about crazy folk in the city, and the danger of being a young woman traveling home at night, alone.

Be careful, Mommy.

She exhaled. She was overreacting. Jamal wasn't dangerous. He was just a brother eager to get to know her. He had a keen stare that made her a bit uneasy, but that didn't mean he was a serial killer.

"So relax," she muttered to herself.

She crumpled the note and tossed it in the wastebasket.

Promptly at eight o'clock, Tonya logged off her computer. She slipped on her snow boots, coat, hat, and gloves, knotted her scarf around her neck, slung her purse over her shoulder, and walked out of the office with purposeful strides. She had about thirty minutes to get to the train station on Canal and Madison streets. She had plenty of time since the station was only five blocks away, but when you were in the city, you moved with purpose, as if you had somewhere important to go and not a lot of time to get there. She loved the city's energy. It was contagious.

Snow had been falling all day, and it had stuck; as the temperature dropped, the snow hardened into an icy crust. Taxis, cars, and buses rushed by, their tires rolling through dirty slush. Harried pedestrians strode along the sidewalks, snow crunching under their heels, frosty clouds billowing from their mouths. The infamous "hawk"—a frigid wind blowing off Lake Michigan—gusted down the city streets, howling and biting, forcing Tonya to pull her gloves more snugly on her hands and yank her hat down over her head to protect her tender ears.

She loved the city, but hated the winters.

She reached the station with fifteen minutes to spare, and headed into a Starbucks. A knot of people milled inside, snow melting off their shoes as they waited for their beverages. She purchased a Caramel Macchiato and carried it to the condiment bar to add a spoonful of sugar.

As she stood there stirring the drink, she saw Jamal walk past the coffee shop. He wore a black quilted bubble jacket and a black scully cap. She saw only his profile, but she was sure it was him. She felt it in her gut.

So what if it is him? Maybe he takes the train home, too, Tonya. That's common for people who live in the city, you know.

But the careful side of her wondered if it was a bit too coincidental that he would happen to be in the train station at the same time as her. He probably knew when she was going home, and the train she would board, too. He'd read the schedule posted near her desk.

Without looking in her direction, Jamal vanished into the streaming crowd. She sighed.

I'm getting paranoid.

The paper cup of Caramel Macchiato was warm, but the warmth didn't transfer to her palm. Her hand was clammy, as if dipped in ice water.

Her cell phone rang—a ring tone from the Gwen Stefani song "Hollaback Girl." Tonya had downloaded the ring tone a year ago because she thought it was funny, and she hadn't changed it since.

She dug the phone out of her purse. Her mother was calling.

"You about to board the train?" Mom asked.

"Yes, I'm at the station now."

"You okay? You sound funny."

She never had been able to fool her mother. Her mom had a nose for sniffing out her emotional states.

No, Mom, I'm not okay at all. Matter of fact, I'm feeling kinda paranoid about this guy I met at work. I think he's following me . . .

"I'm fine, Mom," she said. "Just tired. It's been a long day."

"All right, I was only making sure." Her mother sounded skeptical.

"How's my baby?" Tonya asked.

"He's fine. I can tell he's getting tired, but he's got his little mind set on staying up till you get home."

"I'll be there soon." Tonya checked the time. "I gotta go. The train's about to start boarding."

But her mother didn't hang up. "You want me to pick you up from the train station?"

"That's not necessary. My car is there."

"It'll be buried under six inches of snow," Mom

said. She sighed heavily. "I hate the idea of you being out there at night scraping ice off the car."

"Mom, I really have to go. Stop worrying about me, okay? I'm almost thirty years old."

"I know. But you'll always be my baby."

There was no way to respond to that, so Tonya assured her again that she would be fine, told her good-bye, and hurried to board the train.

The Metra/Union Pacific North line ran every hour from Chicago to Kenosha, Wisconsin, making twenty-five stops in between. It was a double-decker train, with several cars. At peak times, it could be quite crowded, passengers seated shoulder to shoulder and even standing up holding the hand straps. But when Tonya boarded at eight thirty-five, there were a lot of empty seats.

She found a seat in the corner, on the lower level. There were only a handful of other passengers sharing the compartment with her: a couple of businessmen dressed in trench coats, reading newspapers, a college-age girl with a backpack, and two young women laden with shopping bags from stores on State Street.

No dirty old men. No Jamal. He was undoubtedly sitting on a southbound train on his way to Evergreen Park or wherever the hell he lived.

The conductor announced their departure. The train expelled a blast of air as the brakes disengaged, and began to roll away down the tracks.

In retrospect, Tonya was not convinced that she had really seen Jamal at the train station. She had thought it was him, but as she had glimpsed only his profile, it could have been another man. All black people didn't look alike, but some of them looked damn similar.

It doesn't matter, she thought. *All that matters is that I'm finally going home.*

She couldn't wait to see Aaron. She hoped he had managed to stay awake.

She slid her iPod out of her bag, popped in the ear buds, and turned on the player. Then she pulled out the latest issue of *Essence,* and began to read to the soulful sounds of Will Downing.

As the train wound its way through the dark, ice-mantled northern suburbs, the conductor passed through the car to punch their tickets, and then passengers began to disembark. One of the businessmen got off in Evanston. The two shopaholic women detrained in Wilmette. College girl left at Glencoe. The other businessman exited at Highland Park.

She was alone in the car, and there was still about a half hour to go before they reached Zion.

She yawned. She hadn't lied to her mother during their last conversation. She was, truthfully, completely wiped out.

During eight months of commuting to the city, she had mastered the art of the twenty-minute catnap. Her eyes drifted shut. Will Downing continued to croon sweetly into her ears.

She slept . . . and woke with a start.

Someone had entered the compartment.

Jamal.

For a moment, looking at Jamal stride toward her, Tonya thought she was dreaming. She thought she was really asleep, and having a nightmare about seeing this annoyingly persistent and intense man, yet again—and being all alone with him.

"Taking a catnap?" he asked.

This wasn't a dream. His voice was too real—and so was the pounding of her heart.

She straightened.

Jamal settled onto a seat directly across from her. He pulled off his skully cap, twirled it around his finger. He grinned, but his gaze was as acute as ever.

"You boarded the wrong train, Tonya," he said.

"What?"

"You're heading north, not south. You said you live on the Southside."

"Oh, I, uh . . ."

"Hyde Park, maybe?" He chuckled.

"All right, you got me." Embarrassment burned her face. "But you said you live in Evergreen Park."

He nodded. "I do."

"So why are you on this train?"

"Because I wanted to talk to you. Your boss interrupted us earlier."

"Oh." Didn't he realize how threatening his behavior seemed? Following a woman home on a train wasn't charming. It was frightening.

She moved her purse onto her lap, like a shield between them, and slipped her hand inside.

"Why are you so nervous, girl?" he asked. "I just wanna talk to you."

"I'm not nervous," she said, but she heard the shakiness in her voice. *Keep it together, Tonya.* She cleared her throat. "What do you want to talk about?"

"You." He smiled, and rubbed his hands together as if they were getting down to serious business.

"What about me?"

"You seeing anyone?"

"I have a boyfriend."

"Right." It was obvious that he didn't believe her. "Is it serious?"

"He's the father of my son."

The truth was, she and Marcus hadn't been together in two years, and she hadn't been in a serious relationship since. But Jamal wouldn't know that.

"That doesn't mean it's serious," Jamal said. "Just means he gave you a baby."

If she was a different kind of woman—like Benita, perhaps—that comment would have been grounds for her to cuss him out. As if she was some trifling woman who would lie down with a man and have his baby without being in a serious relationship with him!

"Well, it's serious, okay?" she said.

"Your son favors you. That's a good thing, 'cause you're beautiful."

She almost started to ask him how the hell he knew what her son looked like—and then remembered that she kept several photos of Aaron prominently displayed on her desk.

"Dime piece," he said, admiring her from head to toe. "Pretty face. Small waist. Big behind."

The longer he looked at her, the dirtier she felt.

"Can't you say 'thank you' to a compliment?" Jamal asked. He tried for a humorous tone, Tonya thought, but he couldn't disguise his irritation.

"Thank you," she said, tightly.

The train arrived at the next stop: Lake Forest. Still over twenty minutes away from home. An eternity.

Jamal leaned forward. "So you *claim* to have a boyfriend. That's cool. But you interested in having a friend?"

"My boyfriend wouldn't like that."

Jamal laughed. "Of course he wouldn't. But would you?"

He gave her the stare again. Probing into her brain.

She shifted in her seat. She could not remember the last time a man had made her so uncomfortable. She was accustomed to crude compliments—*Damn, girl, the way you looking in them jeans make me wanna give you a baby*—gawking, and the like. And she had learned how to brush them off and keep moving. Any woman knew how to do that.

But this was different. She had never been cornered like this. Jamal was a different kind of male animal—and she felt like potential prey.

I have to get rid of him.

But what could she say that would make him leave? She had to tell him something, or else he wouldn't leave her alone.

She glanced at the end of the compartment. The conductor was nowhere in sight. No help.

She turned to Jamal. "Look, it's been a really long day. I'm tired, and I want to get home. What do you want from me?"

"Can you just give me your number?" he asked. "That's all I want. Then I'll get off the train. I need to get back to the city, anyway."

All he wanted was her phone number? He'd gone through all of this trouble simply to get her number?

It sounded like a lie, but she wanted to believe that he was telling the truth.

"You just want my number?" she asked. "Then you'll go?"

"That's all." He pulled a cell phone out of his pocket. Watched her expectantly.

"Okay."

She rattled off a number—not her real one. He punched the digits into his phone.

"There," he said. "I've saved you at the top of the list, Tonya Washington."

"I'm honored."

"Funny." He smiled. "One day, when we're married, we'll look back on this chat and laugh."

"When we're married? What?"

"I'm kidding." He stood. "Damn, girl, loosen up."

She only looked at him. "You leaving now?"

"I'm going, I'm going," he said. "Gotta go back to the other car and get my bag. I'm hopping off at the next stop."

Good, she thought. But she said, "'Bye."

"See you, sister."

He left the compartment.

She released a deep sigh. She took her hand out of her purse.

She had been gripping a bottle of pepper spray so tightly that it left an imprint on her palm.

"Next stop, Zion . . ."

Tonya was so eager to get home that she was trembling. She hadn't seen Jamal again, but she believed that he was satisfied with what she'd given him, and had left. He'd just wanted her phone number. The fact that she'd given him a fake number should give him a hint that she wasn't interested.

You hope. The man followed you on a train all the way from Chicago. He isn't going to let a wrong phone number keep him down . . .

She shook her head, shut out the voice of doubt.

The rocking train began to slow. She looked out

the window. An icing of snow covered the world, and she heard a shrill wind whipping around the train. The mere thought of stepping out into that cold weather made her shiver. She buttoned her coat, pulled on her gloves and hat, and tightened her scarf.

With a screech of brakes, the train drew to a halt. The doors slid open.

"Zion . . ."

She walked out the car and onto the platform. Pausing, she looked both ways.

The icy wind blew, drawing tears from her eyes, but she saw what she expected: she was the only person disembarking from the train.

Satisfied, she headed toward the steps that led to the parking lot. Salt, thrown on the pavement to melt the ice, crunched underneath her boots.

She heard the train rumble away down the tracks.

The Zion station was located on the far eastern side of town, about a half mile away from a shutdown power plant and the shores of Lake Michigan; an area of open spaces choked with weeds and forest-land. There were no residences. No one came over here unless they were boarding the train. There was nothing else around.

This was the worst part of coming home late at night. The place was so desolate she felt as if she was the only living person in the world. A single street-lamp standing at the edge of the parking lot provided weak, pale light. The light revealed that the snow, thank God, had been plowed from the parking lot, and was now piled in head-high drifts along the edges of the area.

Her Toyota Camry sat in the far corner of the parking lot, a large hump underneath a blanket of snow.

She shuffled toward it. Just thinking about scraping off the snow and ice made her tired. She wished she had agreed for Mom to pick her up—

"Tonya!"

Oh, no, it can't be.

Jamal hurried off the platform steps.

She'd thought she was the only one who had gotten off the train. He must have waited until the doors had been about to close, must have waited until she had turned and started walking away, before he'd jumped off.

What the hell did he want? She had given him a phone number. What else could he want?

Whatever it was, it couldn't be good. Nothing good could come of a man following her all the way from Chicago at night to an empty parking lot.

Anxiety cramped her stomach. Rather than slowing, she increased her pace.

"Tonya, hold on!"

She didn't stop.

She pulled her keys out of her purse. The small black bottle of pepper spray dangled from the key chain. She levered her finger over the SPRAY button.

"Tonya, wait up, girl!"

She glanced over her shoulder. Jamal was running now.

She started jogging, too. Her breath plumed in front of her.

But Jamal was closing in on her.

Adrenaline pumped through her veins. She'd been a track athlete in high school, remembered the feeling of sprinting when her muscles hit their peak and her lungs drew in more air than seemed possible. Her body felt like that now. Invigorated, ready to take on a challenge—ready to fight, if necessary.

She finally reached her car. She punched the button to disengage the power locks. She grabbed the snow-covered door handle. She pulled.

The door didn't open. Ice had sealed it shut.

Dammit!

She banged her fist against the door. Snowflakes fell away. She hammered the door again. Ice crackled.

She tried again to open the door. It loosened, but still gave resistance. Grunting, she slammed her shoulder against it. Tugged harder. Almost . . .

"Why . . . Why are you running from me, Tonya?"

Tonya whirled, her hand on the pepper spray.

Jamal was a few feet away from her. He was hunched over, panting.

"Why are you following me?" she demanded.

"Just . . . had . . . a question for you."

Was this man insane? He'd chased her down to ask her a question?

She didn't know whether to be angry or take pity on him for his stupidity. But anger took over. He had scared her to death.

"What is it?" she shouted. "What do you want? What the hell was so important that you had to follow me to my car?"

"I wanted to know why . . . why you gave me a fake phone number." He unfolded his body to his full six feet. His lips twisted with rage. "I called that number you gave me. Doesn't even exist. Bitch."

Tonya's surging adrenaline had thrown her into fight-or-flight mode. She raised the pepper spray in front of her like a gun.

"Get back," she said. "Or I *will* spray this in your face."

He didn't move. He didn't seem frightened at all.

Her resolve wavered, but she didn't lower the spray.

"Funny thing about women who work in cubes," he said. "They leave so much personal information out in the open . . ."

"What?"

He moved forward.

"I told you to get back!" she shouted.

"And they leave their purses in desk drawers," he continued. "So anyone walking by could fish around . . ."

He took another step.

"That's it," she said.

She mashed the button.

But the button didn't depress. It was stuck. She mashed it again, to no avail.

Jamal grinned. "And put a few drops of glue on a woman's bottle of pepper spray, make sure she couldn't use that nasty shit to hurt a brother."

She remembered him standing over her cubicle, juggling a tube of glue.

A terrible realization came over her. He had anticipated this. He had set her up. This man had been planning to attack her from the beginning.

On cue, a knife appeared in Jamal's fingers, as if by sleight of hand.

"Now, let's talk about why you've been lying to me so much, bitch." He waved the blade in the air like a hypnotist's pendulum. "A blade has a way of cutting to the truth, know what I mean?" He chuckled at his pun.

In a flash, Tonya imagined what could happen. Holding her at knifepoint, he could force her inside the car, making her lie on the backseat. He could rip away her clothes. Rape her. Cut her. And if he decided to let her live, he could leave her in there, weeping and bloody and humiliated, and then she would have to go home and face her child, a beaten woman.

No.

Tonya screamed and kicked him in the groin.

Jamal cried out, doubled over in pain, the knife dropping out of his fingers and landing in the snow.

"Help!" Tonya cried. "Someone help!"

But even as she shouted, she knew her pleas were in vain. There was no one out there who could help or call the police. She was on her own.

She grabbed the door handle.

Jamal lunged at her.

She tore the door loose and swung it open, smashing it into his head, causing a comically loud THUD. Jamal dropped to the ground with a grunt.

She dove inside the car. As she tried to pull her legs inside, Jamal snared one of her ankles in his gloved hand.

Screaming, she smashed her other heel against his knuckles. He yelped, but didn't let go.

He used his shoulder to force the door open wider.

She saw that he had retrieved the knife.

"Ain't getting away, bitch," he said. His nostrils flared.

She thrust her boot into his nose. Bones broke, an ugly sound. Crying out, he let her go.

She drew her legs inside, slammed the door, and locked it.

The interior was coffin-dark, snow blanketing all of the windows. It was so cold inside that she felt her perspiration freezing into a paste on her brow. Her frantic breathing was amplified in the enclosed space, too, rebounding back to her, pounding in her ears, as if she was trapped inside a steel drum.

She fumbled with the key. Praying under her breath.

"Just let me get home," she said, in a fervent whisper. "Please, God, just let me get home to my baby . . . just let me get home . . ."

With a roar, Jamal rammed his shoulder against the window. The car rocked like a canoe hit by a strong wave. But the glass didn't break. Yet.

She jammed the key in the ignition. Turned it so hard it was a wonder it didn't break off.

Dear God, just let me get home.

In the horror movies Tonya watched sometimes, when the heroine was on the run from a killer, the car never worked. A car that had started reliably for five years failed when the woman most needed it. It happened so often in films it had become a cliché.

Her Toyota started immediately.

Thank you, Jesus.

Regular auto maintenance that she could barely afford had paid off. She pushed the gas pedal, revving the engine. Then she slammed the gearshift into DRIVE.

"Now, let's get out of here," she said. She stomped the accelerator.

The tires spun, and the car moved a few inches— and jerked to a halt.

"No, no, no!" She pinned the gas pedal to the floor. The tires ground furiously.

But the car didn't move, and she knew why: she was stuck in the ice. The city had plowed much of the parking lot, but had neglected the corner in which her car was parked.

She should have known better. This has happened to her before. She kept a snow shovel in the trunk for times like this. She'd have to dig herself out.

But at the moment, getting out of the car was out of the question.

Jamal hammered his elbow against the window, and this time, the glass shattered. Shards tinkled to the floor. Frosty air invaded the car.

Growling like a wild animal, Jamal groped inside, knocking pieces of glass out of the window frame.

"Come back here, bitch."

Out of reflex, she punched the accelerator. But the wailing tires were useless against the ice. She was only digging a deeper rut in the snow.

Jamal got a fistful of her coat. She tried to twist out of his grasp, but he had the strength of a lunatic. He yanked her against the door. She hit her head against the door frame, and the collision made her dizzy.

No, I can't pass out, can't pass out, can't pass out . . .

As if from far away, she heard her cell phone chirp. Probably her mother calling to confirm that she was in her car and on her way home, and letting her know that Aaron was still awake, waiting on her to tuck him in.

Thinking of Aaron brought her back to her senses.

Jamal was reaching for the interior door handle. She seized his forefinger and snapped it back.

He howled. He pulled his hand out of the car.

Tonya realized that the cell phone had fallen silent. Good. Maybe Mom would realize that something was wrong and call the police.

As Tonya leaned to grab the phone, Jamal knocked

away the remaining slivers of glass in the window frame. He grabbed her coat again.

She tried to squirm out of his grip. Tried to wriggle to the opposite side of the car.

He got a hold of her leg. He tugged.

She began to slide across the seats. She raised her other leg, to kick him. But he grabbed that leg, too.

"Gotcha!" he said.

He was going to pull her out through the window, feet first.

As he dragged her out, she curled her fingers around the handle of the passenger door, breaking his momentum. He pulled, cursing. She held fast to the handle.

Her phone rang again.

Mom, call the police, dammit!

A sudden, sharp pain bit into her calf, drawing a cry out of her. Jamal had stabbed her.

Startled by the pain, she lost her grip on the door handle. Meeting no resistance now, Jamal hauled her out of the car like a laborer lifting a load of lumber. He flung her to the snowy ground. She landed hard on her shoulder.

The impact knocked the air out of her lungs, almost pulled her under into darkness.

"Goddamn, you're a tough bitch," Jamal said. He dabbed at his bleeding nose with his glove. "I thought you would be, I love that about sistas. I love me a strong black woman."

She didn't know what to do next. This man was relentless.

But she could not—*would not*—allow him to have his way with her.

As she tried to get up, Jamal sat on her knees, to

prevent her from kicking him. Panting with excitement, he lowered the knife to her chest. The blade was about four inches long, and looked sharp enough to cut the air itself into ribbons.

"You're tough, but every woman's got to submit to a man," he said. "The man's the head. That's what the Bible says, sista. You know that, right? You got a Bible on your desk, too."

She didn't respond, unable to take her gaze away from the knife. She saw her own blood staining the razor-sharp tip. Her stabbed calf throbbed; she felt blood trickling across her skin, like ice water.

Jamal sliced open the front of her coat. Buttons popped.

"Please don't do this," she said.

Giggling, like a child opening presents on Christmas morning, he peeled away the edges of her coat to reveal her blouse.

"Ah, here we go now," he said. Saliva had collected in the corners of his mouth, like dried milk. A blood bubble pulsed in one of his smashed nostrils.

Say something to make him stop.

"I have a son," she said softly.

"Yeah, so? I saw those pictures of him on your desk."

"His name is Aaron."

"Like the guy in the Bible? Moses' brother."

"That's right. He's only five, Jamal. He's expecting me to come home to . . . to tuck him in bed." She sniffled, fought back tears.

He ripped open her blouse. The frigid air raised goose bumps on her naked flesh.

"Don't you have a mother?" Tonya asked, striving

to keep her voice calm. "Would you want some man to hurt your mother, to take advantage of her?"

"Someone did. My daddy."

"Oh." She tried to sound sympathetic. "I'm very sorry."

"I ain't." His eyes hardened to black points. "She's a crackhead bitch. She deserved it."

Tonya wished she had kept her mouth shut. She had been trying to tap a sympathetic nerve somewhere in him and convince him to stop what he was doing, but she'd succeeding only in drawing forth the deep-seated hatred he held for his mother—which he might now channel toward *her*.

She had to come up with another strategy, and her time was running short.

He cut away her bra, then pulled it away and tossed it into the snow behind him. He stared at her fully exposed breasts. Something approaching rapture lit his eyes.

She was a well-endowed woman, but a lot of the brothers that she encountered were all about the booty and could have cared less about her breasts. Normally, it was white men—like her boss, Roger—who fell into a trance when they saw her cleavage.

Jamal's fascination presented her with an opportunity.

"You got some really nice titties," he said. He licked his lips. "Not too big, not too small. Just perfect."

She turned her head away and sighed, as though she was giving up. Trying to lull him into a false sense of power. It was hard for her to play docile, but it might be her best chance to strike back at him.

He roughly squeezed one of her breasts. She let out a cry of pain that was more genuine than anything she could have faked.

He backhanded her across the jaw. Her head snapped sideways, and her vision swam.

Don't pass out, don't pass out . . .

"That's right, bitch. You like it rough? I'm gonna give it to you rough."

His threat brought her world back into focus. His eyes hungry, he lowered his head to her breast. She saw the gleam of his teeth, those perfectly straight, white teeth—and she knew he was intending to bite her.

She couldn't take any more.

As his lips closed over her nipple and his teeth started to rake across her skin, she flipped up the rim of his skully cap, to reveal his ear. Surprised, he started to lift his head, but she was faster: she clamped her teeth over his earlobe and bit down as hard as she could.

He yelled. As he jerked away, his ear tore, blood spattering the snow.

"You bitch!" He scrambled away, hand pressed against his head. "You bit my ear like fuckin' Mike Tyson!"

She spat out his bloody earlobe. Rising, she pulled her blouse across her bosom.

With horror, Jamal regarded his chewed-off ear, lying on the snow in a smear of blood.

She noticed that he had dropped the knife beside her. She snatched it up.

Jamal made a move to charge her.

"Get the fuck away from me!" She waved the blade in front of her, made a feint as if to cut him.

Weeping, gritting his teeth against the pain, Jamal scooted backward. He dug his hand into an inner pocket of his coat.

When Tonya saw the cold glimmer of the gun, she turned and ran.

He fired. A bullet zipped past her, plowed into a snowbank. Bits of ice sprayed her.

She started to run in a chaotic, zigzag pattern, to make herself a difficult target. The station was ahead. There was no attendant on duty, but if she could get inside, get to a pay phone . . . *something*. Maybe some kind of plan would become clear. Maybe she could survive this nightmare.

She leaped the concrete steps and ran onto the platform. She almost slipped on a patch of ice that hadn't been covered with salt, regained her balance just in time.

Jamal was rushing across the parking lot, kicking up snow, coming after her.

She hurried inside the station. It was a small, glass-fronted structure, built solely to shelter passengers from the elements. It was full of faded plastic chairs and a trash can. No potential weapons. Not even a telephone.

Jamal had reached the platform steps.

She ran out of the door on the opposite side of the building, onto the boarding platform. The railroad tracks lay beneath her, gleaming in the moonlight like the vertebrae of some ancient beast. No train approached, and none would for the remainder of the night. She had caught the last train home.

Jamal was charging through the station.

She jumped off the platform, landed on the tracks. She raced across them and plunged into the brittle snow on the other side.

There was forestland ahead. Trees, bereft of leaves, twisted into the night sky.

A distinct thought surfaced in her mind: if she entered these woods, one of them would not return alive.

"Bitch," Jamal called, behind her. He fired. Automatically, she dropped to the ground for cover.

The bullet smashed into a tree only a few feet away from her.

Rising to a crouch, praying with every step, Tonya scrambled into the woods.

She didn't bother looking behind her to see if Jamal was following. Inevitably, he would. He was as persistent as he was crazed.

Why had he picked her? What was it about her that made him decide to attack her? She had never been in a situation like this, had never fought for her life against a psycho. Why her? Why now? She didn't want much. She wanted only to make enough money to give her son a comfortable life. Save her mother's helping hand, she was doing it alone. She was a good person, a Christian woman who strived to do the right thing, treated others as she wanted to be treated, read a Bible passage every day at lunch and said her prayers before every meal, and worked hard to impart good values to her son so that he would grow up to be a decent, honorable man. Why was she being put through this? Why did she deserve this? Why did—

Another bullet whizzed past her.

"Can't run from me!" Jamal shouted.

Maybe not, but she'd be damned if she would give up.

As she ran, her boots punched holes in the snow. The effort of slogging forward had her thighs screaming and her lungs burning, and her injured calf ached, too, but she didn't dare slow down. She ducked underneath gnarled branches, brushed past ʒkeletal bushes. Wind gusted, howling through the forest and blowing gritty snow in her eyes. She squinted and pressed onward.

She heard Jamal behind her, fighting his way through the forest. He had a gun, and she had the knife, but the weapons didn't seem to matter much anymore. This had become a pure contest of wills.

She wasn't going to quit. She had no choice but to win. She *had* to survive, for her son.

She stumbled out of a patch of dead shrubs and into a clearing. A large pond lay before her, the perimeter ringed with tall elms. The pond's surface was an unbroken, smooth sheet of ice that looked like molten silver in the moon glow.

She didn't know how sturdy the iced-over pond would prove under her weight, so she began to travel around the edge of it. When she was at the halfway point, Jamal emerged in the clearing.

She was out in the open, an easy target. She ducked.

He fired.

The bullet bit into her shoulder.

She screamed, spun, lost her footing, and slammed onto the ice, the knife popping out of her hand and spinning across the pond.

CRACK!

Pain fanned across her back and shoulder blades. She rolled over, like a log. Her fall had fractured the ice beneath her. But the surface still held.

She touched her shoulder. The bullet had grazed her; she was lucky it hadn't penetrated, or she would be in far worse shape. But blood dampened her coat, and numbness began to spread through her arm. She felt faint; her sheer will to survive was all that kept her conscious.

She pulled her wool scarf from around her neck and pressed it against her wound, to stop the flow of blood.

Jamal strutted around the pond—the same swaggering walk that she recognized from the office.

She suddenly hated him more than she'd ever hated anyone—even more than she'd once hated Marcus, her son's father, when he tried to deny that Aaron was his child. The hatred she felt for Jamal was the hatred she would have felt for anyone who threatened to destroy everything that she held dear. She was a charitable woman and didn't often indulge such negative feelings, but this time she allowed herself to indulge in hatred, knowing that it would give her the fortitude to keep fighting.

She blinked away tears of pain.

"Well, well, well, Tonya Washington." Jamal looked at her, studied the pond, looked back at her. "You're gonna make a brother walk across thin ice for you, huh?"

With a great, agonizing effort, she crawled farther away from him, toward the middle of the pond. The ice crackled beneath her, but didn't break. However, a long, jagged line had begun to spread beside her.

How deep was the pond? Plunging into even a mere two feet of frigid water would probably induce hypothermia. It could certainly shock the hell out of you, numb you to the marrow, temporarily paralyze you.

A plan formed in her mind. A last, desperate attempt to end this.

She rolled onto her back. Above, the cold stars watched her, a thousand indifferent eyes.

She stretched her tired legs in front of her, looked at Jamal.

"You got me," she said. "Come get it. Get it over with."

He frowned, clearly suspicious. Then he saw the knife, lying out of her reach, and his frown faded.

"I'm coming, sista."

He stepped warily onto the ice, testing his weight. The ice emitted a soft snapping sound, but didn't collapse. He began to advance, with growing confidence.

She drew up her legs, muscles tensed.

"Don't try any shit," he said. He aimed the gun at her, moving closer.

Just as she hoped, his boots pressed across the gigantic fracture that her fall had created.

"Why would I do that?" she asked.

As she spoke, she raised both legs high and then brought down her heels, banging them against the ice.

The ice around Jamal broke.

"Bitch!" he yelled. He plunged into the freezing water.

Tonya scooted away from the shattered ice.

The pond was much deeper than she had thought. Jamal sank completely beneath the surface. He thrashed wildly. Screaming.

The gun flipped out of his hand and clattered onto the ice. Tonya crawled toward it. She got her hands around the handle, slid her finger over the trigger.

Jamal suddenly launched out of the water as if shot from a cannon. He flopped onto a shelf of ice, shivering. He saw her, and his face twisted into a mask of rage.

He began to scramble toward her.

She aimed and pulled the trigger.

The bullet ripped into his throat. Releasing a garbled scream, he splashed back into the water.

He flailed for a few seconds . . . and then sank under the surface.

The water grew still. The night, too, was quiet. The only sound was Tonya's tortured breathing.

He was gone. She had killed him.

She felt no remorse, no anger. Perhaps she would, later. Now, she just felt hollow.

She stuffed the gun into her pocket. She located the knife, wrapped it in her scarf. The weapons were evidence.

Then she crawled back to land, slowly got to her knees, and even more slowly, rose to her feet.

Soon after, she began to cry.

When Tonya walked out of the woods and crossed the railroad tracks, she saw her mother's Jeep Grand Cherokee rumbling down the road beside the parking lot.

Heedless of the pain in her shoulder and her calf, Tonya started running.

Spotting her, her mother drove toward her, pulling up close to the station. Tonya saw Aaron sitting in the front passenger seat, bundled up in a coat and hat.

She raced to the passenger door, yanked it open, and pulled her son into her arms, not even feeling her wounded shoulder. Her son was so warm, so alive. She covered his face with kisses.

"Mommy, Mommy!" He giggled. "I stayed up for you!"

Everything she had faced was worth this moment.

"What happened to you?" her mother asked. "I tried calling you on your cell phone, then decided to drive down here 'cause I got worried about you."

"I'll tell you all about it, Mom," Tonya said. She had a long night ahead of her—contacting the police, retelling the incident blow by blow, going through the entire horrific experience one more time, visiting the hospital to get treatment for her injuries . . .

But she didn't want to think about any of that right now.

She stroked her son's hair, kissed him on the forehead, and looked into his eyes. He grinned at her with a child's boundless love.

"First, let's go home so Mommy can tuck you in."

Notes on the Stories

"Daddy's Little Girl"

This is one of the older pieces in the collection—I wrote this one back in 1996. I initially submitted it to *Tomorrow Speculative Fiction*, the magazine that published "Dead the World," the first short story I ever sold. Algis Budrys, the editor and publisher, declined the story—I don't even recall why exactly, but I'm sure his reason was legitimate—and I set the story aside for a while. Then one day, I got an idea for how I could make it better, and I sat down and rewrote it. I never did resubmit it to Mr. Budrys, and decided to store it in the infamous Writer's Bottom Drawer, in hopes that I would eventually find a home for it someday. So, here it is. (Note to aspiring writers: Never throw anything away.)

The story makes no attempt to be profound or thought provoking. But I think it's fun to read, in a campy sort of way. Besides, who doesn't like werewolves?

"The Sting"

I wrote this one a few years ago, too. At that time, I had noticed a trend in my writing: I was always telling stories about nice guys. I like writing about nice guys, mind you, since we supposedly always finish last—but I wanted to write a story about a complete asshole, for a change. You know the type: the kind of person who is absolutely insufferable, in almost every way. The kind of person whom you are *glad* to see get his just desserts at the end. (Because, in real life, the bad guys often seem to win.)

Oh, and I confess to personally having a minor phobia to winged insects with stingers . . .

"After the Party"

One year, I got it in my mind that I should write a story with a Halloween theme, just to see what I could come up with. I think most of us dread getting pulled over by the police—especially when we know damn well that we've done something wrong. I know I do.

But there are things much worse than being hauled to jail. Much, much, worse.

"The Secret Door"

One of the less exciting jobs that I worked in my youth was that of a "corporate housekeeper"—a janitor, in other words. I'll be honest: I hated the job. I felt that it was a misuse of what I believed my talents to be.

But hey, even Einstein had to hold down a gig to pay the bills. You do what you gotta do, know what I mean?

Although I mostly despised the work, it taught me

humility. It taught me that there is honor in a job well done. And it gave me the source material for this story. (And a bunch more that I've yet to write.)

In retrospect, sounds like a fair trade-off.

"Hitcher"

I've always wanted to write a story about a hitch-hiker. (The 1980s film *The Hitcher,* starring Rutger Hauer as the madman, has stayed with me for years.) But as oftentimes happens to me when I'm writing, what begins as one kind of story suddenly metamorphoses into something entirely different. That's what happened here. I was a bit surprised myself at how strange things soon became with these characters.

Talk about one weird, dysfunctional family!

"Predators"

This is one of those far-fetched, but "this could really happen" type stories that I love. I also love to write about independent, tough-minded women who have faced adversity, lived to tell the tale—and decided to do something about it. That "something" usually translates into the woman refusing to live as a victim. She takes action.

The heroine in this story takes action—to the nth degree.

You go, girl!

"Nostalgia"

Growing up, I spent a lot of time with my grandparents. After my grandfather died, in 1991, my family asked me to move in with my grandmother, to keep her company and help her around the house. I ended up living with her for eight years, and during that time, we became—and still are—exceptionally close.

When I moved away to Atlanta, it was hard for both of us. I was twenty-five and wanted to move on and live my life as an adult, in a new city. But I sometimes felt guilty and asked myself if I was abandoning her. She understood why I wanted to leave, but she loved me like a son, and was sad to see me go.

I wrote this story while I was going through that transition period.

"A Walk Through Darkness"

Years ago, I heard a story about one of my great uncles walking along a lonely road at night, through the mountains in the South—he was hitchhiking, so the story goes. And as he walked, he noticed a man-sized shape up in the hills, keeping pace with him. Was it a bear? A man? Something else? He never found out—someone picked him up before too long, and he eventually arrived home.

Anyway, sometimes I will hear a real-life story and *know* that it's a perfect launching pad for a helluva fiction piece. That's what happened here.

"The Monster"

This one is yet another older piece. When I was a kid, I had (and still do have as an adult) what people label an "overactive imagination." Back then, in my darkened bedroom, my imagination would take off on frightening flights of fancy. There was always someone in the closet across the room, peering at me through the slit between the door and frame. That rumpled pile of clothes in the corner was really a giant, grinning face.

And there was a monster under the bed.

Nothing but a child's overactive imagination, of course.

But what if the monster was real?

"Death Notice"

I've observed that when people begin to get up in age, they oftentimes develop an intense interest in death—specifically, in the recently deceased in their town. The devotees of such matters invariably turn to the newspaper obituaries to satisfy their thirst for this morbid knowledge. And who showed up in the day's obits is a regular topic of conversation.

This story is my attempt to understand why the obits are so important. I'm sure that as I grow older, my wisdom will deepen in this regard.

I just hope I don't end up like Mary Pryor.

"The Woman Next Door"

I originally wrote this piece intending to submit it to the *Brown Sugar 4* erotica anthology edited by

Carol Taylor. Then, for reasons that I don't even remember, I changed my mind and gave Carol another story, "Ghost Writer," instead. But this one still resonates with me. It's my first stab at a mix of erotica and supernatural suspense. (I explored this blend in more depth in my novel *Within the Shadows*.)

Besides, in our transient society, you often don't know much at all about your neighbors . . .

"Flight 463"

This is probably the most serious story in the collection. The main character is undergoing a crisis of faith, triggered by the suffering, and eventual death, of his beloved grandmother. The story grapples with the timeless question that has spawned a thousand books and Sunday-morning sermons: why do bad things happen to good people?

I don't profess to have the answer to this question; I'm not sure anyone does. But it haunts me, as it does many of us who have lost a loved one who seemed to deserve more time on earth, or a better life, or a less painful death.

I *wish* I could get a divine confirmation as powerful as the one Sean receives at the end.

"Presumed Dead"

I attended a book club meeting not too long ago—they were discussing my novel *Dark Corner*—and we got into a conversation about people who fake their own death. One of the ladies shared a story about a guy from her hometown who did just that.

He drove his car into the lake, and dropped out of sight. Everyone thought he was dead—until he showed up back in town a few years later, and someone recognized him.

I think this happens more than we realize. People fake their own demise to escape bad marriages, heavy debt, and other burdens that seem inescapable.

However, if I was such a person, I would think that the temptation to go back home—just once, to see how things have changed—would be nearly overwhelming.

This story is my take on why, if you leave town under false pretenses, maybe you should never go home again.

"The Last Train Home"

This is another of those "this could really happen" stories, set in Zion, Illinois, my hometown, in the dead of winter. I used a train station setting with which I'm personally familiar. (However, for the purposes of the story, I took numerous fictional departures in regard to the train schedules and the finer physical details of the station.)

But Tonya could be anyone. The lady at the grocery store, the woman dropping off her child at school . . . the dedicated employee working overtime to help make ends meet. She is an ordinary woman—placed in an extraordinary situation.

During times of extreme adversity, we find out what we're really made of. And if we survive, we're forever changed by the experience. Always, I think, for the better.

Enjoy the following excerpt of Brandon Massey's new thriller,
THE OTHER BROTHER,
*available July 2006 in paperback
wherever books are sold.*

Standing at his bedroom window watching a thunderstorm building in the evening sky, the man touched the glass and thought about Death.

Death comes stealing like a thief in the night, he thought. It comes without warning, without preamble, breaking into mansions and inner-city projects, taking away the young and the old alike. No one is spared. And no one is ever safe.

Indeed, the veil separating life from death is as thin as the dust-streaked windowpane on which his fingers rested.

He pursed his lips, took his hand away from the window. Ordinarily, he did not contemplate such macabre thoughts. But today, he couldn't avoid them.

It was like that when you expected that someone was coming to kill you.

He was dressed in loose-fitting Levi's, black leather boots, and a gray button-down shirt. The ends of the shirt flowed over his waist—concealing, he hoped, the bulge of the Glock 9mm handgun that he wore holstered on his hip.

Mama knew that he owned guns, but she didn't like for him to carry them around the house.

Tonight, he didn't dare go anywhere unarmed, not even in his own home.

There was a rap at the door. He spun, quick as a cobra, hand flicking to the Glock.

"Dinner's ready," Mama said, behind the door.

He relaxed. "Be there in a minute."

He turned back to the window.

The churning May sky, resembling the countenance of a troubled god, offered him no comfort. The brewing storm made him edgy. And the urban wasteland beyond the glass—the dilapidated houses, trash-strewn sidewalks, and pothole-riddled streets of Chicago's Southside—fired up his anger.

We deserve a better life than this. We never should have been here.

A battered oak desk stood beside the window. Photographs—clippings from glossy magazines and newspapers—covered the desktop.

Many of the photos depicted two black men standing together, dressed in expensive business suits, one older, one younger, clearly father and son, the consummate family entrepreneurs. Other pictures featured only the son, a dapper guy in his late twenties who had life by the balls—and his wide grin showed that he knew it, too.

One photograph—framed and placed at the edge of the pile—showed the father when he was younger, with a pretty black woman wearing an Afro. They were sitting at a table in one of those Japanese hibachi restaurants, smiling as if they would be young and beautiful forever.

He didn't know why he'd pulled out the pictures. Looking at them had the predictable effect of stoking his anger. Always had. He supposed that he was in an introspective mood; ruminating on his life and how it was so unfair that it had turned out this way.

He picked up the framed photograph. The glass front was cracked—that had happened when, in a rage, he'd slammed the frame against a wall.

He double-checked that his shirt hid his gun, and then left the bedroom, taking the photo with him. He glanced both ways along the dimly lit hallway before proceeding into the kitchen. Looking for a hidden intruder. No one was in here. It was just him and Mama, like always. Mother and son against the world.

Mama sat at the kitchen table smoking a Newport. The table was set for dinner. But she hadn't eaten. Delicious aromas—fried chicken and other foods—rose from the pots and pans on the counter and stove behind her.

"You didn't have to wait for me," he said.

"It's Sunday," she said, as if that explained everything. And it did. Mama believed in sit-down family meals on Sundays, and he obliged her.

She believed in attending church services on Sundays, too, but he refused to go along with that. He believed in God. But he no longer believed God cared about people like him. His initial awareness of God's indifference to his plight came during his first stint in juvenile detention, when two teenage bullies, beating him, laughed mockingly when he cried out for God to help him.

And his faith hadn't been helped when, as a teenager, he'd seen the pastor of their church—a married man with three kids—hurrying out of Mama's bedroom one night, yanking up his slacks around his waist.

Fifty-two years old but looking much older, Mama

hadn't lured any philandering pastors or other men of note into her bedroom in a long time. She was far removed from the beautiful young thing in the photo at the Japanese restaurant. Years of hard-scrabble living, cigarettes, and drinking had taken the luster off her looks, dulled the shine that had once enlivened her large eyes.

Mama rose, with effort, and began to fix plates for both of them. She didn't normally get his food for him. But ever since he'd been released from prison, two months ago, she'd given him extra care and attention, as if he was a wounded bird that needed TLC before he could spread his wings again. He didn't have the heart to tell her that he'd never flown.

He didn't like for Mama to cater to him, but she'd snap at him if he resisted, so he sat at the head of the table and waited. He looked around at the fancy new things she'd recently bought. The bone china and silverware and glasses. And he thought about the stuff in the other rooms: the suede furniture, the cherrywood tables, the wide-screen Sony television, the opulent draperies and high-priced vases and oil paintings. The kind of stuff she'd always wanted, but never had been able to afford. The items were pathetically out of place in their cramped, crumbling house—it was like putting a new Alpine stereo system in a rust-bucket car fit only for a junkyard—but who was he to tell her what to do with her money? When he'd given her the check for fifty thousand dollars, the stay-out-of-my-life payment that his father had sent to him, Mama had shrieked so loudly you would've thought she'd won the Powerball lottery.

He hadn't taken any of the money for himself. He didn't deserve it. Mama did. She'd sacrificed so much trying to raise him right that she deserved fifty grand times a thousand.

A rumble of thunder barreled through the night, clinking the dishes on the table. Wind tested the windows, like fingers trying to pry inside.

He cocked his head, listening for sounds of an invasion, aware that the thunderstorm might provide covering noise for intruders. But there was nothing. Yet.

Mama returned to the table with his plate. She'd heaped it with fried chicken, spaghetti, turnip greens, and a hunk of cornbread. Good, old-fashioned soul food. She took a glass pitcher out of the refrigerator and filled his tumbler with extrasweet KOOL-AID Lemonade.

"Thanks, Mama," he said. "Looks good."

"Tastes better," she said, her customary response. She got her own plate and sat across from him. Reaching for his hand, she bowed her head to pray.

He bowed his head, too, but only for her benefit. He'd given up praying after his first beating in juvie detention.

Thunder rocked the world as his mother prayed in a steady voice. He never understood how she managed to pray as if she was so certain that God actually listened to her and cared. He wanted to shake her sometimes, scream at her that she was wasting her time. But he kept his mouth shut and allowed her to nurture her illusions. Everyone had to believe in something.

She concluded the prayer and picked up her fork. He reached into his pocket and placed the photograph on the table.

Mama's lips twisted into a scowl. "Why'd you bring

that in here? You know how much I hate that damn picture."

He shrugged. He wasn't quite sure why he'd brought it, just as he wasn't sure why he'd dragged out all of those other photos sitting on his desk. Maybe he was indulging in self-flagellation.

"Put it away," she said.

But he left it there. "Do you ever wonder how things might've turned out if you'd married him?"

She did not look at the photo, or at him. Her gaze drifted to the wall, and her eyes hardened as though she didn't like what she saw there. "Never. He was married to someone else, you know that."

"But what if he'd left his wife for you?"

"Then we'd be living in the lap of luxury in Hotlanta, wouldn't we? You would've gone to college instead of prison, and I'd be spending all day getting my nails done and shopping at Bloomingdale's. Right?" She turned to him. Fire flashed in her honey-brown eyes, and he caught a glimpse of the feisty woman she'd been before life beat her down. "I'm gonna tell you one last time—put that picture away. It makes me so sick I might lose my appetite."

"Sorry, Mama," he said. "Sometimes, I just wonder, that's all."

"Ain't no use in wondering, baby. We'd better be happy he gave us what he did. It ain't fair, but that's life, huh?"

He nodded. He wasn't satisfied with her answer, but there was no other answer to be found. He reached for the photo.

Thunder cracked again, and it almost masked the sound that he'd been preparing himself for: the front door banging open as if struck with a battering ram.

He slid his hand away from the picture, and grasped the Glock.

They had arrived.

"They" were a couple of thugs with whom he'd gotten into a scuffle at a party last Friday night. Held in a cramped project apartment, it had been a typical ghetto house party: a two-dollar cover charge to get in, dark as midnight, music so loud your heart pounded in sync with the beat, blunt smoke thick in the air, drinks being passed freely, and wall-to-wall brothas and sistas, their horny bodies emanating cologne, perfume, and funk.

He had been talking to a fine sista with cocoa skin and a banging body, and she was digging him, encouraging him, devouring his words as if they were the sweetest taffy—when suddenly, a guy with dreadlocks popped up and claimed to be her boyfriend. Dreads ordered him to step the fuck back or he'd knock him flat *on* his back. Never one to back down from a fight or allow another man to disrespect him, he'd gotten in Dreads's face. Threats flew, followed soon by fists. He punched Dreads in the jaw; someone slammed a fist into his ribs; Dreads's baldheaded partner came at him, and he dropped Baldie with a blow to the kidney. Then, someone in the background drew a gun and fired, shattering a window—and the partygoers fled the house like roaches caught under a heat lamp.

The party was over. But that hadn't been the end of it. On the streets, grudges didn't die—they multiplied. He'd known that Dreads and Baldie would be coming for him. It was only a matter of when.

All because of a woman. It was stupid and petty. But black men died over trivial shit every day.

Footsteps hammered across the floor. From the

kitchen, he couldn't see the intruders, and they couldn't see him, either. The kitchen was at the end of the hall, and the table was in the corner, tucked away from the doorway. But they would find him any minute.

Mama looked at him. Her eyes were huge and scared.

He hated that she'd been pulled into this situation. He could have stayed with a lady friend, laid low for a while. But the danger in doing so was that these guys might hurt Mama to get back at him. He'd seen it happen too many times. He had to stay home to protect her.

"What have you done?" she asked, in a whisper that nonetheless held a note of accusation.

He hadn't told her anything about the fight at the party, about the thugs who were coming for him. Trouble had shadowed him all his life. Mama would know from bitter experience that he was mixed up in another mess.

"Go down to the basement," he whispered. He motioned to the narrow door behind the table; it led to the cellar. "I'll handle this."

She shook her head, tears streaming down her face. How many times had she wept for him? It amazed him that she had any tears left.

"Please, Mama," he said. "Hurry."

Choking back a sob, Mama quickly pushed away from the table. She opened the cellar door and descended into the darkness beyond.

He heard the thugs at the front of the house, overturning furniture and tearing through the bedrooms. Something broke. Probably one of those expensive vases Mama had bought.

Anger stitched a frown across his face. Mama

didn't deserve to suffer for his deeds. He was going to take care of these clowns.

Standing, he lifted his shirt and closed his hand around the Glock's cold grip. He'd paid a lot for this piece. Now, it was time to see what it could do.

He moved to the kitchen doorway and peered around the frame.

One of the thugs was coming down the hallway. It was a black man, dark as midnight and wide as a refrigerator, a black doo-rag capping his dome. Not Dreads or Baldie, but a different brother, another member of the crew. Doo Rag's eyes were bits of onyx.

Doo Rag had a gun, too. The gun in his hands looked like a cannon, at first, but it was really a shotgun, sawed-off, probably a 12 gauge, nonetheless an absolutely lethal weapon.

Doo Rag spotted him, and pulled the trigger.

So did he.

The gunfire was deafening in the house.

The shotgun's buckshot plowed into the door frame, wood splinters flying—and part of the buckshot spray ripped into his shoulder. He screamed and staggered sideways, knocking against a counter. He didn't feel any pain yet, but he knew it was coming, an express train of agony on the way.

But he noted with satisfaction that he'd drilled the thug between the eyes. Doo Rag lay sprawled on his back in the hallway, lips parted in an unfinished prayer. Dead.

He felt nothing—no sorrow or pity. Although it wasn't the first time that he'd killed a man, each time he did it, he felt less for his victim, and in his moments of introspection, that bothered him, made him wonder if he'd lost his humanity.

But he didn't have time to think about that right now. There were, by the sounds of it, at least two more men in the house. One of them poked his head into view at the end of the hall. Baldie.

He fired the Glock at Baldie, and the thug jumped out of sight. He'd missed him.

Pain gnawed deep into his shoulder. Dark blood dampened his shirt. Dizziness swam through him, and he gritted his teeth, determined to stay alert.

But he was fading fast. His legs buckled, gave way. He spilled onto the linoleum tile like a drunken uncle. His hand hooked around the table leg, and he pulled it, fuzzily thinking he could use the table as a shield. The table crashed to the floor, hot food and lemonade spattering around him.

He hauled the table in front of him, propped his back against the row of cabinets, and positioned the Glock atop the edge of the table, to steady his aim.

His vision was beginning to get blurry. The pain intensified; it felt as if someone had packed his shoulder with kindling and set it aflame.

Ahead of him, the hallway was dark, a tunnel of death. But he knew they were out there. He felt their eyes on him.

Gotta hold on.

A door creaked open. Mama rushed out of the basement, to his side. Her eyes were red from crying.

"Get away," he said, but his voice came out as only a hoarse whisper.

"Not letting my baby die," Mama said. Her eyes were steel. She wrapped her arm around his waist and started to drag him across the floor, toward the basement door.

Gunfire rang out.

Warm blood sprayed against his face. It wasn't his blood.

Mama.

"No!" he cried.

She slumped against him, her body as limp and heavy as a sandbag. He tried to hold her against him with his good arm, but he was too weak. She slid out of his grasp and thudded to the floor. Blood pooled around her lips, and for an absurd moment, it looked as if she was okay, as if she'd merely fallen asleep wearing too much red lipstick.

He wanted to believe that she was only asleep. The urge to deny what had happened to her was nearly overwhelming.

He crawled to Mama, touched her chest. It was still; she wasn't breathing.

She was gone.

Grief squeezed his heart like an iron fist.

The photo of Mama and his father, happy during their brief affair, stood nearby, mocking him with the dream of what could have been.

He reached out with his good arm and snagged the picture in his quivering fingers. He fixed his gaze on the man, his father.

This is your fault, and I'm going to make you pay.

If his father had done right by them, they never would have been here. They wouldn't have been living here, he wouldn't have grown up in and out of trouble, and Mama never would have led such a hard life. None of this would have ever happened to them.

No matter what, I'm going to get you for this.

A booted foot materialized from out of nowhere and caught him under the chin. He flipped backward against the tile, blinked groggily.

Two faces swam into view above him, like twin moons: Dreads and Baldie. They were grinning.

"Payback's a bitch, ain't it motherfucka?" Dreads asked.

He tried to raise his hand and fire the Glock, and discovered that he couldn't move his arm. He no longer had the gun, anyway. He'd dropped it somewhere.

But Dreads still had his gun.

Dreads aimed the weapon at his head and pulled the trigger.

He spiraled into darkness, his promise of vengeance following him into oblivion.

No matter what, I'm going to get you . . .

Sign up for Brandon Massey's Talespinner

Readers can subscribe to Brandon Massey's Talespinner by visiting his website at www.brandonmassey.com. Mailing list members receive free short stories, a monthly e-newsletter, book signing updates, opportunities to win prizes in exclusive contests, and advance information about forthcoming publications. Go online today to www.brandonmassey.com and sign up. Membership is free!

GREAT BOOKS, GREAT SAVINGS!

When You Visit Our Website:
www.kensingtonbooks.com
You Can Save 30% Off The Retail Price
Of Any Book You Purchase

- **All Your Favorite Kensington Authors**
- **New Releases & Timeless Classics**
- **Overnight Shipping Available**
- **All Major Credit Cards Accepted**

Visit Us Today To Start Saving!
www.kensingtonbooks.com

All Orders Are Subject To Availability.
Shipping and Handling Charges Apply.

Grab These Other
Thought Provoking Books

Adam by Adam
0-7582-0195-8

by Adam Clayton Powell, Jr.
$15.00US/$21.00CAN

African American Firsts
0-7582-0243-1

by Joan Potter
$15.00US/$21.00CAN

African-American Pride
0-8065-2498-7

by Lakisha Martin
$15.95US/$21.95CAN

The African-American Soldier
0-8065-2049-3

by Michael Lee Lanning
$16.95US/$24.95CAN

African Proverbs and Wisdom
0-7582-0298-9

by Julia Stewart
$12.00US/$17.00CAN

Al on America
0-7582-0351-9

by Rev. Al Sharpton
with Karen Hunter
$16.00US/$23.00CAN

Available Wherever Books Are Sold!

Visit our website at **www.kensingtonbooks.com**

Grab These Other
Dafina Novels
(mass market editions)

Some Sunday
0-7582-0026-9

by Margaret Johnson-Hodge
$6.99US/$9.99CAN

Forever
0-7582-0353-5

by Timmothy B. McCann
$6.99US/$9.99CAN

Soulmates Dissipate
0-7582-0020-X

by Mary B. Morrison
$6.99US/$9.99CAN

High Hand
1-57566-684-7

by Gary Phillips
$5.99US/$7.99CAN

Shooter's Point
1-57566-745-2

by Gary Phillips
$5.99US/$7.99CAN

Casting the First Stone
0-7582-0179-6

by Kimberla Lawson Roby
$6.99US/$9.99CAN

Here and Now
0-7582-0064-1

by Kimberla Lawson Roby
$6.99US/$9.99CAN

Lookin' for Luv
0-7582-0118-4

by Carl Weber
$6.99US/$8.99CAN

Available Wherever Books Are Sold!

Visit our website at **www.kensingtonbooks.com**